A man bent o

forge...

The stranger appeared single-minded in his devotion to his craft, as if chained there by the fire and his work, pounding at some inner demon only he could see. Hayley found herself moving stealthily closer, drawn by the rhythmic force of his blows, awed by the beauty they were creating.

She was certain she hadn't made a sound, but without warning he turned. Hayley froze.

"Who the devil are you?" he demanded gruffly. The heat of his gaze was far hotter than his fire. His voice was deep and soft as crushed velvet. A tingle traveled up Hayley's spine.

"I'd be careful calling on the devil if I were you. You already look like you're standing over the fires of hell."

The man blinked in surprise. The corners of his lips darted upward for a second, but the hint of a smile disappeared before it could fully form.

"A good reason for you to run away, little girl."

Dear Harlequin Intrigue Reader,

Beginning this October, Harlequin Intrigue has expanded its lineup to *six* books! Publishing two more titles each month enables us to bring you an extraordinary selection of breathtaking stories of romantic suspense filled with exciting editorial variety—and we encourage you to try all that we have to offer.

Stock up on catnip! Caroline Burnes brings back your favorite feline sleuth to beckon you into a new mystery in the popular series FEAR FAMILIAR. This four-legged detective sticks his whiskers into the mix to help clear a stunning stuntwoman's name in *Familiar Double*. Up next is Dani Sinclair's new HEARTSKEEP trilogy starting with *The Firstborn*—a darkly sensual gothic romance that revolves around a sinister suspense plot. To lighten things up, bestselling Harlequin American Romance author Judy Christenberry crosses her beloved BRIDES FOR BROTHERS series into Harlequin Intrigue with *Randall Renegade*—a riveting reunion romance that will keep you on the edge of your seat.

Keeping Baby Safe by Debra Webb could either passionately reunite a duty-bound COLBY AGENCY operative and his onetime lover—or tear them apart forever. Don't miss the continuation of this action-packed series. Then Amy J. Fetzer launches our BACHELORS AT LARGE promotion featuring fearless men in blue with *Under His Protection*. Finally, watch for *Dr. Bodyguard* by debut author Jessica Andersen. Will a hunky doctor help penetrate the emotional walls around a lady genius before a madman closes in?

Pick up all six for a complete reading experience you won't forget!

Enjoy,

Denise O'Sullivan
Senior Editor
Harlequin Intrigue

THE FIRSTBORN

DANI SINCLAIR

TORONTO • NEW YORK • LONDON
AMSTERDAM • PARIS • SYDNEY • HAMBURG
STOCKHOLM • ATHENS • TOKYO • MILAN • MADRID
PRAGUE • WARSAW • BUDAPEST • AUCKLAND

For Helen Pastis whose caring has no limits.
For Roger, Chip, Dan and Barb.

With heartfelt thanks to
Natashya Wilson and Judy Fitzwater.
You're both terrific.

Special thanks to Judy Boone for answering my questions,
and to her husband, Daniel,
whose family of blacksmiths
traces back fifteen generations.

ISBN 0-373-22730-2

THE FIRSTBORN

This edition published by arrangement with Harlequin Books S.A.

Visit us at www.eHarlequin.com

Printed in U.S.A.

ABOUT THE AUTHOR

An avid reader, Dani Sinclair didn't discover romance novels until her mother lent her one when she had come for a visit. Dani's been hooked on the genre ever since. But she didn't take up writing seriously until her two sons were grown. Since the premiere of *Mystery Baby* for Harlequin Intrigue in 1996, Dani has kept her computer busy. Her third novel, *Better Watch Out*, was a RITA® Award finalist in 1998. Dani lives outside Washington, D.C., a place she's found to be a great source for both intrigue and humor!

You can write to her in care of the Harlequin Reader Service.

Books by Dani Sinclair

HARLEQUIN INTRIGUE

371—MYSTERY BABY
401—MAN WITHOUT A BADGE
448—BETTER WATCH OUT
481—MARRIED IN HASTE
507—THE MAN SHE MARRIED
539—FOR HIS DAUGHTER*
551—MY BABY, MY LOVE*
565—THE SILENT WITNESS*
589—THE SPECIALIST
602—BEST-KEPT SECRETS*
613—SOMEONE'S BABY
658—SCARLET VOWS
730—THE FIRSTBORN†

HARLEQUIN TEMPTATION

690—THE NAKED TRUTH

*Fools Point/Mystery Junction
†Heartskeep

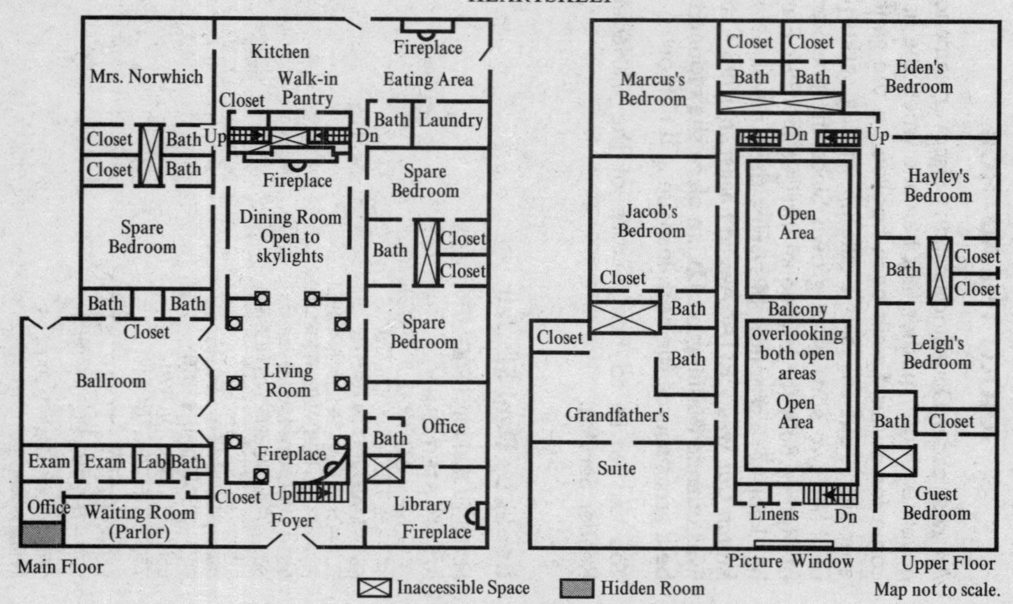
HEARTSKEEP
Mrs. Norwhich
Kitchen
Walk-in Pantry
Closet
Fireplace
Eating Area
Bath
Laundry
Closet
Bath
Up
Dn
Closet
Bath
Fireplace
Spare Bedroom
Dining Room Open to skylights
Spare Bedroom
Bath
Closet
Closet
Bath
Bath
Closet
Spare Bedroom
Ballroom
Living Room
Office
Bath
Exam
Exam
Lab
Bath
Fireplace
Closet
Up
Office
Waiting Room (Parlor)
Foyer
Library
Fireplace
Main Floor
Marcus's Bedroom
Closet
Closet
Bath
Bath
Eden's Bedroom
Dn
Up
Jacob's Bedroom
Open Area
Hayley's Bedroom
Bath
Closet
Closet
Closet
Bath
Balcony overlooking both open areas
Closet
Bath
Leigh's Bedroom
Grandfather's Suite
Open Area
Bath
Closet
Linens
Dn
Guest Bedroom
Picture Window
Upper Floor
Inaccessible Space
Hidden Room
Map not to scale.

CAST OF CHARACTERS

Dennison Hart—He made sure Heartskeep would stay in the family. It didn't occur to him he was setting them up to be victims.

Amy Hart Thomas—When her father died seven years ago, she disappeared without a trace....

Marcus Thomas—He married his nurse as soon as he had his first wife declared legally dead.

Eden Voxx Thomas—She doesn't care what the world thinks. She married Marcus and she intends to run Heartskeep as she sees fit.

Hayley Hart Thomas—As the firstborn, she inherits. But only if she survives long enough to claim her inheritance.

Bram Myers—The sexy blacksmith was hired to put bars on the windows and doors. But is he a safe haven or the source of the storm?

Leigh Hart Thomas—Hayley's twin is in England visiting with friends. Isn't she?

Jacob Voxx—Everyone likes Eden's son. Everyone except Bram.

Odette Norwhich—Eden's newly hired cook has an attitude problem—and total access to Heartskeep.

Paula Kerstairs—Eden's newly hired housekeeper moves like a wraith through the mansion hearing more than she should.

George and Emily Walken—These neighbors and close friends of the family have taken in troubled youths for years.

Helen Pepperton Myers—Did her death in childbirth precipitate a plan for revenge?

Dear Harlequin Intrigue Reader,

HEARTSKEEP is a series I've been developing for several years. The idea grew from an actual home where the front parlor had been converted into a doctor's office. The house fired my imagination. There was a sense of tiredness about the sprawling old building, as if it had seen too much of life over the years. What secrets might it hide?

I don't know about the real house, but Heartskeep has many secrets. When Hayley Thomas arrives to claim her inheritance, she discovers a dark, formidable structure—much like the compelling stranger she finds working with such fierce intensity in the woods out back. Who is this man? Why does he stir such strong emotions in her? Nothing is the way she remembers. Is she losing her mind as well as her heart? Step into Heartskeep and find out for yourself.

Happy reading!

Dani Sinclair

Chapter One

Almost home.

Hayley Thomas suppressed a shudder. Heartskeep hadn't been home since the day her mother disappeared more than seven years ago. The sprawling estate along the Hudson River was the envy of many, but only because it appeared so rich and serene on the surface.

The canopy of tree limbs overhead darkened the final road home, matching her mood as she sped through the sleepy hamlet of Stony Ridge, New York. As she plunged deeper into horse country, the scenery changed yet again, to velvety green fields basking in the fading sun. The unusually intense heat wave of early June hadn't yet taken its toll, but soon enough the lush green would turn a scorched golden-brown.

Rolling her head to stretch the kinks from her neck and shoulders, Hayley was relieved to finally come upon the lane leading to Heartskeep until she turned into the wide-mouthed entrance. She braked the car to a jarring halt.

What had he done?

Hayley tried to still the clamor of her heart as she stepped from the idling car and stared in disbelief. Towering brick pillars had replaced the shorter, crumbling ones on which two stone lions had perched, standing guard for more than sixty years. Spanning the new pillars was an intricately worked, yet formidable wrought-iron gate, closed against intruders.

Marcus didn't really believe he could bar her from her own family home with a metal gate. Did he?

Shaking in outrage, Hayley strode up to the wrought-iron fixture. Both the art major and the business major in her appreciated the fascinating piece. Another time, she would have enjoyed examining the artistry and craftsmanship that had gone into creating this incredible gate. The work was like nothing she'd seen before. But now, its unexpected presence caused a surge of pure anger.

What had Marcus done with her lions?

He had no right!

Hayley rattled the gate in a rare explosion of temper. Only then did she realize it wasn't locked. With effort, the bar that held the massive gates closed could be lifted and slid aside from where she stood. Still, she pulsed with anger as the gates swung open smoothly. She was not a child anymore. She would not let her own father intimidate her by putting a gate in front of her house.

Darn it, *Marcus* was the outsider here at Heartskeep, and it was definitely past time to tell him so. Out of respect for her mother, Hayley had never challenged his right to live here. Not even when he'd remarried. But this was going too far. This gate was a deliberate slap in her face. He was staking his claim and daring her to take exception.

Fine. She would accept his challenge, and she'd be the one to come out the winner. According to the law, Heartskeep belonged to her. Removing the gate and reinstalling her stone lions had just become her first priority when she assumed control of the estate.

The small car bounced hard as she drove recklessly up the tree-lined driveway. If Marcus had finally felt a compulsion to do something around the estate, why hadn't he started by making some badly needed repairs? This driveway was a disgrace. The ruts were deeper and more numerous than she remembered from her last visit. Hayley hoped she didn't break an axle or some other essential item on the car, even as she pushed the compact relentlessly over the pitted surface. She was anxious now for the confrontation to come.

She'd spent most of her life treading warily around the man who was her biological father. She and her twin sister had learned early to stay out of his way. While she couldn't remember when they had started actually calling him Marcus out loud, he had never been anything else in their thoughts.

The sight of the sprawling brick mansion never failed to surprise her as she rounded the last curve. It did even more so tonight as the house appeared, starkly forlorn, silhouetted against the rapidly darkening sky. Had it always looked so eerie?

Hayley shook her head. Once, Heartskeep had been a welcome haven. The past seven years had changed all that. And tonight there wasn't even a welcoming glimmer of light. The structure looked like an abandoned movie set for a slasher film.

''Great. Psyche yourself into a case of nerves, why don't you?'' she muttered.

But it was true. The happy memories the house had once evoked were long gone. They'd disappeared along with her mother.

Hayley and Leigh had been back to Heartskeep only a handful of times since the two of them had started at Wellesley College. The visits had never been pleasant so they'd been careful to keep their stays as brief as possible.

How dare he remove her lions?

Heartskeep and everything connected with the estate belonged to Hayley and Leigh, not Marcus Thomas. As her mother's firstborn child, ownership of the house and grounds would revert to Hayley when she turned twenty-five next year. Didn't Marcus know that?

Of course he did. Wasn't that why he'd put up the gate? She'd known Marcus and his wife, Eden, would not be happy to see her, but Hayley hadn't anticipated anything like this.

Despite this new provocation, she had no real intention of turning them out. She might not like Marcus, but the blood relationship existed, and she would acknowledge and respect that fact, as her mother had done. However, Marcus would have to come to terms with Hayley's ownership of the estate. He was not master here any longer even if she wasn't twenty-five yet. She was no longer a minor under his jurisdiction.

Of course, she'd feel a lot braver with Leigh at her side. The deep bond between them had been forged at conception. But Hayley had wanted to spare her twin the coming unpleasantness.

Too bad she hadn't realized just how unpleasant things were going to be. Still, she wouldn't have asked Leigh to cut short her visit with her friends in England. Hayley could take the brunt of Marcus's anger. After all, there was nothing he could do to alter the situation.

Unless he made her disappear, as he had her mother.

Hayley tossed aside that morbid thought and tried to concentrate on missing the worst of the ruts. No one had ever been able to prove Marcus had had anything to do with their mother's disappearance, no matter what Hayley and Leigh believed. Not that the local police had tried all that hard.

Hayley bypassed the wide, sweeping circle in front of the house and drove around to the back entrance she generally used. She suppressed a shiver. The truth was, she was secretly afraid of Marcus. She always had been. While her grandfather was alive, Marcus hadn't mattered. Her grandfather had taken on the paternal role, since Marcus ignored his daughters most of the time. That had suited everyone just fine. In the beginning, their mother had tried to make excuses for his indifference, but it wasn't long before she'd stopped trying.

Shortly after her eleventh birthday, Hayley had gone looking for her birth certificate, convinced Marcus couldn't really be her father. She had cried uncontrollably after discovering the document said otherwise.

How could a real father be so cold? He was a doctor, of all things. And not just any doctor, a gynecologist and obstetrician for a very select clientele. No one had ever been able to explain his indifference to his own family. Hayley and Leigh had learned to accept the situation. They'd lived with their parents and grandfather on the vast estate for most of their lives, but they often had gone days at a time without seeing Marcus.

Hayley knew Dennison Hart had shared their dislike of Marcus, though he'd never said a critical word in their hearing. He'd even had the front wing of the house remodeled into an office for his son-in-law, after Marcus complained about his long commute to work. Leigh surmised it was her grandfather's way of keeping Marcus from moving his family away from Heartskeep. Hayley thought her sister probably had it right.

Everything had changed when their grandfather died without warning one night. The vast estate seemed to shrink. Teenagers by then, she and Leigh had frequently heard Marcus ranting at their mother. They'd worked harder than ever to stay out of his way, but they couldn't help wishing their mother would toss him out and file for divorce.

Instead, it was Amy Thomas who'd gone away. A few months after her father's death, their mother took a sudden, inexplicable trip to New York City and vanished without a trace. Hayley and Leigh knew something awful had happened when she didn't call home to check in with them after the first night.

Valet parking at Amy's hotel said they'd retrieved her car for her early the morning after she arrived. Neither she nor the car was ever seen again. Though she'd left her luggage at the hotel, Hayley and Leigh had both known their mother wasn't ever coming back to claim it.

The depressing memory of that time accompanied Hayley to the kitchen door—a door now covered by another intricately detailed wrought-iron grill. The door was locked.

Trembling with anger, Hayley pressed the bell, holding it in place. There was no sound from within. Where were Mrs. Walsh and Kathy? The housekeeper and her daughter had rooms right off the kitchen. They rarely went out in the evening.

Puzzled, and more than a little uneasy, Hayley took a step back to survey the house in the rapidly fading twilight. Every ground floor window now sported wrought-iron grillwork. Outrage mingled with fear. What was going on? Bars on the doors and windows? Was Marcus preparing for a siege?

Hayley turned toward the converted garage, which had once been a stable. Perhaps a look around inside would tell her something. She was halfway to the building when a light flickering through the trees caught her attention. Was that a fire?

Dropping her overnight case, she broke into a run, only slowing when she realized the glow was growing brighter, but not larger. A strange, rhythmic hammering sound, carried by the wind, had her edging forward more cautiously. Just short of the clearing she paused.

The original Heartskeep had been built in the eighteen hundreds. A fire had destroyed the main house at the turn of the century, and the current mansion had been erected in its place. Some of the barns and outbuildings were still originals. They included an old forge that hadn't been used in living memory—until now.

The door gaped open, allowing Hayley to see that it wasn't actually being used now, either. The glow was coming from a large, portable forge standing beyond the building. A man bent over the intense heat of a fire, fueled by a massive propane tank. His features were in profile, his face etched with lines made harsh by the glow of his fire. Hair curled around his neck, thick and dark at the edges where moisture had dampened the strands. A sheen of sweat beaded his arms and plastered the dirty white, sleeveless T-shirt to his formidable chest. Stained jeans encased his lean hips. He was a large man, tall and well muscled. The sort of muscles that came from physical labor rather than a gym.

One of his large hands was covered by a thick, heavy glove holding what appeared to be some sort of tongs. He drew a glowing metal rod from the heart of the fire and set it to one side on a mounted anvil. The bare hand wielded an incredibly heavy-looking hammer, making the large tattoo on his upper arm flex and writhe. Transfixed, Hayley watched the intensity of his expression as he pounded away at the glowing length of metal, twisting and shaping it with undeniable skill.

There was something disturbingly sensual about the stranger and his actions. At the same time, he appeared almost sinister in his single-minded devotion to his craft, as if he was chained there by the fire and his work, pounding away at some inner demon only he could see.

Hayley found herself moving stealthily closer, drawn by the rhythmic force of his blows, awed by the beauty they were creating. He thrust the rod back into the flames once more. She moved even closer, determined to see what he was crafting with such intensity.

She was certain she hadn't made a sound, but without warning, he turned. The white-hot piece of metal waved only inches from her face. Hayley froze, unable to utter a sound. She felt as if that glowing tip had actually branded her flesh.

"Who the devil are you?" he demanded gruffly, using the hammer to push back his protective goggles and survey her. The disturbing heat of his gaze seemed far hotter than his fire, but at least it broke the spell holding her mute.

Hayley exhaled and raised her chin. "I'd be careful calling on the devil if I were you. You already look like you're standing over the fires of hell."

The man blinked in surprise. The corners of his lips darted upward for just a second, but the hint of a smile disappeared before it could form fully and the somber, dark mask settled back over his features.

"A good reason for you to run away, little girl."

A strange tingle traveled straight up her spine. His voice was as deep and soft as crushed velvet. He rocked back on his heels, surveying her in a blatant challenge she couldn't ignore.

"Personally, I prefer aerobics to running. I also prefer petite to little. And I haven't been a girl for a number of years."

The momentary softening of his mouth hinted at more amusement, quickly hidden. "Yeah? How many?"

She should have been nervous. At the very least, she told herself, she should be cautious. Yet somehow she sensed no real menace from the man, despite his brooding looks. Instead, she sensed an aura of sadness about him that immediately stirred her curiosity.

"I'm old enough to know you're trespassing on private property." She forced herself to respond lightly.

"Is that so?"

"Uh-huh. Want to put your weapons down, or do you think you'll need a hammer and a poker to ward me off?"

A grin slid across his features so fast she couldn't be sure she'd actually seen one. He set the hammer aside with deliberate care. The glowing metal hissed loudly, sending a vapor stream into the darkness of the night as he plunged the object into a large tin of water.

"I'll risk it," he told her.

"So, who are you? What are you doing here?"

"I don't think you're the one who should be asking the questions. I was hired to be here. What about you?"

Anger washed over her. "Marcus," she cursed.

"I gather you know the owner?" he questioned.

"You're looking at the owner."

Slowly, he began tugging off his gloves, but not before she had the satisfaction of seeing his surprise.

"A little young, aren't you?"

"You seem fascinated by my age."

He watched her, his face mostly in shadow now, giving him an even darker, more brooding appearance.

"You're a fascinating person," he told her softly.

Her breath caught in her throat. A current of awareness arced between them. Disconcerted, she shook her head against the powerful impact he seemed to be having on her senses. Not all the heat seemed to be coming from the forge.

"Look, it's getting late and I've just had a tiring drive," she said quickly. "Is Marcus home?"

"I've no idea."

"Okay. Then do you have a key to get past that fancy gate you put over my back door?"

"Your door," he said mildly, hooking his thumbs in the waistband of those closely fitted jeans.

"Yes, *my* door. The name is Hayley Hart Thomas. As

of two weeks ago, Heartskeep in its entirety belongs to me and my sister.''

It was only a slight exaggeration. Two weeks ago their mother had been officially declared dead. There was no other living person with any legal right to lay claim to the estate.

The blacksmith regarded her steadily while seconds ticked silently past. Full dark descended. The waves of heat emanating from the fire seemed to fill the night, blocking normal sounds. She gave a small start when he finally spoke again. This time, his voice was bare of inflection.

''No keys, Ms. Thomas. You'll have to take that up with Mr. Thomas.''

''Oh, don't worry, I intend to.'' Bitterly she decided she might have to call the police after all. ''Sorry I disturbed you.'' Gathering her anger like a cloak, she spun around. After taking two steps, she paused to look over her shoulder. The stranger hadn't moved.

''And I want my lions back.''

His eyebrows raised at her demand.

''Do you mean the old stone lions that used to be at the main entrance? Mr. Thomas wanted them destroyed—''

''You didn't!''

''No, actually I didn't. I had them taken to my shop.''

Relief swelled inside her. He still had her lions. ''Where is that?''

''Tucked up in the hills about an hour's drive northwest of here. I doubt you've ever heard of the place. Murett Township doesn't appear on most maps.''

He was right. She'd never heard of it. ''I want them replaced the way they were. Excuse me while I go have a nice long chat with my *father*. Have a good evening, Mr.—''

''Myers,'' he supplied. ''Bram Myers.''

''Well, Mr. Myers, it was interesting talking with you.

You'll have to forgive me for running off, but it looks like I need to drive a car through one of your clever gates to get inside my own house.''

He rocked back on his heels. Once again she sensed an underlying amusement. ''Now why do I think you're ready to do exactly that?''

''Good instincts?''

''Try the front door,'' he suggested softly. ''I haven't completed the design for that gate.''

Hayley hesitated. ''I will. And Mr. Myers, I wouldn't waste time creating any more gates or bars for Heartskeep if I were you.''

Hayley plunged back down the pitch dark path toward the house. She didn't dare look back. Bram Myers was entirely too disconcerting for comfort. She had never seen a sexier man in all her life. Too bad she was going to have to fire him in the morning.

She wished there was a moon overhead as she made her way cautiously around the house to the front door. Curiously, she didn't even need her key. The tarnished brass knob twisted easily beneath her fingers. The door swung wide, revealing a black, cavernous interior that was far from inviting. Hayley could barely see to step over the threshold. She searched along the wall for the remembered light switch, relieved when her fingers closed over it. But nothing happened.

A large chandelier hung over the foyer. One bulb might be burned out, but not all of them. Obviously, the electricity wasn't working again. The house had an empty, deserted feeling. Where was everyone?

''Hello? Is anyone here?''

Her voice seemed to echo hollowly.

Straight ahead, the formal grand staircase rose imperiously to the second floor. Beyond it was the incredibly large, one-of-a-kind living room. On her right was the library, and to her left, the narrow, formal parlor her grandfather had converted into a waiting room for Marcus's patients.

Hayley knew a moment of shock when she sensed the door to that parlor standing wide open. Except during office hours, Marcus always kept that door closed and locked.

Despite her unease, she was drawn to the opening. She set down her case and crossed to the entrance, stepping warily inside. The bank of windows on her left was covered by thick, heavy drapes, so there wasn't even a faint trace of light in the waiting room.

"Hello? Is anyone home?"

A whisper of sound slithered to life from somewhere inside. Common sense told her to leave. Fear told her to run. Sternly, Hayley told herself she wasn't a child. This was her home. She had nothing to fear here.

"Hello?"

Shoving back a long tendril of hair that had worked its way loose from her ponytail, she stepped into the dark recess of the room.

"Is someone in here?"

No one answered, but there was a definite slither of sound that sent prickles of alarm straight up her spine. It was impossible to pinpoint the source of the noise, yet she sensed someone standing nearby. Someone who obviously didn't intend to make his or her presence known.

As Hayley stepped forward cautiously, her leg made unexpected contact with a hard object. Her fingers identified the reception desk, even as her eyes strained to pierce the uncanny blackness of the room. Visions from every horror movie she had ever seen rushed to paint images in her mind. There was a feeling of wrongness in here that was almost physical.

A disturbing chill suddenly brushed her skin. Hayley sensed rather than saw a movement in the ominous well of blackness pooled at the opening that had once led into the formal ballroom. The heavy door now led to the corridor her grandfather had created when he'd converted a portion of the ballroom into a bathroom, laboratory and exam rooms for Marcus. The narrow hall ended at an office.

Hayley held her breath. She felt sure someone stood in that pocket of shadow, silently watching her. The sense of menace seemed to swell until she turned and bolted back into the hall.

She noticed the tall, looming shape too late to avoid a collision.

A scream tore from the depths of her soul. Hands closed roughly around her shoulders. Even as dry-mouthed fear enveloped her, she instinctively lashed out with her foot. There was a soft grunt of pain as she connected with a shin. Her attacker released her.

"Take it easy, will you? I'm not going to hurt you."

A core of remaining sanity placed the voice. A powerful shaft of light emerged from a flashlight in his hand. She was momentarily blinded by the beam before he aimed it away from her face. His harsh features wavered into view.

"Sorry if I startled you," Bram Myers said quietly.

"Startled?" Her heart raced as if she'd run a mile. "You nearly gave me a heart attack."

"That would have been a real shame. Not to mention a spectacular problem."

His wry humor steadied her frazzled nerves. "What are you doing in here?"

"I came to be sure you hadn't driven your car through a door like you threatened."

"Very funny." She couldn't stop trembling. It had been such a long day, and he was standing too near.

"What happened to the lights?"

"They aren't working," she bit out.

"I noticed." He swung the beam so it spanned the empty

hall, causing shadows to leap and writhe. "Are you all right? You're shaking."

"Of course I'm shaking. You scared the heck out of me."

"The way you came bursting out of that room, I have a feeling I'm not the only thing that scared you."

Flustered, she struggled for a composure she was far from feeling. "There's someone in there. Whoever it is wouldn't answer when I called out."

He tensed. "Wait here."

Before she could stop him, Bram strode through the opening. Hayley followed on his heels, secretly relieved by his reassuring presence. His flashlight brought the dark room to spooky life. The drapes were of thick, heavy damask. Empty chairs sat in a line in front of them.

"Inviting. I hope you're planning on having a decorator come in," he said mildly.

"Cute."

The beam of light swept behind the desk to reveal the heavy, dark wood double doors that led back to Marcus's lair. They were closed, sealing off the converted rooms. Her stomach lurched.

"One of those doors was open a second ago," she whispered.

Bram spared her a look. Crossing to them, he reached for the knob. "Are you sure?"

"Of course I'm sure."

He rattled the handle. "It's locked now. Want me to break it open?"

Yes, she wanted to shout, but she couldn't push the word past lips that felt numb. Someone had stood in that doorway only a minute ago. She was sure of it.

"I can force it open if you want me to, but are you sure it wasn't your imagination playing tricks? It would certainly be understandable. Without light, this room is as dark as the inside of a coffin.''

To prove his point, he shut off the flashlight, plunging them into a total void. Hayley stifled a gasp. Bram went on talking.

''I'm standing right here and I can't even see the doors, much less tell if they're open or closed. It would be a shame to kick them in if you're wrong. They don't make interior doors of solid cherry anymore.''

Had the door been open? Was it possible her imagination had taken over? It had been a long day, after all. Hayley was tired from the drive and stressed by what she'd found here—to say nothing of how furious Marcus would be if she damaged something.

Why was she worried about that? This was *her* house, a tiny voice shouted inside her head. Still, she hesitated. Could she have been wrong?

''What happened to the electricity?'' Bram asked abruptly. He snapped the flashlight back on, to her intense relief.

''I don't know.'' She cursed the quaver in her voice, but she couldn't even control the shakes that rippled through her body. ''Don't you sense it?'' she whispered before she could stop herself.

He regarded her steadily. ''Sense what?''

The wrongness, she wanted to shout. Instead, she shook her head. ''Never mind. The house feels…empty.''

''You just said someone was in here.''

''Forget it.'' Thoroughly embarrassed, she turned back to the main hall.

''Look, I don't know what's going on, but I think we ought to see if we can get some lights on. Do you know where the fuse box is?''

Gratefully, she nodded. ''There's one in the kitchen, inside the pantry.''

"Show me?"

He moved to within inches of where she stood. She'd known he was a big man, but having him this close made her feel small and fragile.

"Don't patronize me," she warned him.

"That wasn't my intention. Would you prefer I leave?"

"No! No," she said more calmly, drawing a deep breath. "I'm a little rattled. I don't understand what's going on here, either. Where is everyone? Mrs. Walsh? Kathy? Someone should be here. Someone *must* be here. The front door was unlocked."

"It was?" He appeared mildly surprised.

"Yes!"

He held up a palm. "Okay, take it easy. Are you always this defensive?"

"Only since—" Since she'd gotten the lawyer's letter, requesting that she come home to discuss a problem. Hayley could hardly say that to a total stranger. "Since I got here and found everything changed."

"I can see where that might be unnerving. I'm afraid I haven't spoken with anyone in a couple of days now. I've been staying in the old barn by the forge while I complete the work your father hired me to do. I'm afraid I don't know any of the people you just mentioned. I've only spoken with your parents since I got here."

"My father and his wife," she corrected. Then, not wanting to explain, and disconcerted from standing this close to him, she turned away. "The kitchen's back this way."

His light swept the hall ahead of them as she set off quickly. She wondered if he'd ever been inside the sprawling mansion before, and if he had, what he'd thought of the incredible rooms that stretched up to the huge skylights. Normally, moonlight would have made the interior clearly visible, but tonight clouds blocked the light and the house felt like some vast, empty cavern.

"Was your father expecting you?" Bram asked.

"I didn't call to tell him I was on my way home, if that's what you mean."

Bram didn't respond. If he was wondering about her relationship with Marcus, he didn't ask. In fact, now that she thought about it, she was a little surprised he hadn't demanded some sort of proof of her identity. She could have been lying. On the other hand, it wasn't his job to protect Heartskeep—except by covering all the openings with metal grillwork. She should be grateful for his presence, or at least for the presence of his flashlight. And she was—it was just that she was having a strange reaction to being this close to him.

The kitchen was a dark, silent shell. The light switch clicked uselessly. "The pantry is right over there," she told him, pointing to the closed door.

Funny. Growing up here she'd never viewed all this heavy, dark wood paneling as gloomy. The house had seemed a warm, comforting haven in her childhood. The feeling was gone now, just like her mother and grandfather.

Bram opened the pantry door and stepped inside. "Big place," was his only comment.

Hayley couldn't argue. The house was enormous. Rooms, closets—every aspect of the house was large. She watched as he studied the electric panel for a moment. Finally he flipped a large breaker. Nothing happened.

"Power lines must be down."

"That happens when it storms, but it's not storming tonight," she pointed out. "At least, not yet."

"No," he agreed, "but a car could have taken down a utility pole or something. Maybe that's why everyone is gone. Not exactly what you'd call a cozy place without lights. Have you got another place to stay for the night?"

Situated high above the Hudson River, northeast of Saratoga Springs, Heartskeep was a good distance from its closest neighbor and the small town of Stony Ridge. There were neighbors she could call, but Hayley hated the idea of imposing on people she hadn't seen in years.

"Not really, but it isn't as if I'll freeze or something without electricity. I can always light some candles."

"You plan to stay here alone? I'm not sure that's such a good idea."

Neither did she.

"What if someone else *is* in the house with you?"

"I prefer not to think about that." Fear crawled around in the pit of her stomach. He was right. she had a decent imagination, but she was pretty sure she hadn't imagined someone else standing out of sight inside the parlor.

"Have you eaten?"

Startled, she focused on Bram. "What?"

"I haven't eaten dinner yet and I have a steak big enough for two. You'd be welcome to join me."

"You cook?" She stalled, trying to picture herself sitting across a table from him, sharing a meal.

His eyes seemed to glitter. "Why don't you be the judge?"

"No power, remember?"

"I've got a hot forge."

"You cook at your forge?"

His teeth glinted as he smiled. A thrill shot through her. She had the distinct impression that smiles were a rare thing with this man. And the one that creased his face now was every bit as appealing as the man himself.

"I have a smaller tank of propane and a camp stove with me. Hungry?"

The pretzels she'd eaten on the drive from the Boston apartment she shared with her sister suddenly seemed less substantial than they had several hours ago.

"Yes, actually, I think I am. If you'll shine that light over there, I can supply the wine." His flashlight picked up the built-in wine rack. "I'm not much of a drinker, so I don't know much about wines," she confessed. "Do you want to choose something?"

He reached past her with one well-muscled arm. She found herself fascinated by the tattoo on his upper arm as he selected a bottle without hesitating.

"Is that a dragon?"

"Yes. Corkscrew?"

Hayley wondered if the question had bothered him. He didn't look upset, but then she knew absolutely nothing about the man calling himself Bram Myers. Nothing except the fact that she was strangely drawn to him. Even as she found a corkscrew and followed him back through the house, she wondered if she was making a serious mistake. He paused to scoop up the overnight bag she'd left inside the front door.

"Just in case," he told her.

"In case what?" she asked nervously.

"In case there really is someone running around in here."

"Oh."

They stepped outside and he waited while she forced her key into the stiff lock on the front door.

"At least he didn't change this lock," she muttered. "Do you think I should call the police?" How strange that she hadn't even thought of that until now.

"Up to you. It's your house, Ms. Thomas."

"Hayley."

He inclined his head. "Nice name."

"Thank you." She felt disconcerted once again.

"One problem with calling the police is that it will require more than a single officer to search a house this size. By the time a responding officer sends for enough backup to do a thorough job, anyone inside would have slipped away."

"True," she agreed, not certain the police would respond if she did call them. "But if someone is in here, they could do all sorts of damage, not to mention help themselves to any number of valuable items."

The adrenaline rush was fading fast and so was she. Following this man back under the dense canopy of trees no longer seemed like such a good idea.

"Suit yourself," he said. "You can stay here if you like, but I'm going back to have dinner."

She followed him off the porch onto the thick carpet of grass. Nervously, she cast a look over her shoulder. A movement caught her eye. She was almost certain a curtain had twitched in one of the parlor windows.

Chapter Two

''Do you still think you saw someone at the window before we left?'' Bram asked.

He watched Hayley's features tighten. She straightened up in his dilapidated old camp chair and faced him squarely.

''Yes.''

He'd assumed she'd been rattled by the dark, spooky house. Frankly, he was. Heartskeep wasn't a structure he'd want to call home.

''It's pretty dark. You probably saw light reflecting off the window.''

''What light?''

Good point. ''My flashlight?'' Her expression told him what she thought of that suggestion. ''You should have let me go back inside and check around.''

''No, you were right. The house is too big to search without lights. You could have been hurt.''

''Think so?'' Amusement warred with annoyance. Bram watched Hayley shrug as she lifted the paper cup to take another careful sip of wine. She glanced around the clearing nervously. With no moon visible tonight, the setting was perfectly designed to give any smart young woman a case of nerves. The only light came from his camp stove and the citronella candles he'd staked around them to ward off the hungry insect population.

Bram suspected those weren't the predators that worried Hayley. She was alone with a man she didn't know, surrounded by trees and the prying eyes of whatever four-legged creatures resided here. If she yelled for help, no one would hear. Only a fool would feel comfortable with the current situation, but he had to hand it to Hayley, she contained her fear well.

Bram felt a stirring of desire and tamped it down quickly. His reaction surprised him. She was undeniably attractive. Her fitted slacks and casual blouse revealed a trim, lithe, enticing figure. But Bram had worked at being immune to any woman's figure for some time now.

Maybe that was the problem, he thought wryly. Except that it wasn't her figure so much as something in those wide, doelike eyes that held him enthralled. For all her bold talk, Hayley had a disturbingly innocent sensuality.

She tossed back her head, and he followed the shimmery motion of each golden-brown strand as her hair settled around her shoulders and slid down her slim back. Oh, yeah, she was definitely sparking a reaction in him, yet there was no hint of the practiced tease. Just the opposite, in fact. She was tense and wary and trying not to let it show. He admired her guts, if not her intelligence. The problem was, he didn't want to be admiring anything at all.

''Feel better?'' The question came out more gruffly than he'd intended. Hayley didn't flinch at his abrupt tone. Her head tipped to one side.

''Actually, I do. Sorry I was such a glutton. I didn't realize I was so hungry until I started eating. Thank you.''

''You're welcome.'' His social skills might be rusty, but at least he still remembered his manners. ''You weren't a glutton. I'm glad to see you aren't one of those picky eaters.''

Hayley had polished off her share of the food and now she was working her way through a second cup of wine with slow, careful sips. She didn't seem to have noticed that his cup stood untouched.

"I know I should feel like a complete pig, but I don't care. Even if I have to work out an extra hour tomorrow morning, that meal was worth every bite."

An image of her bending and stretching in some body-hugging outfit was not something he wanted to picture at the moment. As Bram searched for a safer topic he felt the slow crawl of her eyes over his chest. They lingered just long enough to stir the unwanted heat simmering in his loins.

"You know, a look like that can get a woman in a lot of trouble," he told her softly. Her gaze flew to his face. He was pretty sure she blushed, but she wasn't the type to be easily intimidated.

"Sorry. I was looking for the cape and the suit with the big *S*."

"What?"

"You know. Blue tights, red cape, big red *S* on the chest?"

He nearly grinned as he caught her meaning. "Sorry, no superhero costumes in my wardrobe."

"Pity."

"But I'll be happy to go back up to the house with you and have a look around just the same."

She shook her head. He found himself captivated by the shimmer of her hair once more.

"I don't think so," she told him. "While that dragon on your arm looks suitably fierce, I doubt it shoots real flames in times of crisis. I'd hate to be the reason you discovered that tough hide of yours isn't bulletproof."

For the third time that night Bram found himself wanting

to grin. She had a way of catching him off guard with her droll sense of humor.

"What I should have done," she continued, unperturbed, "was to follow my instincts as soon as I saw your gate out front, and called the police."

"I didn't think my work was that bad, but, hey, don't let me stop you."

She gazed up at him from beneath her thick eyelashes. "I didn't mean it that way. Your art is beautiful and you know it. Besides, I left calling them a bit late, don't you think? I can just see his reaction now if Marcus came home and found the police searching the house again."

"Again?" Obviously, she and her father were not close.

She ignored the question. "Whoever was inside is probably gone by now."

"Then it should be perfectly safe for me to have a look around—even without the bulletproof hide."

"No, that's okay."

Bram couldn't have said why her abrupt dismissal annoyed him so much, but he had an irrational urge to reach over and touch her. He stood abruptly and reached for a bag to dispose of the trash.

Startled by his sudden movement, Hayley jumped. To cover her reaction, she unfolded herself from the low chair with a gracefulness few women could have managed. Her unease wasn't due exclusively to him, he realized as her gaze wandered past the circle of light to study the darkness that surrounded them.

"It's getting late," she told him. "I should go."

She handed him her paper plate and their fingers collided. Bram felt her touch all the way down to that part of him her presence had already roused to life.

Hayley went still. Her eyes widened as if she felt the charge as well. He took a small measure of satisfaction from the fact that she nearly dropped everything in her hurry to pull back from that casual contact. Her large blue eyes clearly registered consternation.

"Sorry. I'm not usually so clumsy."

Clearly nervous now, she pushed back a strand of hair that skimmed across her cheek. The action unintentionally invited him to take a closer look. Her skin was smooth and every bit as tempting as her fascinating hair. His fingers tightened on the plate to keep from reaching out to see how both would feel.

What the devil was he thinking? She was a kid. And a scared kid at that. Besides, the last thing he wanted was an entanglement of any kind. Hayley was the sort of woman with entanglement stamped all over her. If his libido wanted sex that badly, he could always find a casual partner. She didn't qualify.

"Have a seat and finish your wine," he ordered sharply. "I can handle the cleanup."

He glimpsed a flash of hurt in her eyes as she stepped back.

"I've had enough wine for the evening. I should go back to the house. I'm sure Marcus and his wife are home by now."

Bram took a firm grip on his self-control. He would not let her get to him on any level. "Not fond of the stepmother, huh?"

Her chin came up quickly. "Not that it's any of your business, but his marriage to Eden doesn't bother me one way or another."

Right. That was why her unpolished nails were biting into her palms and her very kissable lips were set in a thin, unhappy line. Well, tons of families were dysfunctional these days. Her problems weren't his. Time to back off before her nails drew blood.

"You're right. None of my business."

"I'm sorry. That was rude. Eden can be...difficult."

"I imagine it isn't easy having a stepmother."

"Oh, she's always been that way. She was Marcus's nurse for years."

"I didn't realize your father was ill."

"He's not. Marcus was a doctor. Eden worked for him."

Bram raised his eyebrows. "*Was* a doctor?"

"I don't think he's practicing medicine anymore. As you must have gathered, Marcus and I don't have much of a relationship. I'm not looking forward to this particular reunion. Marcus didn't know I was coming." She shrugged as if it didn't matter, but her fingers didn't relax.

Bram frowned. A lot of things were starting to bother him about this situation. "So you inherited Heartskeep from your mother?"

"My grandfather, actually. Our family has owned this land since the Civil War."

"Impressive, but I'm confused. If it belonged to your maternal grandfather, why is your father in charge?"

"He's not. He just thinks he is." She tossed her head, drawing his attention to her hair once more. "It's a long story."

"I don't have any pressing engagements tonight."

For a minute, he thought she'd clam up, and he found he really did want to know more about her. He told himself it was because his job might depend on it, but he knew that wasn't the only reason. When she shrugged lightly, he relaxed. She wasn't going to walk away quite yet.

"Family tradition has always passed the land to the firstborn child. My mother was an only child, but my grandfather didn't like Marcus. He bypassed tradition and named my mother's firstborn child as his primary heir."

"That would be you?"

"Yes. Since my sister and I were minors at the time, my grandfather wrote the will so that we wouldn't inherit until we were twenty-five."

"Isn't it usually twenty-one?"

"It's whatever the person wants to make it." She shrugged lightly. "My grandfather had a bad heart. He knew if something happened to him before we were old enough to stand up for ourselves, Marcus might create problems for us."

Again she shrugged. Despite his best intentions, Bram found himself watching the quick rise and fall of her breasts. When he realized she'd noticed, he turned his back and made a production of cleaning away the remains of their meal.

"How did you get interested in working with wrought iron?"

"My father and his brother were both blacksmiths. I used to hang around the forge a lot as a kid, watching them."

Since this was an uncomfortable reminder of his father's illness, Bram quickly changed the subject. "What do you do for a living, Hayley?"

"I'm working as an assistant art buyer for a gallery in Boston."

"Yeah?"

"What?" she demanded.

"What, what? All I said was, yeah."

"There is nothing wrong with being an assistant art buyer. I happen to have a degree in art from Wellesley College." She planted her fists on her hips.

"I never said there was."

She lifted her chin. "I also have an MBA."

"Impressive."

"You're laughing at me."

"Nope. But for someone with two degrees, I sense a little defensiveness about being an assistant art buyer."

Her shoulders slumped. "Marcus and Eden think I've wasted my education, but I'm learning the business. One day I plan to open my own gallery."

"Nothing wrong with that. Are you an artist as well?"

"No."

"That was an emphatic no. Did Marcus and Eden tell you that, too?"

Unexpectedly, she giggled. The strangely appealing sound filled the clearing.

"My art teachers did. They tried to be kind, but I'm utterly hopeless. Ms. Sang suggested the only canvas appropriate to my particular talents would be the outside of a building."

"Ouch."

Hayley grinned, unabashed. "She's right. I've got a great eye for color and design, and I can spot a marketable piece of art a hundred yards away, but they have trained monkeys with more ability to create art than me."

"That bad, huh?"

"Definitely. Did you design the front gate yourself?"

"Yes," he said warily.

"Now that's genuine, marketable art."

She made it a pronouncement of fact.

"Why do I feel I should be shuffling my feet and saying, 'aw, shucks, ma'am'?"

"Did I embarrass you?"

"Hardly. It's a just a gate." And a design he'd been working on for months.

"It's art," she said flatly.

"I seem to remember a threat to drive your car through some of that same art."

He couldn't tell for sure, but he thought she blushed again.

"I was annoyed."

"I remember. Look, I hate to change the subject here, but what are you planning to do tonight if your father isn't back yet?"

"I hadn't thought about it. Where are you staying?"

Desire tightened his body. ''Out here,'' he managed to say neutrally. ''You'd be welcome to join me, but I only have the one sleeping bag.''

Her eyes widened. Then, surprisingly, she smiled and shook her head, creating fascinating ripples in her long hair. ''Thanks, but I've got a nice comfortable bed inside the house.''

''With no electricity and a possible intruder for company,'' he pointed out. He wasn't sure if it was the idea of her going back inside that house alone, or the fact that she didn't seem to view him as a threat anymore that bothered him the most. He told himself it was the former. He definitely didn't like the idea of her sleeping alone in that enormous house, even if he did think she'd been imagining things.

''You don't need to worry,'' she said as if tapping into his thoughts. ''Someone must be home by now. Marcus goes to bed when the sun goes down. This is a late night for him.''

The ice in Hayley's tone every time she referred to her father never ceased to surprise Bram, making it hard for him to stem his curiosity.

''Your father might have gone away for a few days,'' he suggested. ''You said he wasn't expecting you.''

''Marcus seldom leaves Heartskeep and his precious roses. Not since—'' She stopped abruptly. ''Anyhow, you don't have to worry about me. I grew up in that house. I can always lock my bedroom door.''

Brave words, but Bram saw the tiny tremor she tried to conceal. She wasn't nearly as comfortable with the idea as she wanted him to believe. Despite his determination not to get involved, he wasn't about to let her do something stupid.

''I'll go with you,'' he stated.

Hayley stilled. He was mollified by her renewed apprehension. She was entirely too trusting for her own good.

"To the house," he added. "I'd feel better if I had a look around."

"That isn't necessary."

"Maybe not, but I don't see any letter *S* on your chest, either."

Stupid. He shouldn't have drawn attention to her chest again. Her nipples were clearly raised beneath the thin material of her blouse. He'd been trying not to think about that fact, because it certainly wasn't due to the eighty-something degree temperature out here. He darn well didn't want to think about what else might be causing the reaction.

"I appreciate your concern—" she began apprehensively.

"Hayley, if I was going to attack you, I would have done it a long time ago. I'm not into molesting young women."

Her chin raised a defiant notch. "Just older women, huh?"

"Yes," he said bluntly. "You don't qualify. Now, come on."

Acting avuncular went against the grain. His body was not feeling anything close to avuncular. Without waiting, he scooped up her overnight case and set off through the trees, cursing under his breath. What was he doing? Rescuing maidens in distress wasn't part of his job description. He was a loner and he liked it that way. Hayley had permanence stamped all over her.

As the trees parted and the house came into view, Bram was reminded of exactly why he was helping her. Heartskeep should have been an attractive old mansion. It wasn't. Not only was it in need of major repairs, but a brooding air of menace seemed to hover over the place like a cloud. He wasn't given to flights of fancy, but Heartskeep gave him the creeps.

HAYLEY HAD TO TROT to keep pace with Bram's much longer legs. The arrogant man didn't seem to notice or care. How could he be so nice one minute and such a jerk the next? Thank heavens he didn't know about the fantasy that had run through her mind during their quiet meal. Utterly ridiculous, of course, but she couldn't remember ever being more attracted to a man.

Or more annoyed by one.

Bram Myers was a dichotomy she couldn't ignore. He certainly didn't seem to be having any problem ignoring her—except for that one brief moment when their hands had touched. Hayley didn't want to think about that surge of physical awareness. She was used to men finding her attractive, but she'd never felt such a strong reciprocation. He wasn't even her type. She preferred preppy, outgoing blondes, not dark, brooding men.

Fortunately, as the house rose out of the darkness, her thoughts were pulled from the disturbing memory of her physical reaction to the man. She was relieved by his presence at her side as they drew closer. Bram might be a total stranger, but he offered her a much needed sense of security. Her gaze traveled to the window where she was sure she'd seen some sort of motion earlier. She didn't like this scared, sick feeling she had.

Unlocking the door, she stepped boldly into the main foyer and felt around for the light switch. To her intense relief, the electricity was back on. Like everything else in need of repair around here, the huge, dirty chandelier had several burned out bulbs, adding unwanted atmosphere in the enormous front hall.

Hayley called out once more. There was no response.

"You can't stay here," Bram said bluntly. His gaze swept past the grand piano in the far corner and the wide staircase rising to the second floor. The massive living room loomed ominously dark beyond the stairs.

While she wanted to agree with him, she stubbornly shook her head. "I won't be chased out of my own home. However, if you'd like a change of pace, you could spend the night here with me."

She wanted to bite her careless tongue. Bram stared at her in total silence. She knew exactly what he was thinking.

"I didn't mean *with* me," she corrected, practically stumbling over the words. "I meant in a bed. There are several empty rooms. You can have your pick. I thought you'd appreciate a change from a sleeping bag on the ground. You know, since you're worried about me staying here all alone."

Oh, Lord, she was rambling like a schoolgirl on her first date. If she had an ounce of brains she'd get back in her car and leave. What was she doing, inviting a total stranger to spend the night with her? Despite his kindness, and her undeniable attraction, she wasn't sure she even liked the man.

No, that wasn't true. She liked him just fine. Maybe too fine. As weird as it seemed, for some reason she felt safe with Bram. She couldn't say the same about staying in Heartskeep alone.

"Your father wouldn't approve," Bram said mildly.

Her hackles rose. "So what? I'm an adult, not a child. As I told you, *he* doesn't own this house. I do."

"Maybe so," Bram said softly, "but *he's* the one who hired me."

Hayley wavered. Should she stay or go? She glanced around uneasily. She could never remember a time when Heartskeep had been empty. If her mother or grandfather hadn't been home, Kathy or Mrs. Walsh had always been around. Why weren't they here now? The housekeeper and her daughter were practically members of the family. This cold emptiness was all wrong. If only Leigh was with her.

She should leave, only it would take twenty minutes to

drive to The Inn outside Stony Ridge. She was already exhausted from the drive down from Boston, and she'd had two cups of wine. Besides, what if The Inn was full? It often was. The Inn was the only accommodation close by.

Was she going to let a little imagination chase her away from home like a scared little kid? Surely someone would return any minute. She'd told Bram the truth. Marcus seldom left the estate these days, preferring to spend most of his time working with his roses.

The muffled ring of a telephone shattered the ominous quiet. Hayley gave a start and offered Bram a weak smile, relieved at the familiar sound. "Excuse me a minute."

She hurried across the marble foyer to the library. Flinging open one of the heavy wooden doors, she hit the wall switch, relieved when the lights not only worked, but the familiar room sprang into view, exactly as she remembered it. The rest of the house might feel cold and alien, but there were only warm memories in this room.

She lunged for the telephone, afraid whoever it was would hang up before the answering machine kicked in. Even as she picked up the receiver, she was aware that Bram had followed her inside. He lingered near the door, staring around the richly paneled room lined with books.

"Hello?"

On the other end, someone inhaled sharply. Then a voice barked in her ear, "Who is this?"

Hayley recognized Eden's nasal tone immediately. "This is Hayley, Eden."

"What are *you* doing there?"

"Gee, Eden, the last I knew this was *my home.*"

Eden had worked as her father's nurse since before Hayley was born. The woman had never been particularly friendly, but until Hayley's mother had disappeared, she'd never been outwardly antagonistic, either.

"Put Mrs. Norwhich on," Eden demanded.

"Who?"

"The new housekeeper."

"Where are Mrs. Walsh and Kathy?"

Eden sniffed. "They quit. Is Mrs. Norwhich there or not?"

"When did they quit? Where did they go?"

"I don't have time for this, Hayley. Put Mrs. Norwhich on."

Hayley held on to her temper. "As far as I know, I'm the only one here."

"Where's your sister?"

"Leigh's still in England."

Eden sniffed again. "I gather the power is back on?"

"Yes."

"Well, Marcus already went to bed. I'm not going to wake him. It was all I could do to convince him to stay at The Inn this evening as it was. There's no telling how long the power will remain on this time. The electric company is having some sort of problem with a transformer or something. I didn't pay attention to their excuses. We decided it would be best to come here, since The Inn has its own generators. I won't have to worry about having warm water or hot coffee come morning. This has been very annoying, I can tell you. Odette must have decided to stay in town overnight, as well."

"Who's Odette?"

"Mrs. Norwhich," Eden explained brusquely. "Your father and I will drive back after breakfast."

"Wait! Is there anyone else staying here at the house?"

"No. It's a nuisance, but until her lease is up, Mrs. Kerstairs only comes in to clean during the day. Of course, she hasn't been able to do much this week. You can't work without electricity."

Eyeing the dust on the tabletop, Hayley thought Mrs.

Kerstairs hadn't been doing much in far longer than a week, but she kept that thought to herself.

"Oh. There's also that man Marcus hired to put up the new gates. I don't remember his name, but he's camping out by the old barns."

"Yes. I've met Mr. Myers."

Eden sniffed again, this time in disapproval. "Well, if you don't want to stay there by yourself tonight, you'll need to drive out to the highway and find a motel. The Inn is completely booked. This annoying electrical problem has driven many of our neighbors from their homes. If Mrs. Norwhich returns, let her know we won't be needing breakfast. I'll tell your father you're back."

Eden disconnected.

"You just do that," Hayley muttered into the dead telephone. She cradled the receiver, drumming her fingers against the hard plastic. Thoroughly annoyed, she looked up and found Bram silently watching her from across the room.

She'd forgotten about him, hard as that was to believe. Leaning back against the door frame with his legs crossed at the ankles, he looked too sexy to contemplate. Her stomach muscles tightened as her breathing quickened. How could she have forgotten him even for a second?

"Is everything all right?" he asked.

"Marcus and Eden went to The Inn for the night because the electricity keeps cutting out."

He frowned, coming away from the doorjamb in a smooth motion that tripled her pulse rate. "Are you going to join them?"

Hayley couldn't help it. She shuddered. "No."

"I have a feeling I should be glad I'm not one of your father's patients."

Hayley managed a weak smile. "You'd have made medical history. He's an OB-GYN."

The smile started in his eyes before moving to his lips, but it was definitely a smile. A wicked, incredibly sexy smile that sent her pulses leaping.

"In that case, I'm definitely glad I wasn't one of his patients. Come back with me while I secure the rest of my camp for the night, then we can pick out a bedroom."

The invitation sounded deliberately provocative. Blood rushed to her cheeks. What would it be like to kiss him?

The question haunted Hayley as they walked back through the woods at a more sedate pace. Watching him check the forge and put away tools, she decided he did everything with a disconcerting deliberation. Would he make love the same way?

She had no business thinking like that. Her hormones had been acting up outrageously all night. If she wanted to wonder about Bram, she should concentrate on things like what had prompted him to have a dragon tattooed on his upper arm.

The question fascinated her—like the man himself. She wanted to know everything about him, but it had quickly become obvious over dinner that Bram didn't talk about himself. He'd managed to divert every question so that she was the one doing all the talking. She knew almost nothing about him beyond the fact that he was too sexy for comfort and could work absolute magic with cold metal and a little heat.

She watched him gather a few items and a change of clothing with economical movements, before leading the way back to the house with his powerful flashlight. As they reached the yard, Hayley came to an abrupt halt. The lights they'd left on were out once more.

"Another blackout?"

Bram studied the house. "Wait here while I check."

She followed closely on his heels instead of waiting. If he thought she was afraid, he was right. Imaginary or not, she couldn't shake off the sensation that something evil lurked nearby.

Bram flashed his light around the open foyer. Hayley found herself staring at the blackness guarding the top of the stairs. Unseen eyes seemed to peer down at them. When Bram touched her shoulder lightly, she started.

"Take it easy."

He followed her gaze, shining the light into that dark maw. Empty. But she felt no relief.

"Look, those two couches in the library looked pretty comfortable to me. Do you really want to go exploring right now? We could give the couches a try tonight."

Pride almost won out against common sense. She wanted to tell him she wasn't afraid to go upstairs. Unfortunately, he would see right through that lie when her knees buckled on the first step.

"At the risk of sounding like a child afraid of the dark, I think the couches sound like a terrific idea. There's a bathroom we can use down the hall past the library."

She didn't mention that there were two guest bedrooms beyond that bathroom. She could share a room with two couches, but she could hardly ask him to share a room with one bed.

"Mom always kept candles on the fireplace in the library," she told him. "We could even build a fire if you think we'll need more light."

"Let's skip the fire," he said lightly. "Given the fact that it must be at least eighty-five outside tonight, we don't want to lose what cool we have left in the house from your air-conditioning system."

Hayley nodded. With help from his flashlight, she took down several thick, squat candles and holders to set on the coffee table between the two couches. She even found a fat, dripless candle for the bathroom. Her grandmother's handmade afghans were inside one of the built-in cupboards, and while the temperature definitely didn't call for blankets, it was somehow comforting to snuggle beneath the familiar material in a house that felt all wrong.

Hayley knew she wouldn't sleep a wink. For one thing, she was entirely too aware of Bram's large frame sprawled directly across from her. He used the afghan as a pillow. Irrationally, she was disappointed that he found it so easy to be a perfect gentleman.

She studied his features after he closed his eyes and began to relax. In the flickering candlelight, the harsh planes of his face softened. He was actually a strikingly good-looking man. She'd never experienced such a strong physical pull before.

She closed her eyes and tried to relax. She'd put in a lot of overtime recently getting ready for a showing, which was one reason she hadn't gone to England with Leigh. The strain of that, plus the drive here and the past few hours had taken more of a toll than she'd realized. Once she allowed herself to relax, Bram's image slowly faded as exhaustion claimed her.

THE URGENT WHISPER of voices raised her slowly from the depths of a deep, dreamless sleep. The room was in total darkness. It took her a minute to figure out why that was wrong. The comforting sputter of the candles had been extinguished.

Hayley lay motionless. Had those whispers been part of some dream? She didn't hear anything now. It was several minutes before she realized the opposite couch was empty.

Bram was gone.

Tossing aside the afghan, Hayley sat up. Reaching out, she brushed a candle with her hand. Steadying it, she found the wax still warm and fluid. Bram must have just blown it out. Why would he do that?

Hayley heard the faint whispers resume. Someone was

in her grandfather's office, next to the library. She stood silently, straining to hear, but couldn't make out the words. She couldn't even tell if the whisperers were male or female. As quietly as possible, she groped her way to the office door. It had been closed when they'd lain down earlier.

The office was only slightly less dark than the rest of the house. Where was a nice bright moon when she needed one? The drapes on these windows were semisheer, and she might have been able to see something. The whispers stopped abruptly.

She was tempted to call out to Bram, but caution held her silent. Instinctively, she knew it would be better if the speakers didn't realize she was awake. If Bram had blown out the candles, he didn't want her to see who he was talking with. The sense of wrongness she'd felt earlier became a living weight in her chest.

Hayley stubbed her toe on the edge of her grandfather's massive desk. She bit her lip to keep from crying out.

Had they heard her?

She didn't breathe. The absolute silence was more unnerving than the whispers had been. The sense of danger became so acute she wanted to run. Her heart began pounding loudly enough to be audible out in the hall.

Someone knew she was in here.

Her hand sought the edge of the desk to use as a guide. When her fingers didn't find it, she told herself to stay calm. She knew this house. All she had to do was turn around and walk straight ahead. The opening to the library was right in front of her.

So was a large, dark shape.

Chapter Three

"What the devil are you doing wandering around in the dark like this?" Bram demanded as his powerful hands gripped her shoulders.

Relief gave way to a surge of adrenaline-fed fury. She punched his chest, shocked to feel firm, bare skin beneath her knuckles. Instantly, he released his hold.

"Stop sneaking up on me like that! That's twice you've done that to me. It isn't funny."

"I wasn't sneaking anywhere. I was looking for you. Why did you blow out the candles? This place is a tomb."

His description was a little too close for comfort. "*I* didn't blow out the candles! *You* did."

"No. I didn't."

"I suppose they blew themselves out," she scoffed. "Who were you talking to?"

She sensed his sudden caution. If only she could see his expression…

"I wasn't talking to anyone, Hayley. You must have been dreaming. I went down the hall to use the bathroom."

"Don't tell me that. I heard you!"

"I don't know what you thought you heard, but it wasn't me."

Goose bumps rose along her arms. Her teeth began to chatter because she realized she believed him.

"Then we aren't alone in here. I distinctly heard two people whispering together. And I didn't blow out the candles."

Bram muttered something that sounded like a curse. "Let's go. I need my flashlight."

"Why don't you have it with you?"

"Because it fell off the coffee table when I reached for it earlier, and I didn't want to wake you looking for it. I didn't figure I needed it just to go to the bathroom, but I didn't know we were going to be roaming around in the dark like this. Come on, you can help me find it."

Bram reached for her hand. His fingers closed over hers, making her intensely aware of his much larger, warmer hand. He seemed to have cat's eyes as he led her back inside the library without a single misstep. No wonder he hadn't needed the flashlight in the dark hall.

His touch was strangely reassuring. She was almost sorry when he released her again.

"I think it rolled under the table," he told her.

She dropped to the carpeting beside the table while he did the same on the other side. Her hands swept over empty air. A second later, she heard his sound of satisfaction.

"Got it."

A decidedly weaker beam bounced around the room, causing ominous shadows to sway against the walls.

"I don't suppose you have fresh batteries anywhere?" he asked.

"There might be some in the kitchen."

Bram set the flashlight on the table and relit the candles. "Wait here while I have a look around."

"No! There's someone else in here. What if they're armed?"

"I don't think that's likely."

His skeptical tone struck a nerve. "You don't believe me."

"I didn't say that."

"You're thinking it. I can tell from your tone."

"Hayley—"

"There were two voices," she said firmly. "You were one of them, weren't you? You must have been. Why are you lying to me? Who else is in here?"

"Calm down."

Furious, Hayley came around the couch to ram a finger against his chest. "Don't tell me to calm down! I want to know what's going on."

Bram lifted her hand from the rock-hard wall of his chest and reached for his shirt, which he'd draped across the back of the other couch.

"I don't know what's going on, but I intend to find out."

He didn't raise his voice, but there was a reassuring core of steel in his tone. She watched him slip the shirt over his head.

"I'd offer to leave," he said quietly, "but I can't walk away under the circumstances."

"I did hear voices," she insisted.

Bram scraped a hand over the dark stubble on his jaw. "Hayley, have you ever had a dream where you knew you were dreaming, but couldn't wake up? Then, when you did, the dream stayed with you like a fog, making you feel disoriented?"

"I was not dreaming!" She couldn't have been. "If I was dreaming, how do you explain the candles going out? Do you think I blew them out in my dreams?"

Bram regarded her solemnly. "They were lit when I went down the hall. When I came out of the bathroom, I had to keep my hand on the wall to find my way back here. I heard you moving in the other room so I went to investigate."

Hayley shivered. He sounded so sincere. *Could* she have dreamed the whispers?

A muffled sound from the hall stopped his words and her heart. Bram spun around. In a flow of motion almost too fast to follow, he glided into the foyer. The sounds of a struggle came almost immediately. Hayley snatched up the flashlight and tore after him. The weak beam trapped two figures locked together near the front door.

"Jacob?"

Bram had the younger man pinned against the wall. The dragon on Bram's arm looked ready to breathe fire as it pressed against Jacob's throat, holding him in place.

"You know him, Hayley?" Bram demanded softly.

"That's Eden's son, Jacob. Let him go, Bram."

Bram gave the man a hard stare before stepping back. He looked perfectly ready to resume his attack at the least provocation. Jacob rubbed his throat, swallowing hard.

"Hayley?" he croaked, peering into the light.

She lowered the beam so it wasn't shining directly in his eyes.

"What's going on? Who *is* this guy?"

"Jacob Voxx, meet Bram Myers. Marcus hired him."

"As what? An attack dog?" He gave Bram a resentful glare.

"Bram's been creating and installing the wrought iron around the house."

"Yeah? I noticed the gate. What was wrong with the lions?"

Hayley darted an I-told-you-so look in Bram's direction, but his attention remained focused on Jacob. Bram reminded her of some large, fierce predator ready to spring. It was all too easy to envision Jacob as his rabbit of choice.

"Why were you sneaking in here at this hour of the morning?" Bram demanded softly.

"I live here. Or at least, my mother does." Jacob appealed to Hayley. "What's going on? Where is everyone? What happened to the lights?"

Quickly, Hayley explained.

"You weren't expected," Bram said.

"Uh, no. I wanted to surprise everyone." Jacob looked from Bram to Hayley. "Surprise?"

"Oh, Jacob, I'm sorry. It's just that we've had a scare. I think someone is hiding in the house."

"You're kidding!"

It annoyed her when he looked to Bram for confirmation.

"Hayley heard voices," Bram said neutrally.

"Did you call the cops?"

"No," Hayley told him.

"Big place to search in the dark," Bram added, rocking back on his heels. His gaze never left the younger man.

"Well, yeah, but the cops have powerful flashlights. I mean, if someone's in here, we ought to call them, right?"

"Up to Hayley," Bram told him.

Thoroughly annoyed, she glared at both of them. "There isn't much point calling *them* for help. You know that, Jacob."

"Uh, look, Hayley, I know you don't like the local cops, but if someone's in here, we should do something."

She sensed Bram's interest, but she wasn't about to start explaining her relationship with the local police right now.

"We are going to do something. We're going back to the library and to wait for the power to come back on or daylight, whichever comes first," Hayley said firmly. "With all this commotion, any sane burglar is long gone by now."

Jacob looked at Bram, who shrugged. "You heard the lady."

Hayley wanted to stamp her foot in frustration. Instead, she pivoted and returned to the library. Plopping down on the couch, she fumed until Bram came in and sank down beside her, so close their legs brushed. His action was as deliberately challenging as the look he directed at Jacob.

Jacob stared from one to the other. ''Uh, do you two know each other?''

''Not really.''

''Yes,'' Bram said firmly at the same time. ''We were spending a quiet evening together when all hell broke loose.''

''Oh.'' Jacob seemed to have no idea what do to with the conflicting information. ''Where, uh, where's your sister?''

Hayley tried to shift positions but found herself sandwiched between the arm of the couch and Bram's hard body. ''Leigh's in England visiting friends,'' she managed to reply. And if her voice sounded breathless, neither man seemed to notice.

''Oh, yeah. I remember Mom mentioning something about that. A final fling before she starts her new job, right?'' Jacob sank down on the couch across from them and yawned. He looked tired and at the same time unconcerned. ''Lucky her. Say, have you met Mom's newest staff yet?''

''No.'' Hayley tried to nudge Bram. He didn't budge a millimeter. Obviously, he wasn't nearly as pliable as the rigid metal he worked with. ''Jacob, what happened to Mrs. Walsh and Kathy?''

''Beats me. They've been gone for a long time now. I thought you knew.''

''Not until a couple of hours ago, when I spoke with your mother on the phone. She said they had a better offer.''

Jacob's shoulders rose and fell. ''Mom said they quit when you and Leigh stopped coming home. She's had trouble finding live-in help ever since. I think this is the fifth or sixth housekeeper she's hired. Mrs. Norwhich is sort of built like Bram, here. A little older, and she lacks the tattoo, but she's a force to be reckoned with. Sort of weird, but nothing compared with the new maid. Wait'll you meet *her*.

Say, maybe it was Mrs. Norwhich and Paula Kerstairs you heard.''

Hayley shook her head. ''I don't think so. Your mother thought Mrs. Norwhich was staying in town tonight. Besides, wouldn't she have woken me if she came home and found a stranger sleeping on the couch?''

''You'd think so.''

''Maybe she tried,'' Bram offered. ''You're a pretty sound sleeper, you know. You didn't even stir when I got up.''

Bram's words and tone implied an intimacy that made her squirm. He made it sound as if they'd been sharing a couch. Before she could correct that impression, Jacob yawned hugely.

''Sorry. I've been sitting on the Jersey Turnpike for hours thanks to a multicar accident. I think I'm too tired to worry about prowlers or weirdo housekeepers tonight. As far as I'm concerned, they can do whatever they want as long as they let me sleep. Would you mind if I go upstairs and sack out?''

''Take the couch,'' Bram said firmly. ''Hayley would prefer us to stay together.''

''But there're only two couches in here.''

''That's all right. Hayley and I don't mind sharing. Right, Hayley?''

A protest leaped to her lips, but a warning in Bram's expression made her hesitate. She did want them to stay together. Jacob shouldn't go off on his own until they knew what was happening around here. The men might not believe her, but she knew someone else was inside the house.

''Go ahead and take the couch, Jacob. I'm not tired anymore, and Bram's going to sit here and tell me all the fascinating details of his life, including how he got that tattoo. Right, Bram?'' she asked with mock sweetness.

Bram settled back. He had to hand it to Hayley, the

woman had a knack for turning the tables. Too bad for her that he'd had years more experience at it than she had.

"I wouldn't bore anyone with my life story, but I'm sure we can find something more interesting to talk about," he said suggestively. "We can start with all the things we have in common. Don't worry, Jacob. We'll keep our voices down."

"Uh, sure. Okay." But he stared at them, obviously perplexed by the exchange.

Bram was relieved when Hayley settled for glaring at him as Jacob stretched out on the couch self-consciously. The man's arrival seemed entirely too well timed to be a coincidence. If Hayley really had heard people inside the house, Bram suspected Jacob had been one of them.

"If, uh, anything else happens, just wake me," Jacob told him.

"Count on it."

Hayley shifted restlessly. Bram ignored her none-too-subtle hint to move over. He was enjoying the feel of her body pressed against his more than he should. And if there was another incident tonight, he wanted to make sure the only way to reach her was to go through him first.

"Tell me more about the place you work," he encouraged.

"I'd rather hear about you."

"I'm flattered."

"Don't be. I'm making conversation here. Where did you get the dragon tattoo?"

"Thinking of getting one yourself?"

"You're being deliberately impossible."

"Years of practice," he agreed.

"Is it some big secret? Some gang tattoo or something?"

"Interesting opinion you have of me." But the set of her jaw told him she intended to be stubborn on this issue. "If you must know, I woke up after drinking all night and there it was.''

He knew his words sounded clipped, but he hated thinking about that period of his life. Not that he could remember much of it, including how and where he'd gotten the tattoo, much less why. He'd been drinking heavily in those days.

''Oh.''

She traced a finger over one dragon wing. Her touch was featherlight, yet it activated every nerve cell in his body. Desperately, he tried to think of a safe topic, but looking into those wide, innocent eyes seemed to be robbing him of coherency. He should not be noticing how soft and kissable her lips looked.

''You, uh, said your father and uncle were both blacksmiths. Is that how you got your start?'' she asked, fidgeting.

That wouldn't have been his conversational choice, either, but if it helped divert his current thoughts, he was all for a discussion of his work.

''Yes. My uncle used to work with real iron, like they did back before car manufacturers discovered they needed a metal with a more uniform strength.''

He droned on in his best lecture mode, conjuring up nearly forgotten facts on the subject that he remembered from his youth. As a boy he'd watched his father and uncle work the forge for hours, absorbing their tales.

Hayley surprised him by actually listening. Even after she closed her eyes and her head began to nod, she'd throw out a sleepy question to indicate she was paying attention. He was running out of things to say when he realized her breathing had slowed and deepened. Her head slumped against his shoulder.

Unable to resist, he stroked the fall of hair running over his chest. He'd been right, it was as soft as a river of raw silk. Inhaling the light scent of her shampoo, he was pleased to note she didn't favor heavy perfumes. There were far too many things he liked about Hayley.

Jacob snored lightly across from them. Reaching for the afghan, Bram spread it over Hayley and surrendered to the urge to make her more comfortable. He snugged her tightly to his side.

Instead of waking, she nestled against him as if she'd been doing it all her life. Her head fit almost perfectly in the crook of his arm, while her long hair drifted whisper soft against his bare skin.

Something inside Bram tightened—not just with desire, but with a remembered longing. He'd forgotten how good it could be to simply hold a woman like this. While he didn't welcome this protective feeling swelling inside him, he didn't know how to turn it off, either. But he couldn't afford to get involved here. That road led to a pain he had no desire to repeat.

Hayley stirred without waking. Carefully, Bram slid his arm around her, leaning his cheek against the top of her head. She was young. He had to keep reminding himself that he was too old and too jaded for the sort of thoughts he was trying not to have about her.

His father had told him that he'd never really be free until he faced the ghosts that haunted his soul. Funny, he couldn't help thinking that perhaps the time had finally come.

DUST MOTES DANCED amid the sunlit rays filling the room when Hayley woke. She lay on the couch, covered in the familiar afghan. The house no longer felt empty—but the library was.

Where was Bram? Had she really fallen asleep in his arms? She'd felt his lips brushing hers as he'd stretched her out on the couch. Memory? Or a dream-induced fantasy?

Glancing around, she realized her overnight case was no longer on the floor nearby. Jacob must have seen it and carried it upstairs for her. Bram wouldn't even know where her room was.

The thought of him seeing her bedroom was unsettling. She folded and replaced the afghans before stepping into the main hall.

The first thing she noticed was the door to the former parlor still standing open. She needed to use the bathroom, yet she was drawn across the hall by something she couldn't explain. Even in daylight, the room's atmosphere was depressing.

"Looking for something?"

Bram's voice sent her spinning around. Her heart gave a leap at the sight of him. Last night, shadows had dimmed his features, but this morning there was nothing to soften the impact of that firm jaw and those dark brown eyes that seemed capable of reading her innermost thoughts.

He was powerful rather than handsome. Now that she was feeling more objective, it was easy to see why Jacob had looked to him for guidance. There was an aura of leashed power, a sense of confidence, that made Bram a natural leader.

He'd changed into clean jeans and a fresh T-shirt and had even shaved. He looked younger than he had last night, despite the tiny lines at the corners of his mouth and eyes. His hair was freshly combed and still damp, the ends curling, darkly wet against his neck. He must have just come from a shower. He looked perfectly at home and incredibly sexy.

Abruptly, she realized several seconds had passed. Flustered to be caught staring at him, she gestured at the room in general. "I, uh, wanted to see this room in the light."

She stepped forward briskly, though it was the last place she wanted to be.

A row of formal chairs gathered dust beneath the drape-shrouded windows that lined the outside wall. The Danish-modern receptionist's desk looked ridiculously out of place in the formal room, but it did serve to restrict access to the heavy double doors that had once led to the old ballroom and now opened onto Marcus's exam rooms. She had sensed the unseen watcher standing there last night.

''Hitchcock would have loved this place,'' Bram muttered at her back.

Hayley couldn't argue. Even in daylight there was a disturbing wrongness about the room. Moving around the desk, she reached for the door handle. Locked, just as Bram had told her last night. Hayley felt inexplicably cold.

''What are you doing?'' he asked.

''I'm not sure. Searching for proof that I wasn't imagining things last night?''

Bram touched her shoulder, causing her heart to flutter foolishly. ''Do you think you *were* imagining things?''

''No.''

He nodded without expression. What was he thinking? That she was a foolish, emotional young woman?

''I carried your bag upstairs for you.''

''*You* did?''

''Mrs. Norwhich told me which room was yours.''

He'd seen her bedroom, still decorated with posters from her high school days. ''You've met Mrs. Norwhich then?'' she asked, to keep from wondering what he'd thought about her room.

''Uh-huh. She came in around six this morning. Didn't seem at all bothered or surprised to find unexpected company in the house. She told me to help myself to a shower, and offered to fix me some breakfast.''

"How did she know which room was mine? I've never even met the woman."

"Beats me. I put them in the third bedroom down, on the right-hand side."

"That's my room," she acknowledged. "Where's Jacob?"

"He went out—after suggesting to Mrs. Norwhich that she should count the silver." His lips curved faintly. "I don't think your friend Jacob likes me very much."

"You didn't exactly make a good first impression," Hayley pointed out. She tucked several strands of wayward hair behind her ears. "I'd better go up and grab a shower, too."

"I put fresh linens in your room," said a dour voice from the doorway.

Hayley spun to gape at a tall, middle-aged woman dressed in a flower-print shirt and baggy slacks. The clothes hung limply on her bony frame. Her stringy blond-and-silver hair was piled in an untidy mat on top of her head. Bony fingers pushed at the wispy strands trying to escape. Her long, seamed face was pinched and sallow and set in a permanent frown. She held a duster in one hand. A pail of cleaning supplies sat at her feet.

"No one's supposed to be in here. That's what they told me. Don't go in the front parlor, they said."

Once again Hayley was reminded of an old horror film. Didn't those housekeepers always appear out of nowhere? "Mrs. Norwhich?" she asked tentatively.

Beady eyes hardened. "*She's* in the kitchen." The woman turned and glided silently down the hall, her back stiffly erect.

"Now I know why Jacob said to wait until we met the maid," Bram whispered near her ear.

"She moves like a ghost."

"Sort of looks like one, too," he agreed. "Very skeletal. Want me to walk you upstairs?"

"I remember the way."

He was suddenly standing much too close. She felt totally unprepared for the emotions he seemed to evoke in her.

"Then I'd better get back to work," he told her.

His soft, deep voice slid over her, sending all sorts of inappropriate impulses to her nerve endings.

"Thank you. For last night, I mean."

He lowered his head. Her heart thudded crazily in anticipation. He was going to kiss her.

With one knuckle, he gently raised her chin. His gaze held her captive more surely than any shackles.

"My pleasure."

While her lips readied for his, Bram brushed a kiss over the tip of her nose, released her and strode to the front door without looking back.

Hayley could barely climb the stairs to her bedroom. Her legs were weak and her heart was racing as if she'd been running a marathon. For crying out loud. If she reacted like this to a peck on the nose, what would she do if he really kissed her?

Her imagination went to work on that as she showered.

The electricity might be back, but the hot water tank had little to offer. Since a cold shower seemed totally appropriate, she washed quickly and changed into a pair of shorts and a sleeveless top. Although it was still morning, the heat and humidity were already challenging the air-conditioning system.

As she pulled her hair into a ponytail, Hayley couldn't stop thinking about Bram. Trite or not, the fact was he was like no one she had ever met before. He fascinated her on every level. She wanted to understand the man hiding beneath that rigid exterior. A man who seemed as hard as the steel rods from which he forged such beauty.

In the kitchen, Hayley discovered Jacob's description of Mrs. Norwhich hadn't gone far enough. Odette Norwhich was a large, unyielding woman of few words who managed to convey disdain in each syllable, particularly when Hayley bypassed a real breakfast in favor of coffee and toast.

Eden arrived as Hayley was heading for the dishwasher with her cup and plate. Eden didn't bother with pleasantries.

"Good. We have power. We need to install a generator of our own. This situation is intolerable. We'll be wanting dinner at seven, Mrs. Norwhich. Did Paula arrive?"

"Mrs. Kerstairs is making up the bedrooms."

"I want that front room done this morning. How long do you plan to stay, Hayley?"

Hayley forced a pleasant expression. Turning from the dishwasher, where she'd put her cup and plate while Mrs. Norwhich watched with a scowl, she tried for a calm tone. "Permanently, Eden. Where is Marcus?"

Hard as it was to believe that Eden's sour expression could get any worse, it did. Her lips pursed so tightly they disappeared.

"In the garden," she finally spat out. "But don't be surprised by anything he may say."

"What do you mean?"

"He's been diagnosed with the early stages of dementia."

"What?"

Eden pivoted and strode regally from the room, leaving Hayley staring after her. Mrs. Norwhich grunted and repositioned Hayley's cup inside the dishwasher. Crossing to the walk-in pantry, Hayley grabbed a bottle of water from the stash Marcus always kept there. She'd developed the habit of carrying water with her everywhere she went.

Sadly, it was the only thing she and Marcus had ever shared in common.

"Cold ones are in the refrigerator," Mrs. Norwhich said disapprovingly.

"Thank you."

"Don't know what's wrong with the water coming out of the tap," the woman muttered. "Perfectly good water, if you ask me. If it's good enough to cook with, it ought to be good enough to drink."

Exchanging the bottle for a cold one, Hayley ignored her comments and bypassed the kitchen table as she crossed to the side door, intent on the far path that would take her into the vast gardens.

Leave it to Eden to drop a bombshell and walk away. How could Marcus be in the early stages of dementia? He was only in his sixties. Hayley had a ton of questions, but she knew she wouldn't get any answers from Eden without a struggle. She'd have to see for herself what the situation was. She should have waited for Leigh to get back before coming here.

Dementia would explain Marcus's sudden need for bars on the windows and doors. But why hadn't anyone thought to inform her of the situation?

She was stewing over that as she headed toward the entrance to maze three. Her mother and grandfather had worked so hard to establish three distinct mazes filled with cheerful flower gardens and topiary plants. The hedges had always been kept neatly cropped at waist height, but Marcus had let them grow until they concealed an average-size person now. Walking through the overgrown mazes could prove to be a real challenge, since the topiary figures were mostly unrecognizable from lack of pruning.

In the past, the gardens had always brought a sense of peace. Leigh had sworn she could feel their mother's presence here. But today, the garden brought Hayley no solace whatsoever. Her grandfather's death had been bad enough, but her mother's strange disappearance was something Hayley doubted she would ever get over. There could be no closure in her life until she learned what had really happened to Amy Thomas.

Hayley didn't notice the puddle that had oozed across the twisty path until she stepped right into it. She shook her wet sneaker, annoyed that she hadn't been paying attention. Obviously, the underground sprinkler system had been at work this morning. Now that she was paying attention, she saw that droplets of water clung to every leaf and petal, soaking the ground beneath the plants.

The system was just another reminder of her mother. It had been installed the day Amy Thomas had disappeared—the last gift she had given her precious garden. It angered Hayley that Marcus had let the whole place become so overgrown. Everything was a mess except the roses. Flower beds that didn't contain roses were in desperate need of weeding. Vines had begun to cover some of the benches sitting inside the neglected circles.

Marcus's sudden devotion to his wife's roses might have been mistaken for dedication to her memory in another person, but not with Marcus. His unusual interest in them right after their mother's disappearance had rung alarm bells for Hayley and Leigh. The timing was definitely suspicious.

Maybe because she was older now, Hayley suddenly wondered if Marcus had always wanted to tend to them, but had felt unwelcome in the garden when her mother and grandfather had been alive.

It was an odd thought. Her parents had never shared anything that Hayley could recall. She and Leigh had often wondered why the two of them had stayed married. They'd lived very separate lives, sharing only the house and a few social functions.

Her mother's religion didn't condone divorce, but Amy

and Marcus hadn't been married in the church. Hayley suspected her mother's decision to remain married was due more to the fact that she never broke her word once she'd given it. While she must have regretted her decision to marry Marcus, her mother had honored the contract she'd entered into with her husband.

Hayley actually knew very little about the man responsible for her birth. He'd played such a minor role in her life. It was Dennison Hart who had showered the twins with kindness, guidance and love.

Was it possible Marcus had felt crowded out there, too?

Hayley tried to banish the disturbing thought. Marcus had never seemed the least bit interested in them. Try as she might, it was impossible to picture him in the role of some tragically misunderstood figure.

Dennison Hart's death had come a few months before their mother's disappearance. If he'd still been alive, he would have never stopped looking for her—unlike Marcus. Despite his heart condition, their grandfather had seemed invincible—until the morning he simply hadn't woken up.

The low murmur of a man's voice snapped Hayley from her thoughts. Rounding a curve in the path, she came to a dead stop. Marcus was on his knees pruning a bush covered with brilliant red roses. There was no one else in sight.

"Your roses are doing well, Amy. Not a sign of black spot anywhere. You should be pleased."

He stroked a gloved hand over the dirt almost fondly. Hayley darted out of sight. She swallowed hard, trembling all over. Could she and Leigh have been wrong about him all these years? Could Marcus actually be pining for their mother, or was this behavior related to the dementia Eden had mentioned?

Hayley felt badly shaken. This Marcus barely resembled the forbidding man she'd always known. He'd lost a great deal of weight and his thinning hair had become more white than brown. He actually looked more frail kneeling there in the dirt.

His appearance and his words had shaken her resolve to confront him. Hayley took a side path she was pretty sure would lead her back to the house and the stone fountain that had been installed along with the sprinkler system.

Seven years ago, Hayley and Leigh had been so certain Marcus had killed their mother that they'd convinced the local police chief to dig up the newly poured fountain to search for her body. Marcus had watched the proceedings in stony silence. When the police came up empty, Marcus had ordered the landscaper to repour the fountain, and had walked away. He'd barely spoken a civil word to his daughters after that day.

"I'd offer you a penny for your thoughts, but based on your expression I'm not sure I want to hear them."

Startled from her musings, Hayley watched Bram saunter toward her.

"Something wrong, Hayley?"

A flutter of physical awareness pushed aside her bitter thoughts. His hair was mussed, his muscular arms once more naked. Sweat stained his dark T-shirt, and dirt once more smudged a pair of indecently tight jeans. A knot of unwanted need tightened inside her.

"Save your penny," she advised him. "What are you doing out here?"

"I was getting ready to hang a window grill when I saw you walking in this direction."

"Oh." Nervously, she lifted her bottle of water and took a quick gulp. His dark eyes followed the move with an intensity that left her shaken.

"Hot out," he said.

Hayley nodded, suddenly tongue-tied. He was commenting on the weather, not the slow simmer her insides were doing.

"Willing to share?"

She told her heart to stop hammering and her brain to stop jumping to conclusions. He was thirsty. The day was hot and humid. Especially for someone who spent his time over a glowing forge.

"I've been drinking from this bottle."

"I'm thirsty enough to risk a few germs."

There was nothing sensual in his tone, yet pulses of desire accompanied each beat of her heart. She thrust the bottle toward him. Their fingers touched, zapping her with tingles of electricity.

"Thanks." Bram fit his mouth over the bottle's opening and drank deeply, taking his time. Hayley couldn't tear her gaze away as he swallowed, then ran a knuckle across his lips to catch the drops of moisture lingering there.

His eyes darkened to pools of rich, dark chocolate. "You shouldn't look at a man like that," he said softly.

Breathing became a chore. "Like what?"

"You know what I'm talking about. I'm too old to be teased, Hayley."

The rebuke stung, partially because she deserved it. Her thoughts had been inappropriate, but he couldn't know that.

"That's quite an ego you carry around."

"Think so?" He thrust the bottle toward her.

"What do you think you're doing?" an all-too-familiar voice growled from behind them.

Chapter Four

The open bottle fell to the ground, splashing water against their legs. Bram stepped in front of Hayley. The protectiveness he'd felt last night returned in force at the sound of his employer's angry voice.

"I'm not paying you to loiter in the garden."

"Mr. Thomas," he acknowledged, forcing a calm belied by every quivering muscle in his body.

Hayley tried to shove him aside. When she couldn't, she stepped around him. "I offered him some water," she greeted her father. "It's hot out here."

"I'm paying him to work, not stand around," Marcus snarled.

"His work is finished. I don't want bars on the doors and windows of Heartskeep."

Bram tensed, ready to come between them once again. Hayley met her father's fierce gaze without flinching, but the enmity between them was palpable. They seemed to have forgotten his presence.

"I'm not interested in what you want," Marcus snapped.

"You never have been, but that doesn't matter anymore. Heartskeep doesn't belong to you. It belongs to me."

Marcus took an angry step forward. Bram blocked his path. For a moment, he thought Marcus would strike him as they stood eye-to-eye. Youth as well as strength from working at the forge gave Bram an edge Marcus couldn't hope to match. The older man must have realized this, because the fist at his side slowly unfolded. That didn't diminish his vibrating fury, however. He transferred his glare to his daughter.

"You don't inherit anything until you turn twenty-five, next year."

"True. But you stopped being my legal guardian when I turned eighteen. Grandpa's lawyer is the trustee of the estate. He'll respect my wishes."

"We'll see about that."

"Yes. We will," she said firmly.

Marcus scowled at Bram. "Screw her on your own time. We have a contract. Get back to work."

Hayley grabbed Bram's arm. Only then did he realize his own hand had fisted. Marcus took a hasty step back, obviously realizing he'd gone too far.

Mustering his dignity, the older man whirled and strode back to the house without another word.

Bram forced his muscles to relax. "He's your *father?*"

"Hard to believe, isn't it?" Hayley released him, visibly trembling. "I'm sorry you got caught in the crossfire. Marcus may be my biological father, but the paternal role stopped there."

Remembering the close bond he shared with his own father, Bram frowned. "That's too bad."

"No, it isn't. In case you hadn't noticed, Marcus isn't a nice person. Certainly not someone I'm anxious to claim a relationship with."

Bram couldn't think of anything to say to that. He couldn't bring himself to like the man, either, but it bothered him to see such outright hostility.

"Don't waste your sympathy on me. My sister and I didn't suffer from deprivation. My grandfather filled the paternal shoes with all the love anyone could ask for."

For a second, her eyes misted. Then she sighed and looked Bram in the eye.

"I'm honestly sorry, but I have to ask you to stop working on the house now. The estate will pay you for the work you've already done."

He'd seen it coming after what she'd said last night, but at her words, tension coiled in the pit of his stomach, anyhow. "I can't do that."

"Of course you can."

"My contract is with your father."

Determination tightened her features. "It isn't a valid contract. Marcus had no right to hire you. I'm sorry, but you're fired."

Silently, Bram cursed. Based on what he'd just heard and seen, he had no doubt that Heartskeep belonged to her, but he couldn't afford to be fired. He needed this job.

"You can't fire me, Hayley. You didn't hire me."

"This is my home!"

Inwardly, he sighed. He didn't want to be placed in this position, but their conversation could have only one conclusion. "Sorry. I'm a blacksmith, not a lawyer. I was hired to do a job. I've invested a great deal of time and money in this project."

"I told you, you'll be paid for the work you've done, but Heartskeep belongs to me. Marcus has no right to deface my home."

"Deface?" Bram repeated, affronted. He suspected she never noticed his quiet question because Hayley's eyes glittered with the fervor of battle. Even his rising annoyance wasn't enough to keep him from admiring the fire and passion in her. She was older than he'd first thought, but not old enough for him to give in to temptation and try to channel that energy in a more interesting way.

"Do you want to see the letter from my mother's lawyer?" she demanded.

Regretfully, Bram shook his head. "That won't nullify the contract I signed with your father."

"What will?"

He didn't want to fight with her. "Hayley—"

"If you want a legal injunction to stop and desist, I'll get you one."

She whirled around, setting off for the house at just short of a jog. Sunlight bathed her light brown hair, turning it to spun gold.

Bram swore. In the end, Hayley would win. He didn't have the time or money to fight her on this. His father's medical bills were growing right along with his cancer. If Heartskeep was only going to pay Bram for the work he'd already done, he'd just have to work harder and faster to earn as much as possible before the job ended.

Unless he could find a way to convince Hayley to let him finish.

HAYLEY SWIPED AT TEARS of anger and frustration. Darn that sexy, infuriating man. Why did he have to be so stubborn? This was just a job for him. Heartskeep was her family's heritage.

The desire to sit down and bawl was as powerful as it was strange. She never cried, but he made her so mad.

What if Bram called her bluff? She had no idea if the lawyer really would back her wishes or not. In fact, she had no idea what her legal status concerning Heartskeep actually was, beyond being the ultimate heir to the house and grounds.

Another tear escaped and she wiped it away, as well. What was wrong with her? Ever since she'd arrived at Heartskeep, she'd felt emotionally out of control—totally unlike her usual self.

Was she coming down with something?

That was all she needed. She had to be strong and alert to deal with Marcus and Eden—not to mention Bram.

Darn it, she didn't care how attractive he was. Or how protective and kind he'd been last night. She wouldn't think about that. Her brain must have fried in the broiling sun. She wasn't the emotional type. Yesterday may have been an unusually stressful day, but she was used to stress. Why did she feel so weepy and weary?

Thankful to find an empty kitchen, Hayley stepped inside, grateful for the air conditioning. Her mouth was so dry her tongue felt thick. She headed straight for the refrigerator and stood there until she'd gulped down the entire contents of a bottle of chilled water.

There was no sound in the house. She didn't know where Mrs. Norwhich or Paula Kerstairs were, and she didn't care, but she wished Mrs. Walsh was here. Hayley could have talked to her. She desperately needed someone to talk with. The complete absence of noise in the house seemed strange, but not as threatening as it had been last night.

The water quenched her thirst, but a growing lethargy was making it hard to keep her eyes open. Ridiculous. She'd just gotten up. But she hadn't slept much last night. Maybe that was why she was feeling so emotional.

Hayley helped herself to another bottle of water and decided there was no point battling this fatigue. She'd lie down, at least for a few minutes. Then she'd find the lawyer's name and see what needed to be done. Perhaps Marcus's illness and Bram's presence were the reasons the lawyer had been trying to reach her in the first place.

She practically stumbled over her own feet climbing the back stairs. She and Leigh had seldom gone upstairs this way. The steps were narrow and they led to a landing close to Marcus's room. But Hayley didn't have the energy to walk all the way around to the main staircase at the moment. She'd have to risk another verbal battle with Marcus.

While he might look older and more frail now, his nasty disposition hadn't altered any. Fortunately, his bedroom door was closed. If he was inside, he wasn't making any noise.

As soon as she reached her room, Hayley sank down on the familiar blue-green comforter and closed her eyes. She reached out blindly to set the unopened bottle of water on the nightstand, and missed. It fell to the carpeting with a dull thud. Then she heard nothing at all.

IT WAS HER MOTHER'S VOICE, calling urgently to her, that lifted Hayley from the comfortable well of sleep. Couldn't her mother see she was still tired? She didn't want to open her eyes.

But the voice softly nagged until Hayley opened one eye. Her bleary gaze was drawn to the end of the bed. Her muzzy brain told her the distorted figure she saw there was a reflection in the glass-framed poster hanging on the wall. The figure was bending above her overnight case, which sat on the floor beside her bed.

What was her mother looking for?

Hayley wanted to turn her head and ask, but she was too tired. Her eyes closed again and all she managed was a croak of complaint. A cloth fell across her face, covering her nose and eyes.

Hayley came awake at once, batting at the material. She yanked the fabric aside as she rolled off the far edge of the bed, trying to understand what was happening.

The room swam dizzily as a wave of nausea rolled through her. She heard, rather than saw, her bedroom door snap shut.

Someone had been in her room!

Hayley swayed. The room steadied and she saw the contents of her overnight case spread out on the floor. The oversize T-shirt she liked to sleep in lay crumpled on the bed. Someone had tossed it over her face when she'd started to wake up. The person had been right here in the room with her, rifling through her case. And that person hadn't been her mother. If Hayley hadn't dreamed that her mother was calling her…

Staggering around the bed, she lurched to the door. The hallway stretched empty in both directions. Of course it was empty. She'd given the person plenty of time to disappear while she stood there in a fog.

Who had it been? What had he or she been looking for?

Fear overwhelmed her grogginess. Either she hadn't been imagining things last night and someone hiding inside the house had been going through her bag, or someone who belonged in the house had done so. If the person was looking for valuables, he or she was out of luck. Hayley had brought only clothing and makeup with her.

Gripping the door frame, Hayley tried to think. Marcus would have a fit if she called the police, yet she couldn't ignore what had just happened. Still, the last time they'd spoken, Chief Crossley had told her flat out to stop calling his office. Even if the dispatcher did send someone out to investigate, she knew firsthand how hard the police would search for a possible intruder. There couldn't be a man on the small force who didn't know how much the police chief disliked her.

Hayley tried to bring the fuzzy image she'd glimpsed into focus, but it was futile. She didn't know if she'd seen a man or a woman. The sobering thought only added another layer of fear. Why would anyone go through her belongings with her sleeping right there? It made no sense.

She glanced back in the room at her scattered clothing, and drew in a sharp breath as her gaze landed on the bedside clock. It couldn't possibly be almost four o'clock in the afternoon. If that was right, she'd slept away most of the day! No wonder she felt so loggy.

Staring at the oversize T-shirt on the rumpled bedspread,

she felt violated and terribly afraid. She needed to tell someone what had just happened, but she couldn't bring herself to dial 911. She'd be better off calling the lawyer. His letter was the reason she was here in the first place.

What was his name? She couldn't remember. There was a dull ache in the back of her head. She rarely got headaches, but it appeared she was working on one now. She couldn't seem to think. The lawyer's letter was in her purse.

Only where was her purse?

Hayley raked the room with her gaze. The familiar denim bag was nowhere in sight. The thief had stolen something, after all. Her purse was gone!

Hayley rushed down the hall. The eerie silence still embraced the house. Where was everyone?

As she neared the main staircase, she heard muted voices. Her relief was short-lived as she realized one of those voices was shrill with anger. Eden. Hayley paused, peering over the banister. She could just make out the top of Eden's dyed-blond head. The woman was standing near the front door, angrily berating someone. Then she heard the rumble of a low, masculine voice. Bram!

"Either go down or let me pass."

Hayley whirled in surprise at the sound of Paula Kerstairs's nasal voice. The movement sent Hayley reaching for the newel post to keep from falling. She hadn't heard the maid come up behind her. The woman's beady eyes regarded her with something close to loathing.

"Where did you come from?" Hayley managed to croak.

The wraithlike woman jerked her head in the direction of the bedroom near the top of the stairs. The room had belonged to Hayley's mother when Hayley was a girl. The door stood open.

"Cleaning," Paula said tersely. "It's my job."

Maybe fear was replacing Hayley's common sense, but the maid seemed to hate her.

"Were you just in my room?" Hayley demanded.

"No."

The woman's sour expression seemed an open sneer. Hayley straightened in reaction.

"If you made a mess," Paula said, "it'll have to wait. I'm done for today."

Paula Kerstairs was almost a caricature of a cleaning woman with her pail and baggy clothing. A caricature with a number of places to hide small objects. Including a small denim purse?

She made to push past Hayley, who gathered her courage and blocked the way. "Let me have a look in your pail." Paula thrust it toward her and Hayley peered into the pail. The blue plastic bucket contained nothing more than rags and sprays.

"Think I'm stealing the family silver?"

Hayley ignored the question. She refused to be intimidated by this disagreeable person. "Have you seen anyone else up here?" she asked.

"Just you."

With shocking strength, Paula pushed her aside, nearly sending her sprawling. Paula's baggy clothing flapped about her sticklike figure as she glided down the stairs on silent feet. Hayley started to yell to Bram to stop the maid, then realized he and Eden had disappeared. Had they witnessed any part of what had happened?

She couldn't imagine Bram walking away if he'd noticed her. As she descended the stairs behind Paula, a trace movement pulled her gaze to the library. Someone whisked out of sight behind the double doors. Hayley was certain she'd glimpsed Mrs. Norwhich. What was the housekeeper doing slinking about like that?

Hayley's heart was racing so fast she couldn't seem to think. Gripping the banister, she tried to take a similar grip on her imagination. It was starting to run wild with theories that bordered on paranoia.

Taking a deep breath, she told herself to calm down. She would get in her car right now and drive into town to talk to the lawyer. What was his name? *Why couldn't she remember his name?*

It didn't matter. There couldn't be that many lawyers in Stony Ridge. She'd find him.

Except that her car keys were in her purse.

"Hey there, Hayley."

Jacob strode down the hall from the kitchen, munching on an apple. His casual, relaxed greeting sent a burst of relief through her. She'd forgotten about Jacob. His mother might be cold and unfriendly, but everyone liked Jacob.

"Did you get some rest?" he asked.

"No. Yes." She shook her head in confusion.

"Is something wrong?"

She crossed the hall toward him. "Someone entered my room while I was sleeping," she blurted out. "My purse is missing."

Jacob stopped chewing. "It is? I just saw your purse in the library a few minutes ago. It's on the floor beside the couch. You left it there last night."

Hayley rushed past him into the library. Her denim bag was sitting right where he'd said, in plain sight. But she'd taken it upstairs with her this morning.

Hadn't she?

She couldn't remember.

Her hands shook as she reached for the purse.

"Hey. Are you okay, Hayley?"

"No! I told you, someone was in my room." She tried to still the escalating panic inside her. "They were going through my overnight case."

"Who was?"

She opened the purse. "I'm...not sure. I only saw a reflection in the glass of the poster at the end of my bed. The person threw a T-shirt over my face before I could turn to look."

His forehead creased in a frown. "A T-shirt? Hayley, are you sure you weren't dreaming? I mean, you were pretty freaked out last night, not that I blame you or anything, but—"

Keys, wallet, driver's license, credit cards, everything seemed to be inside except...

"It's gone."

"What's gone?"

Stricken, she glared at Jacob. "The lawyer's letter!"

He shook his head. "Someone took your letter? What would anyone want with a letter?" he asked reasonably. "Is your money there? Your credit cards?"

"Yes! Just the letter is missing."

"Hey, take it easy. Are you sure this letter was in your purse?"

"Of course I'm sure!"

Wasn't she?

"Chill, Hayley. A minute ago, you thought your purse was missing, too. Maybe the letter fell out or something." Jacob dropped to the floor and began searching beneath the couch. "Nope. Not here—unless it transformed into a dust bunny." He stood with a small smile, brushing lint from his pants. His smile slipped as he looked at her. "Maybe it fell out in your car."

"Where's Mrs. Norwhich? She was in here a minute ago. I saw her! She must have taken it."

Jacob regarded her earnestly. "Hayley, I don't know what's going on, but Mrs. Norwhich is in the kitchen. I was talking to her."

"I know what I saw!"

"Would you listen to yourself? You sound hysterical."

He was right. Hayley fought against the mind-numbing

fear, clutching the purse to her chest. She was positive she'd seen Mrs. Norwhich in here a second ago, but that didn't mean the woman had taken her letter. If the purse had been sitting here all day, anyone could have taken the letter. She could hardly go storming into the kitchen and accuse the woman.

Like she'd practically done to Paula Kerstairs.

"I didn't dream the T-shirt that was tossed over my face," she told Jacob more calmly. "Someone scattered my stuff all over the floor of my room."

Jacob scratched behind his ear, obviously at a loss.

"Paula Kerstairs was upstairs," Hayley told him.

"Now, that's one creepy woman. I wouldn't put anything past her. You think she was in your room? Is anything missing? Jewelry? Money?"

"I...don't know."

"Let's go have a look. If something's missing, we'll call the cops."

Rattled and uncertain, Hayley followed Jacob up the stairs, clutching her purse.

"How's your job going?" he asked.

"Jacob, I am not stressed out due to my job," she told him sharply.

He spread his hands in a conciliatory way, nearly dropping his apple. "Hey, I didn't mean to imply that. I was just making conversation. You know, trying to lighten things up a little? You look coiled tighter than a spring about to sprong, know what I mean?"

She knew. It wasn't a bad comparison. Her skin no longer felt like it fit. Pausing at the top of the stairs, she stared at the room Paula had claimed to be cleaning. "Hold up a minute, Jacob."

He trailed after her as she entered what was now a guest bedroom. Dark cherry furniture gleamed—dust free. There was no scent of cleaning solutions, but the room was neat and tidy. So was the connecting bathroom.

"Paula said she was cleaning in here," Hayley said.

"Looks like she did. Want me to check for dust over the doorsill?"

Embarrassed, Hayley looked away. "I don't understand what's happening around here."

Jacob shook his head helplessly and followed as she hurried down the hall to her bedroom.

"Jacob, the door's closed!"

He frowned. "Is that bad?"

"I left it open. I'm certain I did. Someone's in there."

Jacob moved past her and opened the door before she could stop him. Hayley followed him inside and jerked to a stop. Her overnight case still sat on the floor beside the bed, but it was closed. Not a thing in the room was out of place. A depression in the pillow and a rumpled bedspread were the only signs she had even used the room.

"Someone's been in here again! They put everything back!" Acid churned in her stomach. "I don't understand," she whispered.

Jacob stared at the perfectly neat room. "Hayley, are you sure you weren't dreaming?"

"Of course I'm sure!"

Could she have dreamed the whole thing? Her head was starting to pound so hard it was difficult to think.

"Look, don't get mad at me, but I've gotta ask. Are you taking something? Maybe you got some bad stuff. How long ago—"

"I've never used drugs in my life," she said fiercely when she realized what he meant. Pushing past him, she hurried down the hall.

"Hayley, stop. Where are you going?"

"To check my car," she yelled without looking back. She felt sick to her stomach and light-headed.

Jacob thought she was using drugs. She supposed she couldn't blame him. Her brain felt numb enough to be in a drug-induced haze. But she wasn't taking drugs, and she hadn't been dreaming, either—except that part about her mother.

Okay, that part had been strange, but understandable. And anyhow, she'd come fully awake the minute that T-shirt had covered her face.

As she raced down the front stairs and out the door, she heard Jacob calling after her. She ignored him and the late afternoon heat and ran to the back of the house. Her car sat exactly where she'd left it.

Some part of her had been afraid it would be gone. Her heart was pounding and she was shaking all over. She'd start to hyperventilate next, if she didn't calm down. It wasn't as if she actually needed the lawyer's letter. Yet it suddenly seemed vitally important that she find it. Like her purse, she wanted something concrete to hold in her hand. Frantically, she searched her car.

The letter wasn't there.

Standing slowly, she closed the door, then her eyes. *Had* she put the envelope in her purse before leaving her apartment yesterday? She remembered picking it up and rereading the message before she'd left. So why couldn't she remember his name? What was wrong with her? Why did she feel so weird?

"Lose something?"

She opened her eyes to find Bram leaning against the trunk of the car. Dressed in tailored slacks and an open V-neck sports shirt, he looked incredibly handsome and solidly real.

"My mind," she told him honestly.

He arched his eyebrows. "Does that happen often?"

On the ragged edge of tears, she found his matter-of-fact

tone was exactly the right note to steady her. Inhaling deeply, she nodded. ''It's starting to seem that way.''

His brow furrowed. ''Want to talk about it?''

Did she? Jacob hadn't believed her, and he knew her. Did she want to see Bram's eyes fill with pity for the crazy woman? Because that was exactly what she was starting to feel like.

''Have you eaten?'' Bram asked.

''What?''

''I was on my way to The Inn for an early dinner. You could come with me if you'd like. I've found problems often have a way of looking different on a full stomach.''

He hadn't moved, so she must have, because she found herself standing only a few feet away from him—close enough to smell a hint of his aftershave. Her body had processed the two slices of toast she'd eaten several hours ago, so at the mention of food, her stomach rumbled in assent. How bizarre to be thinking about food when her whole world was coming apart.

What did it matter? Bram was offering her a chance to escape. A chance to get away and think.

''I'd have to change,'' she told him.

Bram's gaze traveled down her body. ''You look fine to me.''

Her heart stuttered. Sternly, she told herself that he wasn't coming on to her. The words had been said casually. Yet they made her aware of her rumpled shorts and T-shirt and the messy tangle of hair around her face.

''It would only take me a minute.''

''There isn't a woman alive who can change clothing in a minute.''

Some of her tension began to ease. ''Is this the voice of experience talking?''

''It doesn't take experience,'' he told her. ''Men are born knowing that basic fact about women.''

"Really? I'll accept that challenge."

He came off the car. A large, quiet, powerful man who managed to impart a sense of confidence with his very presence. "I was heading for your front porch, anyhow. I left my measuring tape there," he told her. "I guess the heat got to me today. I never leave tools lying around."

She fell into step beside him as they skirted the two rear doors and started around to the front of the building. Mrs. Norwhich was plainly visible through the kitchen window, bustling about the room. There was no sign of anyone else.

"The heat got to me, too. I took a nap this afternoon. While I was sleeping, someone came into my room and started going through my overnight case," she blurted out.

Bram stopped walking. "Who did?"

His instant concern was balm to her shattered confidence. "I don't know. I only saw their reflection in the glass frame of the poster at the foot of my bed. They tossed a shirt over my face and took off."

"Did they take anything?"

"I don't think so."

Bram waited.

"I thought the person took my purse, but Jacob told me it was in the library."

When Bram's eyes narrowed, she started to regret telling him anything, but now that she'd started, she couldn't seem to stop.

"He was right. Jacob went back upstairs with me." She faltered a minute, but decided Bram might as well know the whole story. "I know this sounds crazy, but while I was downstairs, someone went back into my room and repacked the stuff they'd pulled out of my bag. Jacob thought I'd dreamed the whole thing, but I hadn't," she added in a rush.

Bram's features were impassive. She couldn't tell what he was thinking. Did he believe her?

''What were you looking for in your car?'' Bram asked.

''The letter from the lawyer. I was sure I had it in my purse when I drove here yesterday, but it's gone.''

''Is it important?''

Was it? ''Not really. I mean, I don't see how it would be of value to anyone. Except that I can't remember the man's name. I was supposed to call and make an appointment to talk to him.''

''It's after five now,'' Bram pointed out after a moment. ''You couldn't call him today, anyhow.''

She nodded as he resumed walking. ''He has an office in Stony Ridge. I don't imagine there can be too many law offices in a town the size of ours.''

''You wouldn't think so,'' he agreed without inflection.

As they came around the corner, Jacob rose from the front porch steps. His body tensed when he saw Bram.

''Did you find it, Hayley?'' he asked.

Hayley shook her head. ''I must have left it in Boston.'' Not wanting Jacob to say anything else, she looked at Bram. ''Come on in. I'll only be a minute.''

Jacob pinned her with a look of concern. ''Are you going someplace?''

''Bram invited me to have dinner with him at The Inn.''

Bram stepped around Jacob and picked up the metal measuring tape that was sitting on the porch next to the front door.

''Good idea,'' Jacob said. ''Whatever Mrs. Norwhich is making smells like something my roommate used to feed his cat. Mind some company?''

''Another time,'' Bram said, reaching for the handle and opening the door. He waited for Hayley to precede him.

''That was sort of rude,'' she told him as they stepped into the large hall.

''I agree. I was always taught a person should wait to be invited,'' Bram said.

That wasn't what she'd meant and he knew it, but Bram had a valid point, as well. "Would you mind coming upstairs with me?"

His dark eyes studied her face. She forced herself to hold his gaze.

"Are you worried about me or him?" he asked perceptively.

"You can take care of yourself," she told him. "I just don't want to go upstairs alone and find more surprises waiting for me."

It was partly true, and he could think what he wanted. She wasn't going to leave him down here in the hall for another confrontation with Jacob or anyone else.

Bram inclined his head without comment, following her silently up the grand staircase. She wondered what he was thinking as they walked down the darkly paneled hall to her room.

His gaze surveyed her bed, the poster and the overnight bag before he looked at her. "You're sure nothing is missing except the letter from your lawyer?"

"Nothing I noticed." She forced her fingers to open the case. The T-shirt lay folded on top. "I don't fold my clothing like this."

Bram's eyes darkened.

She dropped the shirt with a shudder. She was sure it would never feel clean to her again.

"I'd better change. If it gets too late, we'll have to wait for a table."

Pulling a green sleeveless shift from her closet, she found the matching sandals and entered the bathroom. Glancing in the mirror, she wondered why Bram had even invited her. Her hair was a bigger mess than she'd realized. Heavy shadows rimmed her eyes. She wasn't wearing a trace of makeup, and her clothing was badly wrinkled. She couldn't have looked less attractive if she'd tried.

Hayley skipped the shower she craved and dressed quickly. It suddenly dawned on her to wonder if Bram had a woman he waited for on a regular basis. That might explain why he was fighting their mutual attraction so hard.

Maybe he was divorced. Wondering about that was a whole lot better than wondering about what was happening here at Heartskeep.

Hayley applied makeup sparingly and settled for leaving her long hair loose, brushing it out until it crackled with energy. Her brain still felt oddly fuzzy and she had a dull headache, not to mention the fact that she was terribly thirsty again. Bram was right. She needed to eat something more substantial than toast. Her electrolytes were probably way out of sync or something.

Bram rose from the bed when she entered the room. If she hadn't been watching closely, she would have missed the flicker of masculine approval in his gaze as he looked her over.

"Ready to go?"

A man of few words. But they were enough.

"Yes."

He set something on her nightstand and moved forward. "I'm impressed."

Her heart rate increased.

"Seven minutes flat."

"Next time I'll skip the makeup."

The smile started in the depth of his eyes. Her body tingled warmly and everything else faded away. He might not want this attraction, but it was there all the same. And a smart woman could learn quite a bit about a man over dinner.

Chapter Five

Bram had forgotten that The Inn practically oozed cozy, quaint charm. Its interior was filled with dark, rich wood paneling, much like Heartskeep. Fortunately, the antique furnishings came without most of the fussy, frilly touches that usually accompanied such decor. The Inn not only served good food, it also served as the main hangout for the elite neighborhood.

A quick look at the prices reminded him why he'd been buying his food in town and cooking it on his small camp stove since he'd started this job.

Bram's resolve to talk to Hayley about finishing the project faded away as she was approached by a steady stream of former friends and neighbors. Gracious and friendly, she not only introduced him to each person, she also touted his craftsmanship with an enthusiasm that would have been embarrassing if he hadn't suspected she was trying to atone for her attempt to fire him.

He'd never spent any real time in Stony Ridge so he didn't expect anyone to recognize him, and they didn't. But there was always a chance someone would eventually remember his name and his connection to another prominent family from this area.

Speculation about the two of them didn't seem to faze Hayley. Not even when several people came right out and asked if there was a wedding in the works. Hayley only smiled and said they were just friends.

Unaccountably irritated by the phrase after a while, Bram kept quiet until a man with an expensive haircut and designer clothing sauntered over to their table. He assessed Bram's worth with a scornful glance and dismissed him, turning the full focus of his attention on Hayley. It was quickly obvious that the man Hayley introduced as Sean was the sleazy sort, always on the make. He liked to talk with his hands, but when he used them to touch Hayley's hair, then her shoulder and her arm, Bram had to stifle a strong desire to teach him better manners.

"So, you two planning the big announcement, or what?" Sean asked archly, ignoring Hayley's attempt to pull away. He wasn't the sort to take a subtle hint, so reaching out, Bram clamped his hand around the younger man's wrist. He lifted the offending appendage, speaking softly enough that his voice didn't travel beyond their table.

"If Hayley and I *were* about to announce our engagement, I'd have to take you outside and break every bone in your body." He offered a cold smile. "And if you touch her again, I'm going to start with your hand, anyhow. Just for practice."

He ignored Hayley's indrawn breath, slowly releasing his punishing grip on Sean's wrist. The other man staggered back, rubbing at the red mark Bram left on his skin.

"Take it easy, man. Me and Hayley are old history. Right, Hayley? I never realized you were into the Neanderthal type, babe."

"Go away, Sean," she told him.

When he didn't move, Bram started to rise. Hayley clamped a surprisingly strong hand on his arm. Sean beat a hasty retreat back to his own table and his clearly annoyed companion.

"Don't you dare make a scene in here!" Hayley hissed.

Bram cocked his head, settling back in his chair. "I was planning to take him outside," he said agreeably.

"I am perfectly capable of handling someone like Sean."

"Sorry if I overstepped, but it looked to me like he was the one doing all the handling."

"Sean's a jerk. He's always been a jerk. No one pays him any attention."

Bram leaned back, feeling oddly pleased. "Then you might want to smile. From the looks we're getting, people are starting to think we're having an argument over your old boyfriend."

Hayley glanced around quickly, caught herself, and glared at him. "You're impossible."

"So you've mentioned. Ouch!"

"Oh. Was that your leg?" she asked with saccharine sweetness.

He had to suppress a grin. "My fault entirely. I seem to have bumped my leg against your shoe."

She'd keep a man on his toes—if only to keep himself from being kicked in the shins.

"What a shame. Think how much worse it would have been if I'd been wearing heels." Still smiling, she leaned closer. "You do realize word of your macho scene with Sean will be all over town tomorrow."

Bram might have felt guilty if there'd been any heat behind her words, but there wasn't. He was finding it hard not to respond to the subtle signals she was putting out. His hand itched to tangle in the long mane of her hair. He'd known she was dangerous the moment he'd laid eyes on her. The handful of women who had passed through his life in recent years were nothing like Hayley. He suspected she wasn't like any other woman, period. There was a vibrancy about her that was unique. She could be bold and sassy, or charmingly warm and gracious, but either way, she had an inner core of strength that would always serve her well. He couldn't help thinking that if things had been different in his life, he would have constituted a much bigger threat to her than did Sean, despite the age difference between them.

Troubled by that thought, Bram watched as she tucked her hair behind her ear. He had a feeling that sudden flush to her skin had little to do with Sean, and everything to do with the chemistry that kept bubbling between them like some evil witch's brew.

"You'd be in trouble if you lost that ear."

"What?" Then she grinned impishly. "No, I wouldn't. I'd have my hair cut short."

"Now that," he told her softly, "would be a crime. I can think of a number of interesting uses for that hair."

Instantly, he wished he could call back the reckless words. "I shouldn't have said that."

Hayley studied him. "Are you married?"

"No."

She raised her eyebrows. "That was a pretty strong no. Not interested in marital bliss, huh?"

"There's no such thing," he said flatly.

"Ah, the jaded sort. Maybe I should have asked..."

Silently, he welcomed the middle-aged couple who approached their table with delighted smiles.

"Hayley! We didn't realize you were in town."

"Hi, Mr. and Mrs. Walken, how nice to see you. I drove in last night. May I introduce Bram Myers? He's been doing some work for Marcus. Bram, this is Emily and George Walken. They've been friends of the family and our closest neighbors since before I was born."

Bram rose and extended his hand. George Walken had a firm, solid handshake and a direct way of looking at a person. Bram liked him immediately.

"Bram, was it?" Emily asked. "Unusual name. Short for Abraham?"

"Maybe once. Now it's simply a family name."

"I see. Unusual. I saw you working on that extraordinary gate out front of Heartskeep one afternoon. Is that your own design?"

"Yes, ma'am."

"I'm impressed," Emily declared.

"It is impressive," George agreed, "though I have to admit I sort of miss those old stone lions."

Hayley sent Bram a triumphant look. "They'll be back," she assured the couple. "Bram has them at his place upstate. He's going to have them restored for me."

Bram didn't dispute that, but the fierceness behind her words made him want to smile. He sat back down at the couple's urging.

"Ignore George," Emily Walken said. "He's not much for change, but I'd like to talk to you about doing some work for us when you finish at Heartskeep."

"I'd be happy to talk with you anytime," Bram assured her. The couple chatted a few more minutes before leaving.

"I should have known this would happen," Hayley said. "Everyone shows up at The Inn sooner or later."

"Nice people. I like them."

"So do I. They've always been especially kind to Leigh and me. And they know absolutely everyone. Mr. Walken grew up on his family's estate. His father and my grandfather were best friends as well as neighbors, and George and Grandfather became just as close after the senior Mr. Walken passed away. Emily couldn't have children of her own, so they filled their home with foster kids over the years."

"Good people. Think they were serious about having me do some work for them?"

"I'm sure they were."

He didn't consciously cover her hand with his, but abruptly he realized her skin was warm beneath his palm.

Warm, and exquisitely soft. The impulse to stroke that soft skin with his thumb was hard to resist. Their gazes locked. Anticipation stirred in his gut. Her expression told him that she wanted him, as well. He released her hand and looked away.

"Bram, we need to talk."

No. What they needed to do was to get out of there before he did something completely crazy, like give in to his desire to kiss her at least once.

Hayley reached for her wineglass, draining the last of it as the waiter set pie and coffee on the table.

Bram didn't like feeling so intrigued by this slip of a woman, yet when she peered at him over the rim of her glass, his body wasn't interested in hearing from his common sense. Hayley was getting to him whether he liked it or not.

He'd been feeling muzzy and out of focus much of the day. He'd put it down to the unusually hot June sun, but now he realized it had begun shortly after he'd made the mistake of going over to talk to her this afternoon. Oh, yeah, she was definitely getting to him.

The pink in her cheeks deepened as if she was reading his thoughts. If he didn't do something, the attraction sizzling between them would turn the room incandescent. She was wealthy and young, but not so young she didn't know what she was doing, despite that beguiling hint of innocence about her.

"Why were you and Eden arguing earlier?" Hayley asked, twisting the stem of her empty glass.

Startled by the question when he'd been thinking about how she would look stretched out naked beneath him, he had to work at shifting mental gears.

"How did you know about that?"

"I saw the two of you at the bottom of the stairs. It was

right after...'' she looked around quickly and lowered her voice ''...what happened in my bedroom this afternoon.''

That reminder was just the dose of reality he'd needed to regroup and pull his mind from where it had no business going.

He swept the nearby tables with a quick glance to see if anyone was listening. No one appeared to be paying them any attention.

''Someone left a note on the windshield of my truck that said I was wanted at the house. When I got there, Eden pointed out that as the hired help, I should remember my place and keep away from you.''

Hayley expelled an outraged breath. ''She actually said that?''

She'd also warned him to forget any aspirations he might be harboring toward marrying a potential heiress, but Bram decided it might be more prudent not to mention that part—or the fact that Eden had apparently lined up her son, Jacob, for that role.

Oddly enough, that last bit had bothered him far more than the warning. The truth was, Bram didn't like Jacob. It had been a gut reaction the moment they'd met.

''Look at it from her perspective, Hayley,'' he said mildly. ''I know you don't like her, but as your stepmother, Eden is probably trying to act in your best interests. I *am* the hired help, and a stranger to boot.''

''My best interests?'' Hayley's glass clunked against the tabletop. Her blue eyes glittered in anger. ''Eden doesn't care a thing about my best interests and never will. Not unless there is something in it for her.'' Her fingernails tapped absently against the tablecloth. ''But I wonder...''

''Wonder what?''

''If she was the person going through my bag. How long was she down there in the hall with you?''

Bram shook his head. Hayley wasn't going to like what

he had to say next. "While you were getting ready tonight, I lay down on your bed and tried to see a reflection of the room in that glass covering your poster."

Her fingers stilled. Hayley straightened in her chair. *"Tried?"*

Her affronted tone made him wince. "Maybe I wasn't in the right spot, or maybe the sun needed to be coming in from a different angle, but—"

"Or maybe poor Hayley was hallucinating?" she asked with poisonous insincerity.

"Don't put words in my mouth."

"Why not? I took them straight from your thoughts."

Bram swore softly.

She leaned toward him, and the vee of her neckline dipped recklessly low. Far lower than she realized. Or did she know exactly what she was doing? Bram ripped his gaze back up to her face. Her blue eyes sparkled more intensely than her crystal earrings.

"You've already decided Jacob was right, haven't you? Poor little Hayley must have dreamed the whole thing."

"I didn't say that." But it was exactly what he had concluded.

"Yes. You did," she said angrily. "Just not out loud." She dropped her napkin beside her untouched dessert. "I'll wait for you outside."

He grabbed her wrist before she could rise, exerting enough pressure to hold her in place. "If you want to make a scene, Hayley, let's make it a good one. I don't go for half measures."

Her eyes widened.

"I've got years more experience at shocking people than you do. I know exactly how to give all your friends and neighbors a scene they'll talk about for years. Is that what you want?"

"You're hurting me."

"No, I'm not." But he released her wrist and signaled for the check, far more ready than she was to get them out of there and away from prying eyes. Despite his harsh words, the last thing he wanted was a scene here in Stony Ridge with yet another member of a socially prominent family.

Hayley sat perfectly still. Bram cursed under his breath as he counted out money and added a tip.

"I'm sorry," she said, surprising him.

"No problem."

Her fingers closed over his hand. "Yes, it is a problem. I've got a temper. Leigh's the calm one. It's just that I wanted you to believe me. I know the whole thing sounds crazy. It is crazy. And after the panicky way I behaved last night—"

"I'll be right back with your change, sir," the waiter interrupted.

Hayley's hand fell away.

"I don't need any change," he told the man. "Are you ready, Hayley?"

She nodded and immediately rose to her feet. He had to hand it to her. Not a trace of emotion from the past few minutes showed on her face as she moved through the busy dining room with all the grace and poise of a queen. She had more facets than a diamond, with twice the allure. Bram had to remind himself that even if she'd been older, there were more than a million reasons not to let her get to him—and most of those reasons were in her bank account. He wasn't falling into that trap ever again.

As they stepped outside, they were both surprised to find low scudding clouds had turned the evening prematurely dark.

"I didn't realize it was supposed to storm tonight," Hayley said.

"It wasn't. I had the radio on earlier. They never mentioned a storm."

"Too bad they don't look out a window once in a while."

His lips quirked. "Come on."

They'd used her car rather than his messy truck, and she'd surprised him by handing him the keys and asking him to drive. Now, as he opened the passenger door and waited, Hayley turned to face him instead of getting inside. He expected her to ask for her keys back.

"Thank you for dinner."

So prim. So proper. So incredibly lovely.

"You're welcome."

She didn't move.

"Did you want to drive?" he asked.

"No."

"Then we should go before it starts raining," he prompted.

"*Do* you think I dreamed the whole thing?"

Bram sighed. "Get in the car, Hayley."

She still didn't move. The woman had a real stubborn streak. Resigned, he faced her. "You said there was nothing of value in your case."

"There wasn't."

He shook his head. "Why would anyone sneak back into your room and repack?"

"I don't know! Maybe they had a neat streak. Or maybe they wanted everyone to think exactly what you're thinking right now. I know it doesn't make sense, but I didn't dream that shirt in my face!"

The force behind her words was troubling. She believed what she was saying. Could she be using drugs? Bram searched for a way to ask without riling that temper of hers even more. She climbed into the car, angrily tugging at her skirt, but not before he got a good eyeful of a shapely thigh and leg. Darn it, she was making him nuts. He'd be howling at the moon at this rate.

Whether she'd seen someone or not, he knew she was scared. There was something going on at Heartskeep. He'd sensed the dark undercurrents even before she'd arrived. It was no good telling himself not to get involved here. He'd been involved from the moment he saw her watching him with such rapt attention last night. The question was, could he keep from getting any more involved in the situation?

Hayley drew several deep breaths while she watched Bram walk around the car. What did it matter what he thought? She wasn't crazy. She knew what she had seen.

But—it did matter. She didn't want Bram to think she was crazy like Marcus. The truth was, she was feeling more than a little scared and alone. Bram felt like the only safe anchor in her world at the moment. He was right. None of what had happened made any sense.

Hayley was so frustrated she wanted to scream. Tonight, for the first time since she'd arrived home, she was feeling almost normal instead of loggy and exhausted. Bram had been right about that, too. She'd needed to eat. But even with food in her stomach, she knew she hadn't been dreaming. If only he believed her.

He slid behind the wheel, a brooding, intense man whose strength and competence were openly conveyed in the quiet, self-assured way he carried himself. Hayley had been powerfully drawn to him from the start, yet she still didn't know a thing about him—like why he had such a strong aversion to marriage, and why, although he was attracted to her, he'd made it plain he had no intention of acting on that attraction.

Inserting the key, he started the engine and drove out of the parking lot without looking at her. "I think you should head back to your apartment in Boston tonight," he said quietly.

Startled, she snapped her jaw closed to keep from gaping at him. "Do I disturb you that much?"

He flashed a hooded look in her direction. "Your situation worries me that much," he said firmly.

"I thought you didn't believe me."

He hesitated, as if searching for the right words. "You're too alone in that house."

"It's full of people."

"People filled with antagonism. You need an ally."

"You're forgetting Jacob." She sensed his instant dismissal. "And yourself."

His fingers tightened on the steering wheel. "I realize you're attracted to me—"

"Good. I realize the same thing about you."

"I'm too old for you," he said flatly.

"Really? I didn't know you were sixty-five."

He didn't smile and his voice held no inflection to tell her what he was thinking when he asked, "Is that your cutoff point for eligible men?"

"Depends on what I want them eligible for."

Hayley was gratified to see his control slip a notch.

"I'm almost thirty-five, Hayley."

"As old as that, huh? Do your bones creak when you walk?"

He set his jaw. "I've got more than ten years on you."

She tossed back her hair and sniffed loudly in an imitation of Eden. "That would be physical years," she told him breezily. "In case you hadn't heard, women mature mentally much earlier than men. I figure that should make you almost the right age for me."

"Cut it out. Do you want me to put it in plain English? I'm not interested in you."

"Liar." She tossed her head haughtily, but the words hurt, as he'd intended.

"You're playing with fire, you know," he said softly.

"You play with fire all the time. I don't mind a little heat. Why do I scare you?"

"You don't scare me. Are you always this forward?"

Hayley tried not to flinch. "If by forward you mean do I always go after what I want, the answer is yes."

"And you've decided you want me. Is that it?"

His bitter tone caught her off guard. Someone had hurt him. "There goes that ego of yours again," she said lightly. "I'd like a chance to get to know you better. Is there something wrong with that?"

Rain began to fall. The large drops looked like tears on the windshield. Bram reached out and turned on the wipers. It took Hayley several minutes to realize he had no intention of answering her question. They rode the rest of the way in silence.

He drove through the open gate, down the long drive to Heartskeep. Instead of going around to the back, he pulled her car into the turnaround in front of the house. The structure towered above them, eerily forbidding in the rain-shrouded night, just like his mood.

"Go home, Hayley."

His unexpected words flayed her heart. Pride kept her voice steady. "This is my home."

"You know what I mean." Turning off the engine, he faced her. "Let your lawyer handle this ownership battle before you get hurt."

Her jaw clenched. "Thanks for the advice. I'll take my keys now." Thrusting out her hand, she was proud that there wasn't even a tremor.

"I'm thinking of your safety, Hayley," he said, dropping them on her palm. He was careful not to touch her. That she could affect him so strongly should have been some solace, but it wasn't.

"Don't lose any sleep over me. I can take care of myself." She opened her door and stepped out.

Bram swore as he climbed from the car. She couldn't look at him, not with this hurt gnawing on her insides.

"Good night, Mr. Myers. Thanks for dinner." She sprinted for the porch, half expecting him to follow.

He didn't.

Foolish tears thickened her throat. Inside the vast hall, she was thankful no one was nearby. The last thing she wanted was a run-in with Eden, Marcus or Jacob right now. She flew up the stairs and down the hall to her bedroom. Not until she reached it did she remember that her room wasn't necessarily a safe haven, either.

The memory was enough to stop the threat of tears as well as her headlong flight. Standing in her bedroom doorway, she reached for her light switch and was relieved when it worked. She let her gaze comb every surface before stepping inside. The room looked exactly as she had left it.

Except for a piece of paper sitting on her nightstand.

Fear knotted her stomach. Then she remembered Bram placing something on the table right before they left. She'd been preoccupied at the time. Now, she walked over and saw that it was a photograph.

Lifting the picture, she was shocked to see her own features looking up at her. The background was out of focus, but the building didn't look familiar.

Confused, she bit her lip. She didn't remember anyone taking a candid shot of her like this one. It was probably her twin. A younger Leigh, sixteen or seventeen at a guess. Except neither of them had ever worn their hair that short. Had they? Hayley couldn't remember.

Where had Bram found this picture? Why had he set it here without saying anything?

Puzzled, she tapped it against her hand. The photo slipped from her fingers and fluttered to the floor. Bending down to retrieve it, she saw something jutting out from under the bedskirt. She'd forgotten about the unopened bottle of water she'd dropped earlier.

Recovering both items, she set the picture on the nightstand and opened the bottle. The water was warm, but she let it trickle down her dry throat, anyhow. She had to stop feeling so jumpy. She never used to be this way. If she wasn't careful, she'd turn into squirrel fodder.

Somewhere nearby, a door slammed.

Hayley gave a start, spilling some of the water down the front of her. No door had ever slammed in this house that she could remember. Holding her breath, she listened tensely, but the house had returned to its former ominous quiet.

It hadn't come from Leigh's room, next door, but the sound had definitely come from one of the doors in this wing. That left the empty bedroom near the front of the house, Eden's room or the attic. Since the guest room was unoccupied and no one ever went up into the locked attic, logic said it must have been Eden's door.

Setting down the bottle of water, Hayley eased open her door and peered into the hall. Someone had switched off the overhead lights there. Her bedside lamp barely penetrated the gloom. And where were the night-lights that her mother had always kept at each end of the hallway?

Hayley felt a sudden chill. Either someone had deliberately turned off the lights or a circuit breaker had tripped for some reason. The light switches were on the wall at either end. The closest one to her was next to the attic door near Eden's room.

Eden again.

The woman never had liked her. Did she think slamming doors and turning off lights was going to frighten Hayley?

Okay, it had for a moment, but Hayley had lived in this house since she was a baby. She could walk the place blindfolded if she had to. To prove it, she ignored her leaping pulse and stepped into the hall.

As she headed toward the switch, she told herself there was nothing to fear. No one stood in the darkness watching her. Leigh was supposed to be the imaginative twin. This was a heck of a time for Hayley to start developing a vivid imagination.

Still, her breathing was ridiculously fast and shallow by the time her groping fingers found the switch. She turned it on, but nothing happened.

Okay, so a circuit had tripped. That explained the absence of the night-lights as well. Nothing to panic over. She'd go back to her room, grab a flashlight and go downstairs and check the panel.

She always kept a flashlight in her nightstand. Power loss this far from town had been a relatively frequent problem over the years. One that had never bothered her before, because there had always been someone else nearby. Someone she could call to and joke with. Not someone lurking in the blackness, watching her.

Stop it! What was the matter with her? There was no one standing in the darkness watching her!

Still, a surge of relief swept through her once she stepped back inside her lighted bedroom. Her flashlight was right where it should have been. Lifting it, she turned around as someone stepped into her doorway.

Chapter Six

"Hey, Hayley, I didn't know you were back already," Jacob said. "I just saw your light on. Everything okay?"

It would be once she stopped shaking and her heart went back where it belonged. She mustered a weak smile. "Everything's fine."

"How was your date? I didn't mean to try and horn in on anything tonight."

"It wasn't a date. Bram just invited me to join him for dinner. I wanted to talk to him about his work here."

"Oh. You planning to put some of his stuff in that art studio where you work?"

"I'm only an assistant buyer, but I plan to suggest it. His work is pretty spectacular."

Jacob shrugged. "Hey, look, I want to apologize for that drug crack earlier. I know you don't use drugs."

"No, I don't."

Jacob quickly changed the subject. "So, what happened to the lights over here?"

"I don't know. I was just going downstairs to check the circuit breakers."

"Someone probably hit the wall switch."

"I already tried that."

"Huh. The lights are on in my hall. I guess they must be on a different line. I'll go down with you."

Relieved to have company, she preceded him out the door.

''Look, Hayley, I know it's none of my business, and you can tell me to butt out if you want, but I was wondering—is something going on between you and the blacksmith?''

Hayley stopped walking.

''Raw heat and no flame,'' was the answer that immediately sprang to mind, but that was hardly the sort of answer she could give Jacob. However, if he'd wanted to divert her thoughts, he'd succeeded. His question left her at a loss. Thinking about Bram confused her. She couldn't believe how strongly she'd come on to him earlier. It was so unlike her to be that forward. She did have a tendency to go after what she wanted, but her behavior was completely out of character when it came to Bram.

''It's just...he doesn't seem your type, if you know what I mean,'' Jacob added.

''Why don't you like him?''

''I've got nothing against the guy, it's just...well...he seems a little strange. You know? A little too tightly wired, if you ask me. Look how aggressive he was when I came home the other night.''

''He was trying to protect me from a possible intruder.''

''Maybe so, but Mom caught him sneaking around inside the house earlier today.''

Hayley's pulse quickened.

''He claimed he was looking for you, but Mom said Paula and Mrs. Kerstairs didn't let him in. She was pretty sure you hadn't, either. You didn't, did you?''

Hayley shook her head and tucked a strand of hair behind her ear. She didn't want to tell Jacob his mother had sent for Bram to warn him off. But why hadn't Eden told Jacob the truth?

''You can see why she was worried. Your dad hired him

to make that metal stuff. He's supposed to be working outside, not in here. Look, I don't want to scare you or anything, but we don't know a thing about this guy. I never thought about it before, but Mom reminded me today that you're going to inherit a lot of money once you turn twenty-five. Suddenly this blacksmith is...well, hitting on you,'' he said, sounding uncomfortable.

''It's okay, Jacob. Bram wasn't hitting on me.'' Just the opposite, in fact. She'd been the aggressor, and she'd struck out big time.

Jacob shifted and Hayley rested a hand on his arm. ''Thanks.''

''For what?''

''For caring. You don't have to worry. We had a nice dinner together, but we won't be making a habit of it.''

''Oh. Well, I only wanted to suggest you be careful, you know. Some girls would fall for that dark-mysterious-stranger bit. I should have known you had more sense.''

Hayley cringed mentally.

''Besides, he's too old for you.''

''He's not even thirty-five,'' she felt obliged to protest.

''Really? He looks lots older. Every time I see that cheap tattoo of his, I think of a motorcycle gang member.''

She didn't. The tattoo had only made her more curious about him. ''As I said, we just went to The Inn for dinner. I ran into a lot of people I haven't seen in ages, including our next-door neighbors, the Walkens.''

''You know, I always want to laugh when you refer to people living a mile down the road as your next-door neighbors.''

''City boy.''

''And proud of it. What Mom sees in this old mausoleum of a house out here in the middle of nowhere is beyond me. No offense,'' he rushed to add.

Jacob was nothing if not likable. ''None ta—'' Hayley

froze. Something moved in the darkness near the end of the hallway. Jacob grabbed her arm, yanking it up so the beam of her flashlight shone on the figure standing there.

"You're blindin' me," Paula Kerstairs complained garrulously. She raised a bony arm to shield her eyes.

"What are you doing up here?" Jacob demanded, releasing Hayley's arm.

"Lost my wallet," she complained, holding up a slim black wallet in her other hand. "Had to drive all the way back out here to find it. I told Odette I must'a dropped it making beds, but could she be bothered to look? 'Course not. I've got to drive out here in all this heat and find it myself. What'd'ya'go and turn off the lights for, anyhow?"

She reached for the switch and flicked it up. The hall lights sprang to life.

"What did you do?" Hayley demanded.

"You don't want them on?" Paula asked, sounding disgusted. Before Hayley could protest, she switched them off once more.

"Turn them back on," Jacob demanded.

"Make up your minds," Paula barked, restoring the lights. "I don't have time to stand around here all night." With amazing swiftness, she vanished around the corner.

Goose bumps ran straight down Hayley's arms. She hurried forward, but Paula was already out of sight. She hadn't made a sound.

"That woman gives me the creeps," Jacob said.

"This wall switch didn't work a minute ago," Hayley said. She flicked the lights off and back on again.

Jacob rubbed the back of his neck, frowning. "Are you sure?"

"Of course I'm sure!"

"Maybe my mother beat us downstairs and tripped the breaker."

Possible, of course, but that knowledge didn't stop the

shaky feeling inside Hayley. ''Did you hear a door slam a few minutes ago?''

''In this house?'' he asked incredulously.

Jacob used the bedroom next to Marcus's when he stayed here. If he'd been in his room, he might not have heard the door slam. Eden? Or Paula?

Or someone else?

''Hayley?''

''It's okay, Jacob. Never mind. What happened to the night-lights?''

''What night-lights?''

''The ones my mother always kept plugged in at either end of the halls.''

Jacob shrugged. ''Beats me. I guess Mom had them removed or something.''

''Why would she do that?''

Jacob spread his hands. ''Who knows? I've never understood my mother. Ask her.''

''I will.''

She stared at the darkly paneled stretch of wall.

''No offense, Hayley, but you've been acting a little...''

''Stressed?'' she suggested. ''I'm sorry I snapped at you, Jacob. I am a little stressed. I've got some things on my mind.''

Shrugging, Jacob offered her one of his boyish grins. ''Would you like to go downstairs and watch a movie or something? I brought some new video releases with me. Your dad already went to his room and there isn't a thing on television.''

Hayley hesitated. She wanted to question Bram about the photograph, but Jacob had raised some disturbing possibilities. She was pretty sure his assumptions were all wrong, but they nagged at her all the same. Despite her attraction to him, Bram was a stranger.

She glanced at the light switch uneasily.

She was suddenly tempted to ask Jacob about the picture on her nightstand, but that would lead to all sorts of explanations she didn't want to make. She'd seen Bram set it there, so she decided to wait and ask him.

"Hey, we don't have to watch a movie. I mean, if you're too tired, I understand," Jacob said.

Focusing on his anxious expression, she realized she'd never answered him. "Actually, a movie sounds like a terrific idea." Anything that would stop these crazy thoughts was a terrific idea.

Jacob grinned. "Great. You choose the movie while I make the popcorn."

"I just ate," she protested.

"There's always room for popcorn."

He was right. The smell was impossible to resist. They settled on an action-adventure comedy. Hayley turned down soda in favor of cold bottled water because her mouth felt like cotton. She'd been terribly thirsty ever since she'd come home. This heavy heat, coming so early in June, was really getting to her. Of course, eating salty popcorn wasn't helping. It wasn't long before she found her eyes drifting shut. She woke to find Jacob shaking her gently.

"Hayley?"

"Huh?" Disoriented, she stared at his features without comprehension.

"You need to wake up and go to bed. The movie's over."

Rubbing her eyes, she tried to focus. "It is? I'm sorry, Jacob. I don't know what's the matter with me lately. My brain feels like mush."

"Don't apologize. I understand. Come on. I'll walk you back to your room. Do you want this other bottle of water I grabbed for you?"

"Yes. Thanks. I'm really thirsty." She tried for a smile,

so tired it was hard to think. "I'm sorry I fell asleep. I'll make it up to you."

"I like the sound of that. A beautiful woman in my debt."

A beautiful woman? Hayley stumbled dizzily. Jacob steadied her.

"You really are tired, aren't you?"

Was it her imagination, or did his hand brush her skin in a light caress before he released her?

"This is embarrassing."

"Nope. Embarrassing would be if I offered to carry you," he said with a lopsided grin. "Unlike your muscular friend, Bram, who's used to lifting bars of steel, I'd probably drop you."

Bram's arms lifting her, guiding her body over his... Hayley shook her head at the crazy image and stumbled over a step. Jacob caught her arm again.

"Whoops. Easy there."

"Were you by any chance comparing me to a ton of steel?" she asked, trying for a light tone as she shook off his arm and hurried up the steps.

"Hey, that wasn't what I meant at all. You're the last person I'd think of as cold and hard."

His tone was all wrong. If she didn't know better, she'd swear Jacob was coming on to her. Hayley hurried down the hall, suddenly wanting to be inside the familiar room with her door shut.

"Good night, Jacob," she said when she reached her room. "Thanks for the movie. I'm sorry I was such lousy company."

"That's okay, I understand."

She wished she did.

Without warning, he pressed his palm to her cheek. His expression sent a panicky flutter of unease straight up her spine. Before she could move, he kissed her forehead chastely and stepped back.

"Sleep well. I'll see you in the morning."

"Y-yes. Good night."

Shutting the door, she twisted the lock, feeling foolish. What was the matter with her? She'd known Jacob forever. She was so tired she must have misread the signals. He'd been acting like the boyhood friend she'd grown up with, that was all.

There must be something wrong with her. She felt as if she hadn't slept in months. Only firm resolve kept her awake long enough to change into a faded, oversize T-shirt from her dresser drawer before crawling beneath the covers.

Oddly, as she burrowed her face in her pillow, she was reminded of Bram. His scent clung to the pillow. He'd told her he'd lain down while he was waiting for her. She turned the pillow over and closed her eyes. As she surrendered to the grogginess, she had the nagging feeling that something wasn't right.

She awoke to bright sunshine and a parched throat. When she reached for the bottled water, the disturbing dreams she couldn't quite bring into focus dissolved instantly. Hayley gulped down half the bottle, sitting there on the side of the bed. As she set the bottle back down, fear wormed its way to life once more.

Leigh's picture was no longer on her nightstand.

Hayley leaped to her feet. It wasn't on the floor, under the bed or beneath the nightstand. Her door was still locked, and so was the bathroom door connecting to Leigh's room. But the photograph was gone.

Remembering the way the T-shirt had been flung over her face yesterday, Hayley felt fear explode inside her. She wrapped her arms across her chest, chilled to the bone.

Someone must have come up here while she and Jacob had been downstairs watching the movie.

Bram?

That didn't make sense. Why take a photograph that he'd set there in the first place?

"There's a rational explanation. Calm down and think."

The sound of her own voice brought no comfort, but it did help her push back the panic.

Paula had been up here last night, Hayley reminded herself. What if she hadn't left the house as they'd thought? What if she'd waited for Jacob and Hayley to go downstairs before coming back in here?

But what would Paula want with an old picture of Leigh? What would anyone want with that picture?

Hayley gathered clean clothing at random and walked into the bathroom, turning on the shower. She couldn't afford to give in to the panic clawing at her insides. If only Leigh was here. Hayley had never needed her sister more. England was five hours ahead of the current time. If she called soon, she might be able to reach Leigh and find out when the picture had been taken. And, more importantly, why it might have some special meaning.

After showering she dressed quickly and found the telephone number for her sister in her purse. Her call was answered by a woman with a heavy British accent. Leigh and her friends had gone out for the afternoon, the woman explained. They weren't expected back until later. Thanking her, Hayley hung up without leaving a message.

She stared out the window. She had to talk with Bram and demand some answers. After that, she'd look in the phone book until she found the name of her grandfather's lawyer. Their talk was overdue.

Outside, a movement drew her attention. She was startled to see Eden practically crouching beside a hedge near the opening to the closest maze. There was no one else in sight.

What was she doing?

Hayley stared in amazement as Eden disappeared behind

a tree. Without stopping to think, Hayley raced down the back stairs, determined to find out why Eden was sneaking into the maze like that.

Odette Norwhich looked up from the vegetables she was chopping. "I suppose *you're* wanting breakfast now?"

"No time." Hayley sprinted for the side door.

"Are the gardens on fire?" the woman muttered. "First the mister, then the boy and the missus, even Paula and the handyman."

Hayley ignored her mutterings as she flung open the door and stepped outside. Heat slapped her in the face. Yesterday had been hot. Today, the temperature was going for a record. Good thing she hadn't wasted her time under a hair dryer.

Sprinting toward the maze, she slowed as she reached the tree where she'd last seen Eden. The air was not only hot and humid, but curiously still. Hayley glanced skyward. Not a cloud in sight this morning, yet the sense of an impending storm was reinforced by the hushed silence.

She moved rapidly until she reached a fork in the path. There was nothing to tell her which way Eden had gone. One way would take her deeper into the garden, close to the cliff overlooking the Hudson River. The other path wound around and would eventually bring her back to the entrance she'd just used. Tossing a mental coin, Hayley plunged deeper into the labyrinth.

She hadn't been in this part of the maze in years and hoped she could remember the way. She generally stayed near the fountain. As Hayley moved along the overgrown path, she decided hiring someone to restore order to the grounds had just moved up on her mental list of things that needed immediate attention. Anyone not familiar with the mazes could actually get lost back here now.

Hayley slowed her brisk pace, starting to feel distinctly uneasy. Uselessly, she wiped at the sweat tricking down her face and neck. Her blouse clung like a second skin. Despite the trees shading much of the path, the air was miserably humid. She could barely draw a breath.

She must have chosen wrong. Whatever Eden was doing, Hayley wasn't going to find her by blundering around like this. It was time to go back inside before she melted.

Abruptly, Marcus's voice, raised in anger, shattered the quiet. "No!"

Hayley stopped, wiping at the sweat trickling into her eyes.

"I won't pay another cent!"

If someone answered him, it was done too quietly to be heard over Hayley's labored breathing. She inched closer to another fork in the path.

Marcus laughed, but there was no humor in the chilling sound. "Threats won't work anymore."

She'd heard Marcus angry on more than one occasion, but she'd never heard this particular viperous tone before. Carefully, she peered around the next corner. The path led to one of the many dead ends. Marcus stood in the clearing there, surrounded by a profusion of colorful roses. An empty stone bench sat nearby.

He appeared to be completely alone.

Hayley was struck once more by how much he'd aged. In memory, he'd loomed like an angry giant. The reality was a tall, gaunt man with receding gray hair and harsh, bitter features.

Was Eden on the other side of the hedge? There was nothing to indicate anyone else was nearby. Even the birds and insects seemed to be in hiding.

Marcus began to pace in agitation. He seemed unaffected by the heat. He wasn't even sweating, though he wore long pants, a short-sleeved shirt and heavy dark shoes. A pair of soiled gloves hung from his belt.

Abruptly, he bent over to lift the petal of a blood-red rose.

"You don't scare me, you know," he said conversationally.

For a second, Hayley feared he was talking to her.

"If I wanted to, I could snap your neck like this."

He twisted the perfect rose, ripping it from its stalk with a viciousness that nearly made her gasp out loud. He pulled a thorn from his finger. Blood welled from the spot, as red as the rose he held.

With a horrible smile that chilled her to the core, he dropped the flower to the ground. Lifting his foot, he crushed the delicate petals beneath his shoe with deliberate savagery. Then he turned his head.

Hayley jerked back. Had he seen her? Her body quaked from head to toe. There'd been madness in his eyes, but a calculating look as well. She felt as if she'd just witnessed a cold-blooded murder. The malice behind that action left her breathless.

Was that what he'd done to her mother?

Unable to rid herself of the idea, she turned and began to run. She had to get away from such vile evilness. He'd wanted her to witness that action, she was certain of it. Abruptly, she stopped again, suddenly sick to her stomach. Doubling over, she heaved until the taste of bile burned the back of her throat. She swiped at the sweat running down her face. It stung her eyes, blurring her vision.

The main path lay straight ahead. All she had to do was put one foot in front of the other and she'd reach the house and the blessed air-conditioning. She could make it. She just had to concentrate. But the house seemed so far away.

"Hayley?"

Bram's voice seemed to travel down a long tunnel to reach her. At least the tunnel was providing merciful shelter from the too-bright sun. She barely felt the heat now.

But that seemed all wrong. She *should* be feeling hot.

Dizzily, she tried to focus, afraid she was going to pass out.

''Hayley!''

Bram gripped her shoulders. That was good. He wouldn't let her fall. She could depend on Bram. She clung to him, needing him to understand the horror of what she'd just seen.

''He killed her, Bram. I know he did. He wanted me to know it.''

Bram dropped his tools, supporting Hayley as she suddenly went limp. Her face was cherry-red and she was sweating profusely. Lifting her in his arms, he realized her skin was cool to the touch.

Not good. Not good at all.

Her eyes fluttered open. ''I'm all right.''

''No, you aren't, but you will be. I'll have you out of this heat in just a minute.''

He started for the back door. The housekeeper stared at him through the kitchen window. Her glare was darker than ever, but Bram was in no mood for any comments from her. Mrs. Norwhich, however, surprised him by holding open the back door.

''Straight ahead,'' she said, pointing the way with a paring knife. ''Second door on the right.''

To his relief, he discovered she'd sent him to a bedroom.

''Jacob was right,'' Hayley murmured. ''You didn't drop me.''

Bram had no time to wonder what she meant by that as he laid her on a brightly colored quilt. He pushed back the damp tendrils of hair that clung to her flushed cheeks.

''Hayley? Stay with me.''

Odette Norwhich bustled over, a damp cloth in her outstretched hand. ''Fool girl went running outside with nothing in her stomach. This house is like a refrigerator and it's a sauna out there. You can't treat a body that way. I'll make her some lunch. You see to it she eats every bite.''

''She's suffering from heat exhaustion,'' he told the woman. ''We need to bring her body temperature down right away. Is there a shower or bathtub down here?''

''Both. Through there.'' She pointed to an open door beyond the bed.

Bram nodded his thanks and lifted Hayley again.

''Sick,'' she muttered.

''I know. You'll feel better in a minute.'' But when he set her down, she promptly turned to the sink, clutching it tightly as dry heaves racked her body. He steadied her.

Turning the shower on cool, he let the spray fill the tub. Not bothering to remove her clothing, he lifted Hayley and stood her beneath the shower fully dressed.

''What are you doing? This is cold!''

''Yes,'' he said firmly as she wriggled. ''We need to lower your body temperature. Stop struggling before you fall.''

Water splashed, soaking his shirt. He ignored it and began peeling her out of her drenched blouse.

''Just like a man,'' she muttered, her teeth chattering. ''Taking advantage of the situation.''

Amazed that she still had a sense of humor, he offered her a phony leer as he tossed the blouse into the sink. ''You got it. Any excuse to get you out of your clothing.''

Her nipples were tight, hard points, clearly visible beneath the lace of her bra. Bram ignored the enticing sight as well as the feel of her slick skin, and reached for the button on the waistband of her shorts.

Hayley batted at his hand weakly. ''I can do it.''

''And deprive me of the pleasure?''

''Are you planning to join me?''

His body hardened, despite his best intentions. There'd

been no real emotion behind the question. He sensed she was using banter to cover her embarrassment.

"Nothing would give me more pleasure," he assured her. The zipper parted, allowing him to skim the shorts down her legs. They landed in the pooling water with a noisy splash. "But I'd rather have you panting from desire than panting from heat exhaustion."

Her panties were simple white nylon. Soaking wet, they left nothing to his imagination.

"If you keep looking at me like that," she muttered, "you're going to get both."

The haze was lifting from her eyes. The flush of her skin was being replaced by a more natural color. Her long hair lay plastered against her head and shoulders. And Bram found himself aroused despite his best intentions.

"Sit down, before we both fall," he ordered. "If you don't behave, we're going to shock Mrs. Norwhich."

Hayley smiled weakly. "I doubt anything would shock her." But she let him lower her into the water. "I'm cold."

"That's the general idea."

"Freezing me to death?"

She was so lovely. "No, but we have to lower your body temperature as quickly as possible."

"You've achieved success. Can I get out of here? I already had a shower this morning." She pushed weakly at wet strands of her hair. "Have you any idea how long it takes to dry this stuff?"

"Stop complaining." But when he saw her shiver, he adjusted the water to a slightly warmer setting. "You either soak here or go to the hospital. Your choice."

"How about if I pick neither of the above?"

"Hayley, heat prostration is nothing to fool around with."

"I wasn't outside long enough for that."

"Tell it to your body."

"I'm just tired. And a little sick."

"I noticed."

Mrs. Norwhich entered, thrusting a large, frosty glass into his hand. "Orange juice," she said tersely. "Make her drink all of it. It will restore the fluids and give her an energy boost." Plopping a pile of fresh clothing on the sink, she left.

"You heard the lady."

"I don't like orange juice."

"You sound like one of my brother's kids. Drink it anyway."

"I didn't know you had a brother."

"I have three of them. Now drink."

"You must have been the oldest. You're bossy." She took a tentative sip, then quickly drank the juice. "I'm not always a baby," she said quietly.

He didn't like her change in attitude. A subdued Hayley wasn't normal. He dropped to his knees beside the tub and removed the glass from her hand. His wet shirt dripped on the floor and his denim shorts. He ignored the unpleasant feeling, cupping her chin until she met his gaze.

"You aren't being a baby." He tried to stem his desire by placing a chaste kiss on her forehead. Hayley spoiled the effect by running a wet hand timidly across his chest. The sensation was highly erotic, particularly when her eyes were issuing such a soulful invitation.

"Stop it. Mrs. Norwhich could return any minute."

"Let Mrs. Norwhich find her own man," Hayley retorted. But she stilled her hand.

"You could tempt the halo from an archangel," Bram told her.

"Yeah? What would it take to tempt you?"

Setting the glass on the floor, he gathered her into his arms, pulling them both upright. Her body slithered wetly against his as he lifted her out of the tub.

Hayley's eyes widened in surprise. He snatched up the bath towel, wrapping it snugly around her quaking body before he could give in to the urge to carry her back to that fussy bright quilt and give her the satisfaction they both craved.

"Get dressed."

"I'm not sure I can."

"Then I'll call Mrs. Norwhich to help."

Her eyes searched his face. "Why?"

Ruthlessly, he clamped down on his desire. "Because I'm nowhere near as strong as an archangel. Now, get dressed."

Chapter Seven

Mrs. Norwhich entered the bedroom as if cued. She held out a shirt to him. ''I thought you might want to borrow this,'' she told him knowingly.

Bram felt a flush move up his throat, but she turned away and disappeared. How much had she seen?

Tugging off his dripping shirt, he replaced it with the new one. Faintly warm, it must have come straight from the dryer. It had a subtle, clean smell, and Bram wondered if it belonged to Marcus.

He killed her, I know he did.

What had Hayley meant by that? What had happened before Bram found her?

''Do you have a comb?'' Hayley asked as she came forward, her hair wrapped in the bath towel. She was dressed in a bright cotton sundress.

''Sorry.''

''That's okay.''

''Want to tell me what happened out there?''

''Truthfully? I'd rather forget the whole thing. But I never will.'' She sank down on the end of the bed. ''Marcus killed that rose the way he must have killed my mother.''

Glancing at the doorway, Bram was relieved to see it was empty. He could hear Mrs. Norwhich moving around in the kitchen.

"Are you saying your father killed your mother?" he asked softly. Sitting beside her, he resisted an impulse to touch her again.

"We could never prove it, but we always knew."

"Tell me."

Haltingly at first, she did. Bram found he remembered the general story. The missing woman had been headline news once. He hadn't paid much attention at the time, but hearing the tale now made a number of things more understandable. Things like his employer's paranoid insistence on bars on every window, and even Hayley's somewhat erratic behavior. No wonder Heartskeep felt so eerie.

He'd thought Hayley was merely part of a dysfunctional family, but this went much deeper. As she described the scene in the rose garden, real apprehension stirred to life.

"You believe Marcus was talking to Eden?"

"There wasn't anyone else around."

Bram tensed. "But there could have been. You said you never actually saw Eden after she entered the garden."

"I followed her out there! Who else could it have been?"

All sorts of people—including himself. Bram had seen Jacob slip into the maze and had followed, but had lost the other man at one of the forks. He decided it wouldn't be prudent to mention that to Hayley right now.

Dishes rattled and Paula Kerstairs slipped into the room with a tray. There was something distinctly unsettling about the woman. Bram had a feeling she'd been standing outside the door listening for several minutes.

"I'm not hungry," Hayley told her.

Paula ignored her and addressed him. "I'm to tell you to see to it she eats every bite." She set down the tray and melted away.

Hayley started to shove the food aside, but Bram stayed

her hand. "You'll hurt Mrs. Norwich's feelings. Eat a little, all right? Then we'll talk."

Hayley stared at the omelette, the stack of buttered toast and the bowl of sherbet. "I can't eat all this."

"Just eat a little."

The omelette dripped with cheese as she cut into it with her fork, making his mouth water. It had been several hours since he'd had breakfast.

"Do you have any idea how many calories are in this?"

He covered a wry smile. "You can stand to gain a few pounds."

"Sure. You say that now. But when my arteries clog from all this cholesterol, where will you be?"

She swallowed the bite, cocking her head to one side. Bram managed not to grin.

The towel would have slipped from her head if she hadn't caught it with her hand. "Are you implying I'm too skinny?"

"Nope. I'm not stupid." Besides, she wasn't skinny. She was round and firm in all the right places. And before he could take that thought any further, Mrs. Norwhich appeared, holding a second tray.

"You might as well eat, too," she said gruffly.

Surprised by the gesture, he thanked her with genuine gratitude.

"The soda's yours. The bottled water's for her," Mrs. Norwhich announced. "She and the mister live on that stuff. Though why anyone would pay good money for something they can get right out of their own sink for free..."

His lips twitched as she bustled away, still muttering. "Now who would have guessed there was a tender heart under that grumpy exterior? Want me to open your water for you?"

"Yes, thank you."

Bram handed her the open bottle, then carried his tray to the small writing desk. "I'd better wash my hands first. Keep eating while it's hot."

When he returned, Hayley was making serious inroads on the meal. After the first taste, he understood why. "Mrs. Norwhich can cook."

Hayley nodded. She took a long swallow from her bottle of water. Her color was much better, he was relieved to see, but shadows haunted her eyes.

"You look tired."

"Bram, I'm not crazy."

A bite of toast threatened to lodge in his throat. "Where did that come from?"

She nibbled on a bit of sherbet, then set her spoon down. "Last night you didn't believe me."

"When did I say that?"

Guilt had left him sleepless and angry last night, until in desperation, he'd sought refuge in his work. He knew it was partly guilt that had kept him standing over the anvil as the uncomfortably hot night surrendered to an even hotter new day. He was feeling pretty tired himself this morning.

"Why did you leave that picture on my nightstand last night?"

Bewildered, he started to shake his head in confusion, then stopped. "Are you talking about that photograph I picked up off the floor in your room yesterday? What does that have to do with anything?"

"That's what I want to know."

"I don't understand."

"Where did you get it?"

"It was on the floor by your nightstand. I assumed you'd dropped it."

"You found it in my room?"

"Yeah. What's so important about that picture, Hayley?"

"That's what I'm trying to figure out. Someone took it from my room while I was downstairs last night."

A shaft of apprehension slithered down his spine. "What?"

"It was a picture of Leigh," she added.

"Your sister?" Remembering the image, he shook his head. "I thought it was you. You two could be twins."

"We are."

His stomach lurched. "You never told me you were a twin."

Hayley frowned. "Sure I did."

"I'd remember something like that, Hayley. Trust me. The fact that there are two of you would have made a lasting impression."

"Why? Does it matter?"

"Not to me. I'm just surprised, that's all. What's the significance of that particular picture?"

"I don't know. I've never seen it before. I tried to call Leigh to find out when it was taken, but she was already gone for the day."

"She looked about fifteen in the picture."

"Closer to sixteen," Hayley corrected.

"Where was it taken?"

"I can't tell. The background didn't look familiar to me."

"I don't like this, Hayley. It seems to me that someone's playing a sick game with you. I really think you should go back to your apartment in Boston. If you honestly believe your father killed your mother, you're a fool to stay here. Look around. You're surrounded by people acting strangely. Staying would be stupid. You need a lawyer. Maybe a bodyguard."

There was a noise at the door and Bram spun, automatically putting himself between Hayley and the door. Paula Kerstairs stood there with an annoyed expression.

"You have a phone call," she told Hayley grumpily.

"Would you take a—"

"She say's she's your sister, calling from England."

"Leigh? But I told the woman she didn't need to call me back. Never mind. I'll take it in the office."

Pursing her lips, Paula disappeared from sight. Grabbing her water, Hayley shoved the tray aside and started for the door. "Excuse me, Bram."

"No problem. I need to get back to work, anyhow."

Hayley hesitated. "Thank you."

"You're welcome. And, Hayley? Think about what I said. You should get away from here."

"I'll think about it."

He watched her run down the hall before he lifted the two trays and started for the kitchen.

"I can get those," Mrs. Norwhich said, looking up from a recipe book. "It's my job."

"You're very good at your job, Mrs. Norwhich. That really hit the spot. Thank you for lunch."

Bram was aware that her gaze followed him as he set down the trays and walked outside. Jacob stood in the yard, lounging against an expensive sports car. He watched as Bram bent to retrieve his tools. Bram was sorely tempted to confront Hayley's stepbrother, but settled for giving him a hard look before heading in the opposite direction.

Glancing up at the house, he saw a curtain drop quickly into place. Eden, Marcus or Paula Kerstairs?

Or was someone else inside Heartskeep?

"LEIGH?"

"Hayley? Is that you?"

"Yes." She tried to inject her voice with enthusiasm.

"How's your visit going? The woman I spoke with earlier said you wouldn't be back until late."

"We just stopped back to change clothing. This connection is terrible. I can barely hear you. Can you hear me?"

"Yes. I can hear you perfectly."

"Must be on my end, then. Is everything okay?"

"Of course," Hayley lied. "I just wanted to say hi."

"Oh. Well, I'm glad you called. We were talking about you this afternoon. I wish you had come with us."

So did Hayley. "Next time. Leigh, do you know a man by the name of Bram Myers?"

Her sister fell silent. Static or no static, Leigh must have realized the question was important.

"No," she said thoughtfully. "It's an unusual name. I'm pretty sure I'd remember a guy named Bram. Is he cute?"

Hayley gripped the receiver more tightly. "*Cute* isn't a word I'd use to describe him." *Sensual, incredibly masculine, dangerously sexy,* but never *cute.*

"Hayley? You sound funny. *Should* I know him?"

"No! Not at all. I just wondered. He made a wrought-iron gate for Heartskeep." She decided not to mention the rest. "His work is brilliant."

"But?"

"No buts. I just wondered if you'd heard of him, that's all. Marcus hired him."

"Darn it, this static is terrible. Did you say Marcus hired him? He's putting up a fence around our house?"

"Basically, yes."

Leigh's voice changed. Hayley pictured her sister worrying her lower lip. "Do you need me to come home, Hayley?"

More than anything.

"Of course not. I want you to take a ton of pictures to show me."

"I miss you, too."

"Thanks. Speaking of pictures, I found an old one of you the other day. I'm not sure where it was taken—"

"Hayley? Are you still there?"

"Leigh? I'm here."

"Hayley? Can you hear me? Darn it! Look, if you can still hear me, I'm going to hang up now. All I can hear is static, and the girls are waiting. I'll call you when we get back tonight. Maybe I can get a decent line out then. Okay? Darn this thing. Love you. Bye, for now."

"Bye," Hayley whispered, clutching the receiver against her cheek tightly before setting it down. She felt more alone than she ever had in her life.

"Was that your sister on the phone?"

Hayley whirled. Jacob stood there, though she hadn't heard him enter.

"Yes," she snapped.

He took a hasty step back, a hurt expression on his face. "Hey, sorry. I just wondered. Is everything okay? You look upset."

Adrenaline still poured through her body and her nerves felt raw. "I'm fine. I just miss Leigh, that's all. If you'll excuse me—"

He held out a hand, stopping her when she would have risen from the desk.

"Wait! I was looking for you."

"This isn't a good time, Jacob."

"Please. It's important." He shifted nervously. "Look, maybe I shouldn't be sticking my nose in your business, but...well, I just saw your buddy Bram leaving the house."

"We were talking."

"Yeah? Well, did he happen to mention his wife while you were 'talking'?"

Bram was married?

But he'd told her he wasn't. He'd lied to her? Hayley

didn't want to believe it, but that would certainly explain why he didn't want to talk about himself.

She found she had braced her hands against her grandfather's walnut desk. The polished wood showed its years of use. If she lifted the heavy blotter, she could probably still find the spot where she and Leigh had tried to carve their initials with their grandfather's silver-and-malachite letter opener.

"I see he didn't tell you about her. I went into town this morning and talked to a few people." Jacob eased into the green leather chair across from her. "Mom was uneasy about this guy so I didn't think it would hurt to do some checking. I mean, your father isn't... That is, Mom says..."

"Dementia or not, Marcus probably wouldn't have done much checking once he decided to hire Bram," Hayley agreed. "What else did you learn?"

Jacob arched his eyebrows in surprise. "You're taking this pretty good. I was worried you'd be mad at me. You know, for sticking my nose in or something? But I don't like the way he acts all possessive around you. So when I found out..."

"That he was married," she finished for him when he shrugged uncomfortably. A numbness settled over her. Having a foggy brain was actually a relief at the moment. If this was shell shock, she was all for it. Her emotions seemed to have retreated to some safe haven, as they'd done when she'd realized her mother wasn't going to come home ever again. Sooner or later they would ambush her, but for now, she could handle whatever Jacob had to say. And it was obvious there was more to come.

"I thought you'd be upset. I guess maybe you will be when I tell you the rest. I don't know what Myers did for a living before, but he and his wife used to live in New York City, so I'd say it's a safe bet he wasn't always a blacksmith. His wife was related to the Peppertons.'' He named one of the area's old, socially elite families. Everyone knew of the Peppertons, of course. They were very active in breeding and racing horses, but Hayley didn't know the family personally.

''Was?'' she asked.

''She's dead. So is the baby.''

Amazingly, Hayley's mind processed those blows, as well. Only the fine tremor of her fingers betrayed any emotion at all. She lowered her hands to her lap, out of sight.

He hadn't lied, but it came as a surprise that Bram had been a husband and a father.

''According to my sources,'' Jacob continued, ''Bram's wife showed up at The Inn one day. She was real pregnant. She moved in with her cousin, Betty Pepperton, and made an appointment with a local OB.''

''Marcus?'' Hayley made an effort to control her breathing. If she wasn't careful, she'd hyperventilate, which would destroy this artificial calm.

''Beats me, but I wouldn't be surprised, given he was the closest local OB-GYN back then. And it might explain a lot, if any of the wilder rumors are true. I mean, uh...I don't know if, uh, you've heard any of the stuff people say in town. You know, about Marcus?''

Jacob shifted restlessly and the supple leather chair made soft noises of protest.

''I never listen to gossip, but nothing anyone says about Marcus would surprise me,'' she assured him.

''Oh. Well, you know how people like to talk. Most of the stuff you hear isn't true, anyhow.''

''Jacob, just spit it out.''

''Yeah. Okay. Well, they say Marcus lost more than one infant during a delivery. The nastier rumors say he may have lost some on purpose. Now, I'm not saying it's true, but lots of women wait too long to do things about a pregnancy. You know, women who don't want another kid?'' Jacob shrugged again, looking even more uncomfortable.

''Are you saying Marcus killed Bram's wife and child on purpose?''

''No! Of course not! A few people might want to think that, but Helen Myers delivered in a hospital and everything. Someone would have noticed if he'd done anything wrong on purpose. Most of the stuff I heard was about babies he delivered that didn't make it to the hospital. But heck, the people in town don't...you know, really like Marcus. He isn't exactly considered a good doctor, if you know what I mean. They say he graduated last in his class. I mean, if that's true, I don't imagine he'd be particularly good if there were complications during a delivery. And from what I heard, Myers's wife had a lot of complications. She had to have a cesarean section and there was trouble getting the baby out. Then she went and bled to death. Some people say he cut something he shouldn't have, but who knows?''

Hayley tried not to shudder, but was only partially successful. ''Bram wasn't with her?''

''He showed up the day her cousin drove her to the hospital, but she was already dead when Myers got there. He went berserk. They say it took four security guards to calm him down.''

Hayley drew in a sharp breath.

''You know the worst part? The baby lived for almost four days. A lot of people wondered if it was really Bram's baby, but I guess it must have been because he stayed with it the whole time. Everyone thought he'd go ballistic when it finally died, but the guy I talked to said Myers just sat there holding the little thing. He didn't say a word for a long time and he wouldn't let them take it away until he was good and ready.''

She could see the scene in her head. Those strong, capable hands holding that tiny infant. How he must have hurt. She ached for him. For all three of them.

"Afterward, he just got up, walked out and disappeared," Jacob was saying. "No one saw him again. Until now. I think you have to agree it's real strange, him turning up here like this. I mean, working for your dad and all?"

Hayley forced herself to concentrate on his words. "You think Bram came back here for retribution?"

Jacob shifted, looking toward the window at her back instead of meeting her eyes. "Like I said, you know how people are. They like to talk. Especially when a socially prominent family is involved. There were lots of rumors flying around back then."

"About Bram?"

Jacob hesitated. "You sure you want to hear this?"

He threw up his hands at her impatient scowl. "Okay, okay. There was talk about Myers. You know—was it really his baby, did his wife pick a doctor who might screw up, hoping to get rid of the child? That sort of thing. Other people wondered if she came here to have the baby because she was afraid of Myers. He's a big guy, and she was a small woman, from what I heard. And it is pretty strange that she left her husband when she was so pregnant and all. They eloped when her family demanded she stop seeing Myers. She was only eighteen at the time. Lots younger than him, you know. People figured he married her for her money."

Hayley twisted her hands together tightly in her lap.

"Anyhow, what really surprised everyone was that no lawsuits were filed over their deaths. Even her family didn't sue anyone." Jacob shrugged. "Apparently, the Peppertons blamed Myers instead of the doctor. Chester Pepperton caused a big scene at the hospital after his sister died. Security threw him out."

"Threw Bram out?"

"No, Pepperton. They say Myers just stood there like a stone and let him yell. Security had to drag his wife's brother out."

Hayley's hands were now clenched so tightly she could no longer feel her fingers.

"The thing is," Jacob continued, "I'm not sure if Marcus was Helen's doctor or not, but after I heard all this stuff, I got to wondering, you know? I mean, it strikes me as real odd that Myers would come back here for any reason. When you introduced him around at The Inn, a few of the old-timers remembered the story and started talking. I started wondering if maybe he had decided to get some of his own back from Marcus. I mean, he was real upset about the baby, and if Marcus was to blame..."

There was a buzzing in her head. Vaguely, Hayley wondered if she was in danger of passing out again. Since she was sitting down, at least she wouldn't have far to fall.

"I'd ask Mom about it, but you know how she is." Jacob shrugged once more. "Patient confidentiality is a religion with her. Still, the more I heard, the more I thought you ought to know about these rumors. You need to be careful around him, you know? I mean, it's possible he's playing up to you in an effort to strike back at Marcus."

"Thanks," she muttered weakly.

"Maybe I shouldn't have told you. You aren't mad at me, are you? You look sort of upset."

Devastated would have been a better word choice, but it wasn't Jacob's fault she'd fallen for a man who might be using her to get revenge against a father she didn't even like. Talk about irony.

Hayley shook her head. "I'm glad you told me. How long ago did this happen?"

"I'm not sure, exactly. Around ten years or so."

Hayley stared at him. She would have been thirteen, wearing braces and just starting to take an interest in clothes and makeup. She'd considered most boys jerks, and she wouldn't have looked twice at someone as old as Bram back then.

But she'd lived here ten years ago, and even though she and Leigh went to a private school, she would have thought she'd have heard about a scandal like this. Of course, her mother and grandfather always went to great lengths to shelter them, and that was the summer they had gone to camp, wasn't it?

Hayley realized Jacob was regarding her oddly.

"Maybe Myers really did come here for revenge." He scooted forward to the edge of his seat.

The room started closing in on her. Dizziness hovered on the edge of awareness. She focused on Jacob's worried expression in an effort to keep the room from reeling.

"No one would wait ten years to take revenge for something like that," she said.

"Sure they would. There are people who plan their revenge for years."

"Only in movies."

But, she conceded, Bram was the cautious, deliberate sort. She'd noticed that about him from the first, probably because she tended to plunge headlong into everything. Still, it would be in character for him to take his time and plan carefully if he wanted something. But to wait ten years to take revenge?

Hayley didn't buy it. She could see where Jacob's thoughts were leading him, but the explosive chemistry between Bram and her had nothing to do with Marcus or revenge. She was the one who'd been pushing Bram, not the other way around.

It seems to me someone's playing a sick game with you.

Not Bram. Please don't let it be Bram.

"Bram isn't here for revenge."

As soon as she said the words, she knew they were true.

If he'd plotted to use her, he would have done his research. He would have known she was a twin. He hadn't faked his surprise when she'd told him. Nor was his concern for her phony. She might be going crazy, but her instincts couldn't be that far off base.

Jacob stood, leaning across the desk. "Geez, Hayley, at least think about the possibility. You didn't fall for this guy, did you? I mean, he'll only hurt you, even if the rumors have it all wrong. Myers is scary. He's nobody to fool around with. I don't want anything to happen to you."

"It won't."

Hayley's gaze swept the room and landed on a silent figure standing to one side of the library door. Like a wraith in a horror movie, Paula Kerstairs watched them intently.

Hayley lurched to her feet, thankful her legs were still willing to support her. "Can we help you?" she demanded harshly. Jacob twisted around.

"His mother wants him." Paula inclined her head toward Jacob, then, like any self-respecting ghost, faded from sight.

"Geez! That woman gives me the creeps," Jacob said.

Hayley knew exactly what he meant. "You'd better go."

"Yeah. Okay. Look, I'm sorry I told you all that stuff. I probably should have kept my big mouth shut. You aren't mad at me, are you?"

"Of course not."

"Are you sure you're okay, Hayley?"

"I'm fine."

His expression altered abruptly. He looked her up and down with a smile that changed everything.

"Yeah," he said huskily. "You really are fine. You're a beautiful woman, Hayley. I'll catch you later."

"Later," she agreed faintly. Much later.

Never once in all the years she'd known him had Jacob ever looked at her like that. Watching him saunter from the room, she told herself she must have been mistaken. That couldn't have been a gleam of sexual interest she'd seen in his eyes.

She liked Jacob. She always had. But she had absolutely no romantic interest in him. How could she, when all she could think about was Bram? Besides, Jacob had never given any indication that he was attracted to her.

Until last night.

Now that she thought about it, she remembered worrying about the way he'd touched her. Then there was that inexplicable animosity between Jacob and Bram. Had she been missing subtle signals for years? The last thing she wanted to do was hurt Jacob.

The rumors and innuendoes he'd told her about Bram were disturbing, but she didn't believe for a minute that Bram had returned to town for revenge. Still, it was disconcerting to think Marcus might have been his wife's doctor. Why would Bram come here to work for the man responsible for his wife's death?

Why would Marcus let him?

There was only one way to find out. She'd ask Bram. But first, it was high time to start being proactive. She needed to talk to the lawyer and get some advice. Since she must have left his letter back in her apartment, she'd have to hunt through the local telephone book for his name. She was pretty sure she'd remember it when she saw it again.

Hayley pulled the phone book from the shelf across the room and returned to the desk. Exhaustion was pulling at her, but she was determined to do this now. She'd at least find his name and write down his phone number, then maybe catch a quick nap before she actually called him.

There were more legal listings than she'd expected. Was everyone in the county a lawyer? Her eyes were drooping when her finger literally landed on a small ad to one side of the page. Rosencroft and Associates. That was it! Ira Rosencroft had signed the letter.

Grabbing a pen, she opened the desk drawer for the pad of paper her grandfather always kept there. The usually tidy drawer was a jumbled mess.

Someone had been using her grandfather's desk.

Annoyed, she delved inside, but the pad of paper was missing. The middle drawer was even worse. Envelopes and papers had been shoved inside with no order at all.

Frustrated, Hayley decided to use the back of a blank envelope. Pulling one out, she discovered it wasn't empty. A photograph landed on the desk faceup. Another, more recent picture of Leigh. But it couldn't be. Unlike the one Hayley had found in her room the other night, this appeared to be a current photo—except for Leigh's hair.

The shorter bob was flattering, but neither she nor her sister had ever worn their hair exactly like this. In the picture, Leigh was laughing, looking up at a man with his back to the camera.

Hayley studied the image, trying to make sense of what she was seeing. The background was clear in this picture. It had been taken on the street outside a familiar coffee shop in New York City. In the background was the bank building with one of those signs that flashed the time, date and temperature. The date was showing in the picture.

"Impossible."

She tore through the drawers, hunting for her grandfather's magnifying glass. She had to be wrong. The sign couldn't possibly say what she thought it said.

But it did.

The picture had been taken two days ago.

Chapter Eight

The photograph couldn't be of her sister, then. Leigh was in England.

Wasn't she?

Hayley set the magnifying glass on top of the phone book. Of course Leigh was in England. Hayley had just spoken with her. She'd driven Leigh and her friends to the airport the other morning. She hadn't actually watched them board the plane, but Leigh wouldn't lie to her. They never kept secrets from each other.

Tears pricked at Hayley's eyes. Her entire world was suddenly upside down. If she couldn't trust her own twin, who could she trust?

Bram. Except he was keeping his own secrets.

Until a few minutes ago, she would have said she could trust Jacob, but that hadn't been brotherly interest in his eyes just now. Eden disliked her, Mrs. Walsh and Kathy were gone, and the new staff didn't bear consideration. That left Marcus.

Yeah, right. The father who seemed to despise his twin daughters and had spent twenty-four years trying to ignore them completely.

Hayley rested her head on her arms, dislodging the towel from her head. She'd forgotten all about her wet hair.

"I am going crazy," she whispered.

"No, but you might if you keep talking to yourself."

Hayley jerked up her head, quickly blinking back the unshed tears. Bram filled the doorway leading to the hall.

"What is it? Did something happen to your sister?"

"I thought you left," she managed.

"I came back. What's wrong?"

Wordlessly, she shook her head and slid the picture across the desk to him.

Bram picked it up, frowning. "Leigh again? What's wrong? You don't like the guy she's with?"

"I don't know the guy she's with. Apparently, I don't know my sister, either. She's supposed to be in England, not New York. I just got off the phone with her. She said she was having a great time over there."

"So what's the problem?"

"Look at the date on the sign in the background. Here's a magnifying glass if—"

"I can read it."

He studied the picture, turning it over. His frown lines deepened.

"How do you know this wasn't taken in London? This could be any city street."

"Well, for one thing, how would a picture taken in England two days ago be in a blank envelope inside this desk today? For another, I recognize both the street and that coffee shop. Leigh and I have eaten there several times."

Bram tapped the picture against his open palm. He turned it over, then surveyed the room thoughtfully. "Does all that equipment work?"

Hayley followed his gaze across the room to what her grandfather had called his technology center. He'd loved gadgets and was always buying the latest computer, the latest printer, the most up-to-date software.

Bram crossed to the computer and turned it on.

"What are you doing?"

"I'm going to show you how your sister can be in London and New York at the same time."

Hayley rose stiffly. She wanted to tell him what Jacob had said. She wanted to hear Bram tell her he hadn't come here for some sort of twisted revenge. She wanted reassurance that he wasn't using her for some reason of his own. But nothing was as it should have been. Everything Jacob had told her was starting to seem more possible.

Bram sat down before the bank of machines.

I don't know what Myers did for a living before, but he and his wife used to live in New York City, Jacob had told her, *so I'd say it's a safe bet he wasn't always a blacksmith.*

"You know computers?"

"Doesn't everyone these days? How do you think your father found me?" Bram asked. "Every good businessman needs a Web page."

"I never thought about it." She couldn't see Marcus searching the Web for a blacksmith.

Bram's fingers fairly danced over the keyboard. She'd always been a pretty good typist, but she doubted she was in his league.

"Nice system," he said approvingly.

"It belonged to my grandfather, but it's at least seven years old."

Bram looked at her sharply. "Not this machine. They only put this chip out last year."

Hayley stared from him to the machine. She studied it for a minute and realized he was right. This wasn't the computer her grandfather had owned. Before she could wonder about that, Bram's next words captured her attention.

"If we knew where to look, I'm betting we'd find a copy of this photograph stored in one of these files. I could do a search, but it's probably quicker just to show you what I meant using this picture."

"I don't understand." Her head was starting to throb.

"Watch."

Taking the photo, Bram worked with quiet efficiency, moving easily from one program to another as he scanned the picture into the machine and began to manipulate the image. Obviously, he was more than a little familiar with this sort of work. Unease formed a lump in her stomach.

He zeroed in on the date until it filled the screen.

"What day would you like it to read?"

He could have been speaking Chinese. Her tired brain could barely focus on the screen, let alone his words.

"How about tomorrow?" he asked when she didn't answer.

Minutes flew past as he changed the date on the image. Hayley pulled over a chair, afraid that if she didn't sit down, she'd fall down. She wasn't familiar with the graphics program he was using. Leigh was the computer whiz. She'd probably understand exactly what Bram was doing.

He rose and began checking through packages of printer paper before selecting one. Minutes later she held the same-size photograph printed on an 8½x11 sheet of photo-quality paper. The only difference between the two photos was the date on the bank's display screen.

"That's how it was done, Hayley. If we use that paper cutter over there, you'd never be able to tell which was the original."

Why wasn't that knowledge more reassuring?

"But Leigh's hair is long like mine—unless she just got it cut."

Bram shook his head. "Changing a hairstyle is almost as simple. There are even programs that do that. Watch."

He began searching file listings, stopping when he found one called Hayley. She immediately recognized the picture he opened. Jacob had taken it with the digital camera he'd gotten for his birthday. She had been mugging for the camera at a restaurant in New York where they'd met him for dinner to celebrate. As she watched, Bram erased the hair spilling past her shoulders. Before her eyes, the picture was transformed. Her long hair vanished, replaced by a shorter length.

"It would take time to clean this up completely, but trust me, I could finish this picture so you'd never be able to tell I had altered it. Want to see what you would look like with bangs? I could add them. Want your hair red? No problem."

The knot of unease was growing in direct proportion to her headache.

"That's how it was done, Hayley. Simple, for those who know how. The question is, who in this house knows how?"

Helplessly, she shook her head. "Leigh might be able to do that, if she was here."

"What about Jacob?"

"Probably. This could even be his machine, now that I think about it. I know he's taken computer courses. He and Leigh talked about them once. Computers don't hold much fascination for me so I've never paid much attention. But why go to all this trouble? What's the point?"

"An excellent question."

And one that was starting to really scare her. She reached for her hair, mildly surprised to find it damp. The events of this morning seemed a lifetime ago. She threaded her fingers through the tangled strands. Bram had already seen her at her worst, but if she didn't comb it soon, she'd have a heck of a time getting rid of the snarls.

"Whenever you start toying with your hair like that I know something's on your mind," Bram said.

Immediately, she dropped her hands. There was no point in beating around the bush. "Is it true you were married?"

The question netted a flicker of surprise. "I suppose I have Jacob to thank for that question?"

Hayley nodded.

"My wife died more than ten years ago."

"In childbirth?"

Their gazes locked. If eyes truly were a window to a person's soul, she was gazing into a soul filled with torment.

"Yes," he said tersely. "I assume Jacob didn't omit the fact that my daughter died, as well."

Remembering what Jacob had said about Bram's vigil with his daughter, Hayley laid her hand on his biceps, touching the tip of the dragon's tail. His muscles were knotted tighter than steel. "I'm sorry."

"So am I," he said simply.

"Was Marcus your wife's doctor?"

"What, exactly, did your pal tell you?" he asked softly.

Hayley flinched, but she refused to look away. "Jacob said you married into a wealthy local family. He said your wife showed up in town one day, pregnant and alone. She began seeing a local doctor. Something went horribly wrong with the delivery. I just wondered if Marcus was that doctor."

"How is it that good old Jacob managed to omit that part?"

"He didn't know who the doctor was."

Bram's jaw was clenched so tightly she was afraid he'd crack a tooth.

"I'm sorry," she said.

"Are you?"

Her hand fell from his arm. She felt his grief and his anger as if Bram and she were physically connected somehow.

"Let me guess. Jacob suggested I must have returned seeking vengeance. Right?" Bram swore. "Is that what *you* think? That I'm here planning some sort of convoluted revenge ten years after the fact?"

He stood so fast the chair rolled across the floor, smashing against the desk. Hayley couldn't prevent a tiny gasp.

"Of course you do. You don't want to believe it, but

you do. Why shouldn't you? You barely know anything about me."

"That isn't true!"

"No? Deep down inside aren't you wondering? Isn't there a small part of you that is worried Jacob might be right?"

She couldn't stand to see his pain. "Stop it, Bram."

"Rest easy, Hayley. I'm not some tragic figure seeking belated justice."

"I know that."

He ignored her as if she hadn't spoken. "Do you want to know the truth about why my wife came here instead of staying in New York, where she had doctors she trusted and medical care only minutes away?"

"You don't owe me any explanation."

"She came here so she wouldn't be alone when our baby came. She was angry with me because I was seldom around. You see, I was busy trying to build an empire so I could give her the sort of life and things she was used to having. I was hardly ever home."

He closed his eyes briefly, opening them before Hayley could find any words in response.

"Helen died at the hands of an incompetent doctor who missed a pre-existing condition and botched an operation most doctors could have performed in their sleep. I wanted revenge, all right, but you know what I discovered?"

She shook her head, her throat too thick to speak.

"It's damn hard to take revenge against yourself. Not that I didn't give it a good try, you understand, but it really isn't all that easy to drink yourself to death. I spent four and a half years trying."

"Please. You don't have to tell me this."

"Sure I do. You'll need my version for comparison when you try to decide which one of us is lying."

"Stop it!"

"Your father wasn't Helen's doctor, it was some old man

who should have retired years earlier. Want to know who the real victim was in all this? My daughter.'' His voice thickened. ''She was so tiny I was afraid to touch her. I've never been a religious man, Hayley, but I prayed she would live. Even when they told me she'd be permanently damaged due to oxygen deprivation, I prayed for her to live. But God wasn't answering prayers that day, nor any of the days that followed. I got to watch this tiny little infant hooked to machines, struggling for each shallow breath until—'' His voice broke. ''Until she died, too tired to struggle anymore. And all because I'd put business ahead of my wife and child.''

His pain was unbearable. Hayley's throat ached as silent tears rolled unchecked down her cheeks. ''Don't you think you've blamed yourself long enough?'' she whispered.

Dry-eyed, he stared at her. ''Eternity won't be long enough.''

He strode from the room without another word, a proud, strong man filled with bitter regret. She sat in her grandfather's chair and wept, not sure if the tears were for his pain or her own.

She'd fallen in love with a man who had no room left for love. She was not only crazy, she was a fool.

HAYLEY WOKE with a raging thirst and absolutely no idea where she was. She lay perfectly still in the dark room, breathing rapidly until her sluggish brain remembered. She was curled on the couch in her grandfather's office. The damp towel she'd used on her hair was still damp, from her tears now.

After locking all three doors to avoid conversation with anyone else, she'd given in to a crying jag totally unlike her. She had actually cried herself to sleep. The result was a stiff, puffy face and a raw sore throat.

And for what? Rumors and speculation? She'd caused Bram to relive all that pain when she didn't even believe he'd come here for revenge against Marcus. Bram hadn't needed to answer, but he'd said Marcus hadn't been his wife's doctor, and Hayley believed him.

Staggering to the bathroom, she switched on the light and then blinked, her eyes scratchy. Her face was a mess, but worse, it was going to take forever to remove the tangles from her hair. She'd have to sneak up to her room and hope no one saw her. Hayley had no idea what time it was, but sensed it was late.

Her stomach growled in assent, feeling as empty and hollow as her emotions. Gulping tapwater from the tiny paper cup, she realized she was going to have to risk Mrs. Norwich's disapproval by raiding the kitchen. But she'd better clean up the mess she'd made in the office first.

Hayley stepped back into the room and turned on the lights. Fear chased goose bumps over her arms. The room was as pristine and neat as it had been when she'd first entered to take her sister's phone call.

"This can't be happening. Not again."

The open phone book was gone from the desk. The chair Bram had sent rolling across the carpeting was tucked in its usual spot. The computer was turned off. Only her bottle of water, sitting on the edge of the desk, was out of place. Without that and the towel and the depression on the couch where she'd been lying, she would think she had dreamed the entire thing.

Her heart thundered in her chest. Hurrying to the workstation, she hunted for the picture Bram had printed. It was gone. So was the one from the desk. The wastebasket was empty. There was nothing on the floor.

Someone had entered the room after she'd fallen asleep, and they'd wanted her to know. A quick check proved all the doors were still locked. Even the windows were locked. With extreme care, she searched every inch of the workstation and each one of the desk drawers for the pictures.

They were definitely gone.

If it wasn't for their absence, she might have been able to convince herself Mrs. Norwhich had used a master key to unlock the door so she could tidy up. But Mrs. Norwhich would have no use for those pictures.

Who did?

Picking up her water, Hayley drained the rest of the bottle. Bram had left with nothing in his hands, she'd swear to that. She was not losing her mind and it had not been a dream. He'd been here. They'd talked. And she hadn't cleaned up when he left.

Turning on the computer, Hayley tried to convince herself the pictures weren't important. But they must be or they wouldn't be missing. Bram had thought the one she'd found in the drawer was in a file on the computer somewhere. Maybe she could find that file.

Except the computer wouldn't open without a password.

Hayley battled the encroaching fear that rose like bile to poison her mind. The computer hadn't requested a password earlier.

"A fluke," she told herself. "Or maybe Mrs. Norwhich did come in to clean and something happened when she turned the computer off."

Rebooting the computer netted the same results. The machine wanted a password.

Hayley felt cold right down to her bones. Could Bram have done this? Why would he?

So that she couldn't search the computer for the pictures.

Hayley drew in a long, shaky breath. Darn it, she was tired of feeling scared in her own home! No matter how late it was, she was calling that lawyer right now. He must have an answering service or something. Weren't they like doctors, with clients calling them at odd hours? She was not going to let some faceless person terrorize her in her own home!

Only the phone books were gone.

Panic left her standing there, squeezing the empty water

bottle. A gap marked the space on the shelf where the phone books should have been. Acid fear gnawed her stomach lining. Someone didn't want her calling the lawyer.

Hayley took several more deep breaths. She would not panic. Whoever wanted the phone books could keep them. That wouldn't stop her from talking to the lawyer. She wouldn't let it stop her. She didn't need telephone books. She could get his number by calling information.

Except there was no dial tone.

Teetering on the brink of hysteria, Hayley strove for calm. Cowering in fear wasn't going to help a thing. This was a deliberate attack. Someone wanted her to panic. That was the one thing she mustn't do. How many times had her grandfather told her that the best defense was a strong offense?

She could control this suffocating fear. She *would* control it. If the person had wanted to physically hurt her, he could have done so easily while she was asleep and defenseless. Later, she'd worry about how she could have slept through someone moving around the room like this. Right now she needed to think. This was a game of nerves and she was determined to come out the winner.

I'm not some tragic figure seeking belated justice.

Had Bram been lying?

She didn't want to believe that. So she wouldn't. Did she have the nerve to go and talk to him again? Just the thought of stepping outside this room was scary. Out there waited someone who was trying to make her crazy—and coming uncomfortably close to succeeding.

Hayley exhaled hard and shoved back a tangle of hair that had fallen forward. "They can only win if I let them. And I won't!"

She turned off the light and stepped into the hall. Across from her, the living room looked like a vast, dark cavern filled with deep, shadowy menace.

"Imagination is Leigh's department, remember?" she whispered.

Was her sister really in London? Or in New York?

No. Hayley wasn't going to consider the second possibility. Leigh had promised to call her back tonight, but the phone was out of order. Hayley needed to calm down and concentrate, only she wasn't sure she could do either one. Her mind kept racing.

Muted light drew her toward the kitchen. Her stomach reminded her that it was on empty, and she was terribly thirsty again.

She'd start by facing Mrs. Norwhich's displeasure. She could ask why the woman had been in such a hurry to clean her grandfather's office.

But it was Marcus, not Mrs. Norwhich, who stood at the counter drinking a bottle of water and eating a slice of pie.

"I didn't realize it was you," she said uneasily when he looked up as she entered. "I thought it would be Mrs. Norwhich."

"She went to bed," Marcus said around a mouthful of pie.

"What time is it?"

He squinted at his watch. "Almost nine."

She'd slept away the entire afternoon and evening? What was wrong with her? Truly frightened, she tried to breathe slowly. Marcus finished his bottle of water and opened a second one. When he didn't offer her any, she opened the refrigerator and helped herself. He watched her in silence.

"We need to talk," she told him as she twisted off the cap.

"I've got nothing to say to you." He finished the pie and set his plate in the sink.

"You never do," she said sadly, "but this time you don't have a choice. I'm going to talk to the lawyer tonight about the house. I want you to stop Bram from putting any more bars on the windows."

"No."

"You have no right. You know you don't. This is *my* house."

Hayley shuddered at his expression. Cold and as gray as death, his eyes practically glowed with hatred. For the first time, she was truly frightened of the man who was her father.

"You think so, little girl?" He advanced toward her. "So uppity. A real Hart, aren't you? Harts never learn, do they?" He lowered his voice, the menace even stronger now. "You should, you know. I could snap your neck like a twig." His fingers flexed. A trace of spittle ran from the corner of his mouth.

"What's going on here?" Eden demanded from behind them. "Marcus?"

Hayley nearly sagged in relief.

Marcus faced his wife without losing any of his anger. "I should have got rid of the lot," he said emphatically.

Eden crossed to the counter, picked up his water and held it out to him. She didn't appear concerned by the crazy expression on her husband's face. "Your show starts in a few minutes."

He snatched the bottle from her hand. "Then you deal with her."

"I will."

Marcus muttered under his breath as he disappeared around the corner. Eden eyed Hayley with lips pursed in disapproval. "I won't have you upsetting him. Your father isn't well."

"He's insane, Eden! That isn't dementia. He's truly crazy. And he's dangerous."

"He's tired," Eden countered. "You upset him. He was doing quite well until you arrived."

"How can you say that? He's turning Heartskeep into a fortress! And he's violent!"

Eden sniffed dismissively. She walked to the counter to

wipe away some imaginary crumbs. "You're overreacting, Hayley. I suppose you came in here wanting something to eat now that everything's cleaned up and Mrs. Norwhich went to her room for the night."

Baffled by the woman's reaction, Hayley strove for calm, but she couldn't entirely suppress the shock that still edged her voice. Eden was going to ignore the whole scene. Hayley couldn't let her do that. "Didn't you hear him? What doctor is Marcus seeing? I want to talk to the man."

Eden whipped around, holding the dish towel in her fist. "Why?"

"Because as his daughter, I need to know exactly what is wrong with him."

"I am perfectly capable of looking after *my husband.*"

"Are you? If you hadn't come in just now, I honestly believe he would have struck me. I intend to find out what's going on around here," Hayley continued. "Let's start with who has copies of the master keys to the inside door locks."

"What are you talking about?"

Was that a trace of fear? "Someone cleaned my grandfather's office tonight."

"So what? That is why I employ Paula and Mrs. Norwhich."

"Did you give them passkeys to all the rooms?"

"Why are you dithering about passkeys?"

"Because the office was locked, but someone entered anyhow."

"There are several doors to that room," Eden reminded her haughtily.

"I know. Three. They were all locked. I locked them myself."

Eden's eyes narrowed. Hayley couldn't tell what she was thinking, but her dislike of Eden was increasing with each passing minute.

"Was something taken?" Eden demanded.

"Yes, as a matter of fact, the telephone books."

"Oh, for heaven's sake. Now there's a major crime. I'll have Paula arrested right away. Did it ever dawn on you someone might have wanted them to look up a number?"

"Both of them?"

"Hayley, if you need the phone books, knock on Paula's door and tell her so."

"You told me she didn't live in."

"I convinced her to move into the room next to Mrs. Norwhich yesterday. She isn't reliable at the best of times, and I want her right here where I can supervise."

The thought of ghostly Paula Kerstairs living in the house with them was unnerving, but Hayley decided to deal with that issue later. "You're missing the point, Eden. The phone books aren't important. They won't do anyone much good tonight anyhow, since the phone is dead. What's important is how sh—"

"What are you talking about? When did we lose the telephone? I just made a call a short time ago." Eden strode to the wall phone and lifted it. Glaring at Hayley, she thrust the receiver in her face. "There's nothing wrong with this telephone."

Hayley's stomach tightened another notch. She could hear the dial tone humming loudly. "There's no dial tone on the one in the office," she said weakly.

Eden shook her head in disgust. "Really, Hayley, you're becoming as paranoid and bizarre as your father. I guess I shouldn't be surprised. They do say mental disorders tend to run in families." Eden replaced the instrument smugly.

Hayley decided not to let those disquieting words get to her. But a tiny niggling fear began stirring at the back of her mind all the same.

"What would you call your own behavior this morning, Eden?" she demanded. "I'd say it was pretty bizarre, as well. Crouching down and following Marcus into the maze. I saw you, you know."

"I have no idea what you're talking about."

Eden put so much disdain in her voice Hayley didn't know what to think.

"I'm starting to wonder if you're as insane as your father," Eden continued. "Look at you! You're a mess! Jacob told me how strangely you've been acting since you got here. For your information, I wasn't in the garden at all this morning. It was much too hot to go running around outside. And I never go into the mazes." She shuddered.

"But you did. I followed you, Eden. I heard what Marcus said to you. Are you blackmailing him?"

"What?" Eden looked truly astounded. "What exactly did you hear?"

"Marcus said he wasn't going to pay you another dime."

Eden's demeanor changed once more. For a minute, she looked thoughtful, almost as if she'd forgotten about Hayley. Then she looked directly at her. "You listen to me, Hayley. Stop trying to cause trouble. I promise you, you'll be sorry if you don't."

She pivoted, striding briskly past the walk-in pantry. Hayley heard the distinctive snick of the pantry door shutting tightly.

Someone was hiding in there!

Chapter Nine

Hayley forced herself to open the door. Paula or Mrs. Nor-which might be hiding inside, embarrassed to come out after being trapped into listening to a private family quarrel. But even without hitting the light switch, Hayley could see the pantry yawned, deep and empty.

But she'd heard the door close! She knew she had!

They do say mental disorders tend to run in families.

"There you are, Hayley," Jacob called out, cheerfully bounding into the kitchen. "I've been looking all over for you. You missed dinner. Your car's still out front and I—" He blinked rapidly. "What happened to you? You look..." He stopped, clearly trying to find a kind way to tell her she was a mess.

Hayley pushed at her tangled hair self-consciously while trying to slow the slamming of her heart. Jacob looked so reassuringly normal—even if his usually cheerful face frowned at the sight of her.

"A woman should never fall asleep with wet hair," she explained. Adding a smile was beyond her capabilities at the moment.

"Uh, is something wrong, Hayley? You look...you know, upset about something."

"I just had a disturbing conversation with Marcus and then your mother."

Jacob groaned. "Now what has my mother done? Honestly, if we weren't related I'd be tempted to strangle her at times. She means well, Hayley, but she's extremely protective of your father, especially since he's been...you know, not quite himself lately. Look, why don't you sit down and tell me what happened while I fix you something to eat."

"No. Thanks just the same but..."

Jacob came forward with an expression she recognized. *No. Please. Not now.* Her mind was spinning. She could not possibly deal with an amorous Jacob right now.

"I don't mind. Really. I like doing things for you, Hayley." His voice lowered seductively. "In fact, I'd like to do a lot of things for you."

"Jacob, no. Please. I can't deal with—"

"I've been thinking about this for some time now. Why don't we get married?"

The question exploded into the air, without any warning whatsoever. The absurdity of it made her gasp out loud. *"What?"*

"We've got lots in common," he added quickly, "besides impossible parents. We like a lot of the same things, including each other. No, don't interrupt, hear me out. I'm worried about you, Hayley. You've been acting really, uh, stressed since you got here. I think you need someone to take care of you. You've always been the strong one. Why not give me a chance to play that role?"

"Jacob, stop it! This is crazy."

"No, it isn't. You must know I've been half in love with you since we were little kids."

"No. *No!*" She pushed his hands away when he tried to draw her into an embrace. He dropped his arms to his sides. Breathing was suddenly difficult for Hayley. Thinking was even harder.

"I didn't mean to upset you again. I'm rushing you,

aren't I? I'm sorry, Hayley. It's just that I've been waiting so long to tell you how I really feel. You can be pretty intimidating, you know? I promise I'll take things a little slower, but at least consider it. Give me a chance. I really do care about you."

Too many shocks. She was on overload.

"I can't...I'll talk to you later. Good night, Jacob."

"Hayley, wait. You haven't eaten anything yet."

Hayley fled around the corner. The door to Paula Kerstairs's room snapped closed. Hayley raced up the stairs to the safety of her room, locking the door behind her.

"But this room isn't safe. Nowhere is safe," she said aloud. "Not when someone has keys to get inside each room."

Surveying the bedroom, she grabbed the chair from her desk and shoved it under the doorknob. It wouldn't stop anyone determined to get inside, but she didn't think Jacob would break down her door.

But he could come in through Leigh's room! Hayley flew through the connecting bathroom and used Leigh's chair to block that door, as well. Jacob rapped on her door, calling her. Hayley stood there, waiting. To her surprise, he didn't try her sister's door. As the minutes passed, she realized she could hear him talking to someone in the hall. Eden, no doubt. Her room was on the other side of Hayley's.

And Hayley realized she was breathing as if she'd just run two miles. What was the matter with her? Jacob hadn't attacked her. Why was she cowering in here?

She clutched her stomach and rocked silently back and forth. Jacob had just proposed to her. It was unreal. They'd grown up together. He'd spend a lot of time around the house when they were kids and his mother was working. The whole idea was insane.

Okay. His offer had come out of nowhere. So deal with

it. She'd been handling the male of the species for years without resorting to hiding in her room.

Slowly, she gathered the strength to move away from the door. A glimpse of her reflection in the bathroom mirror made her cringe. How could Jacob or anyone else be interested in her at the moment? She was an utter disaster.

Stripping off her clothing, she locked both bathroom doors and turned on the shower. The warm water took a long time to penetrate the chills quaking through her. The growling of her empty stomach finally sent her reaching for a towel. As she worked a comb through the wet snarls of her hair, she couldn't help thinking the shorter style in the picture she'd found had much to recommend it. The cute, simple wedge style looked easy to manage. Maybe Hayley would give it a try.

If Marcus didn't kill her first.

She shook off that crazy thought and tried to keep her mind a blank, then realized she needed Bram. He was an anchor in a world gone mad. She had to make him understand that she hadn't really believed he was here for revenge.

Hayley pulled a lime print skirt from her closet. She was reaching for a bra to go under the matching T-shirt when she hesitated. She dropped the bra, refusing to think about her sudden decision as she pulled the shirt quickly over her head. If he wouldn't listen, maybe she could show him that she trusted him.

Pausing to listen at her door, she slipped into the hall and hurried down the back stairs. There was a waiting silence about the house that was unnerving. The kitchen was mercifully empty and dark save for the light over the stove. Hayley didn't need much light to raid her own kitchen.

Her stomach growled in happy assent as she munched on a cracker, quietly stuffing crackers and cheese into a plastic bag. Slipping out the back door, she remembered too late that she hadn't thought to bring along a flashlight.

Too bad. She wasn't going back inside to get one. In fact, unless Bram turned her down cold—and he might—she wasn't going back inside tonight for any reason. She actually felt safer out here where the night was alive with the reassuring sounds of insects and small animals getting on with their lives. Hayley hurried along the remembered path, her gaze fixed on the distant glow from Bram's forge.

She wasn't surprised he was working. It made a whole lot more sense to work at night. The temperature had dropped with the sun and there was a slight breeze coming in off the Hudson River. It was a simple, dark summer night, the sort she used to enjoy once upon a time.

Short of the clearing Hayley paused, fascinated anew by the sight of him at work. Bram wore a pair of ragged, cutoff jeans, shoes and the heavy gloves he needed to handle the hot metal. His broad chest was totally bare and glistening with moisture as he pounded a large metal rod with fierce concentration—as if his life depended on each precise fall of the hammer.

He was magnificent, a man at the height of perfection. Hayley savored the sight, trying to commit every detail to memory. His bared muscles bunched and flowed with the energy and rhythm of his work. An unruly lock of hair drifted over one eye. He forced it back absently with a forearm.

Hayley's body stirred as it had the first time she'd seen him. The difference was she now understood the burning need inside her. This was a man she could never dominate. He would meet the challenges she presented head-on.

Bram was a man she could rely on. But he also had a softer side. She'd sensed it from the start. He exposed that silent part of him in the beauty of his art. But she'd experienced his gentleness firsthand. Look at the tender way he'd ministered to her today. How could she have questioned his intentions, even briefly?

Bram stopped working and looked up. There was no way he could see her standing here, concealed in the deep shadows. Yet his brooding gaze went right to the spot where she stood, sending her pulses racing. Slowly, deliberately, he slid the large steel rod deep into the heart of the fire as he stared at her.

Excitement pooled low in her belly. Her nipples tightened in anticipation and she couldn't seem to draw a breath. Without turning away, he withdrew the rod from the flames, holding it so she could clearly see the tip glowing an angry red-orange.

"Did you want something?"

His voice seemed to travel over her body with the impact of a caress. Hayley stepped into the clearing, uncharacteristically nervous.

"I...yes. Can we...talk?"

"Talk?"

His gaze swept over her, lingering a moment on her unconfined breasts. The flimsy material of her shirt became an erotic stimulus against her nipples.

"Go back to the house, Hayley. I'm not in the mood to...*talk* right now."

She almost asked him what he was in the mood for, but he turned and savagely plunged the red-hot metal into a pail filled with water. The sizzle of the cool water on the hot metal rose in the air along with a burst of steam.

"I'm not very good company at the moment, Hayley."

"I know. It's my fault. I'm sorry."

He set down his tools, peeling the heavy gloves from his hands. "What do you want from me?"

Everything.

She set the bag of crackers and cheese on one of his rickety folding chairs and crossed to where he stood. Bram was a hard man, as unbending as the metal he worked. But metal could be softened by heat.

"I need you," she said honestly.

"You mean you want sex," he rumbled darkly. The glow from the fire bathed the sheen of sweat on his chest.

"That, too. But first I need your help." She swallowed, suddenly unsure how to proceed. Her bravado faded. "I'm scared, Bram. Really scared."

His expression remained unyielding. "Of what?"

If he'd shown even the tiniest bit of softness, maybe the truth wouldn't have tumbled past her lips. But his unyielding countenance sent her deep-rooted fears spilling into the warm night air.

"Something's wrong with me. I don't know what's happening and I don't know what to do. I can't seem to think. I'm easily confused and distracted. I'm exhausted all the time—when I'm not asleep. My brain feels like sludge and I don't know why."

She bit off the litany, hearing the threat of tears in her voice.

"I never cry. Never. Yet all I want to do is sit down and bawl like a baby. Maybe Eden's right. Maybe I am insane like Marcus."

"Don't be a fool," he snapped.

"I think it's too late."

"See a doctor."

Hayley nodded, but she didn't move.

"Why come to me?"

Because I think I've fallen in love with you.

"Because you're the only person I trust. You were right, you know. Someone is playing a nasty game with me—and I don't understand the rules."

Unexpectedly, her stomach growled, a loud, distressing sound in the quiet clearing.

Bram scowled. "What did you eat for dinner?"

"I slept through dinner."

He stood there glaring. He wasn't going to help. She would have to get in her car and drive away, after all. She closed her eyes, opening them when he grabbed her forearms.

"Sit down before you fall down." His eyes were twin coals, burning hotter than the flames. His voice softened. "You're trembling."

"I do that a lot lately, too."

Bram swore. With a gentleness that threatened to fill her eyes once more, he guided her down on the other rickety camp chair. "You need to eat."

She nodded. "I have crackers and cheese. I brought enough for two."

"I ate dinner," he said gruffly, turning away.

Hayley closed her eyes so he wouldn't see how much the rebuff hurt. She sensed him moving about the camp, but she didn't watch. It didn't matter what he was doing. He didn't want her here. The attraction had only been sexual on his part, after all. And now he wasn't even interested in that.

She'd rest for a minute, then get in her car and leave. If there was no room at The Inn, she'd sleep in her car tonight.

"Hayley? Wake up!"

She forced her eyes open. "I wasn't asleep." But her voice was thick and her eyes were heavy.

"Yeah," he said more gently, "you were."

She started to protest that she'd only closed her eyes for a few minutes, but he was not only standing there holding a plate, he'd taken the time to rinse away the sweat and grime from his work and to don a clean shirt that buttoned down the front. Minutes must have gone by and she couldn't remember them!

Starkly, Hayley looked at him, her heart pounding in

fear. "Something is wrong. No one is this tired all the time. I'm so thirsty. Would you hand me a bottle of water from the bag?"

"Hayley, are you using drugs?"

"No!"

"Not even some sort of prescription drugs?"

"I don't even drink caffeine."

Bram studied her impassively. "But you do drink a lot of water. I don't think I've ever seen you without a bottle."

"It's healthy."

He handed her the plate. In addition to the cheese and crackers, he'd added some fruit. "Eat this. I'll get your water."

She stared at the plate and knew she'd never get a single bite past her dry throat. Why had she come here? How many times did Bram have to tell her to get lost before she took the hint?

He handed her a bottle of water, but it slipped from her fingers and rolled across the hard-packed dirt. "Sorry. Did I mention I've been unusually clumsy lately, as well?"

Picking up the bottle, Bram suddenly stood unnaturally still. He stared hard at the bottle, then he disappeared for a minute and returned. He thrust a large paper cup into her hand. "Drink this."

"What is it?"

"Club soda."

"Yuck."

"Drink it anyway."

"I'd rather have my water."

"I don't think so."

He moved out of the light and returned with a much larger lantern. Turning it on, he held the unopened bottle of water close to the light and began turning the plastic container slowly.

The food sat forgotten in her lap as she watched him

examine the bottle. He squeezed gently. A tiny trail of moisture trickled down one side.

"When I picked it up just now, it felt wet," he said quietly. "When did you first start to notice all these symptoms?"

She began to tremble. "Shortly after I got here."

Bram nodded. "The other day, I had a drink from one of your bottles."

"I remember."

"I was tired and muzzy all afternoon. I put it down to the heat."

"Are you saying there's something wrong with the water I've been drinking?"

"The seal isn't broken, and I need better light than this to be sure, but if I'm not mistaken, there's a tiny pinhole right here under the bottom lip. The sort a syringe might make."

Her brain emptied of all thought. She could only stare at the bottle in his hand.

"How much of this have you drunk today?" Bram demanded.

"I—I don't know. I can't remember."

"Try, Hayley. Did you have some after you woke up?"

"Yes. But only one bottle."

"On an empty stomach," he said grimly.

"You don't know there's anything wrong with the water."

"I think a few assumptions are in order here. Come on. We need to get you to a hospital."

"No!"

"Hayley, if the water was drugged..." Bram strove for patience when every molecule in his body cried for action.

"They'll call the police," she said, so softly he had to strain to hear her. "The police will say I tampered with the bottles to get them to reopen an investigation out here."

"What sort of investigation?"

"When my mother disappeared, Leigh and I convinced the police to dig up the newly poured foundation for the fountain out back. We were so certain Marcus had something to do with Mom's disappearance that we convinced them to look for her body, even though it appeared she vanished in the city. I was...vocal."

"You raised a stink."

Hayley nodded. "The media picked it up. Marcus was forced to close his practice and send his patients to other doctors. The police tore up the fountain, they even checked the house and grounds without finding anything, but I kept insisting that Marcus was responsible. Chief Crossley finally lectured me on what would happen if I continued making accusations without proof."

"Let me guess. You stopped making accusations but kept hounding them."

"I had to! I won't let them forget about her!" She looked away. "Chief Crossley won't even take my calls anymore. He'd love an excuse to toss me in jail. If the water is drugged, he'll have the excuse he's looking for."

Hayley was nothing if not determined, and she had plenty of guts. Those were just two of the things Bram admired about her.

"We need to get this analyzed," he told her.

"If it was poisonous, I'd be dead by now."

"I hate to burst your bubble, but there are slow-acting poisons out there."

Her eyes widened. She looked so fragile. He didn't want her to see how worried he was, but it was all he could do not to lift her up, toss her in his truck and take her to the hospital whether she liked it or not.

"Isn't there someplace private we could take the water to have it tested?" she asked.

"Probably."

"At least there's a reason I seem to be going crazy."

"You aren't crazy."

"Don't be so sure," she said with grim humor. "I haven't told you what happened a few minutes ago."

"Tell me in the truck."

"I told you—"

"No hospital," he agreed. "The other night when we went for dinner you introduced me to a nice older couple."

"George and Emily Walken."

Bram nodded. "Let's go pay them a visit."

"What can they do?" She shoved at her hair as he helped her to her feet.

"I've no idea, but you said they know practically everyone. I'm out of my depth here, Hayley. I don't know this area well enough to find us a lab that could run an analysis on the water, and it's late. We'd never find anyplace open at this hour. Maybe they can suggest someone to help us. Get in the truck while I secure the area. You can eat something on the way. Food might help absorb whatever's in that water."

"Are you sure? Maybe I should throw up."

Looking into her stricken eyes, he saw just how scared she really was. He felt exactly the same way. Fear for her was gnawing away at his insides. It was all he could do to remain calm. He laid his palm against her cheek. Her skin was incredibly soft and cool to the touch.

"No fever. Do you feel sick?"

"Not unless you count the butterflies doing aerial dives in my stomach."

"Let's go talk to the Walkens."

There was total trust in her expression. "Okay. Oh. Wait! I have to go back to the house for my purse."

"Forget it. You aren't stepping another foot inside that place until we find out what's going on." He wasn't budging on that issue for any reason. She must have recognized that fact because after a moment she nodded slowly. He helped her into the passenger's seat.

"I'll be right back."

When he slid behind the wheel several minutes later, her head was back, her eyes were closed and the plate of food was sitting in her lap untouched.

He shook her gently, relieved when her eyes popped open. "Come on, Hayley, fight it. You have to stay with me. I'm going to need directions to their house."

The Walken estate proved to be considerably larger than Heartskeep, but designed along more traditional lines. Emily Walken answered the door right away. If she was startled to see them at this hour of the night, her innate graciousness covered the fact.

"Hayley, Mr. Myers, what a nice surprise."

"Mrs. Walken," Bram said, ushering Hayley inside. "I'm sorry for barging in unannounced this late, but we have something of an emergency."

As George Walken entered the spacious foyer Bram got right to the point. "Hayley's been drinking bottled water that appears to have been tampered with."

"What sort of symptoms are you having?" Emily Walken asked. Her calmness was reassuring.

"Exhaustion, mental confusion—anything else?" Bram asked Hayley, who stood there half-asleep.

"Maybe auditory hallucinations," she said nervously. "I was sure I heard the pantry door close, but when I looked inside, it was empty."

George met Bram's gaze. "The hospital—"

"No!" Hayley said adamantly.

He nodded soothingly. "All right, Hayley. We have some friends who may be willing to help. Saul is a doctor. His wife is a chemist."

"Saul's a pediatrician, dear," his wife corrected. "But unfortunately, the world being what it is, he's had to treat more than a few youngsters for drug ingestion and overdose. Come inside and sit while I call Rhea. You'll like the Levinsons."

They did indeed like the couple. Saul was a short, jolly man who made up for his lack of stature with a big heart and a cheerful disposition. Rhea was a foot taller and on the quiet side, but it was quickly apparent she knew her profession.

Hayley sat reassuringly close to Bram on the comfortable sofa. Maintaining physical contact seemed to steady her as well as him.

"My patients are generally younger and smaller than you, but let's see what we can discover," Saul told her. "I'll need a urine sample as well as some blood, and as much information as you can give me."

Emily escorted the couple and Hayley upstairs, leaving Bram to pace the warmly inviting family room restlessly. George Walken watched from his chair near the enormous fireplace.

"I understand her concern over involving the police," George told him. "Hayley's been a thorn in Chief Crossley's side ever since her mother disappeared. The lead investigator on that case was out of New York City. He and the local boys didn't get along, so the situation has been difficult for everyone."

"Do you think Marcus had something to do with Amy Thomas's disappearance?"

George sighed. "I've never known what to think. Everyone took Dennison's death hard, but no one more than Amy. She adored her father, and when she disappeared so soon after his death, her state of mind was called into question."

"I don't imagine that sat very well with Hayley."

"No. None of us ever believed Amy went to New York

on a shopping expedition so soon after her father's death, but we don't know why she did go there.''

George took his measure thoughtfully for a minute. He eyed the tattoo on Bram's arm, the open-necked shirt and the clean jeans Bram had quickly changed into before joining Hayley in the truck. There was no censure in his expression.

''Hayley will never admit it, but it is remotely possible that grief made Amy behave out of character to some degree. She was never a careless person, but the city police are probably right that she was killed for her money and jewelry and dumped in a shallow grave somewhere.''

''Do I sense a but in there?''

George continued to look him in the eye. ''But I agree with the girls that there is more to the story. Unfortunately, Amy was an intensely private person. She always faced her problems head-on and dealt with them on her own.''

''Hayley's her mother's daughter.''

George nearly smiled. ''Yes, she is. Thanks for bringing her here tonight. When Dennison was first diagnosed with his heart condition, he confided in me. He was worried about Amy and the girls, especially if anything should happen to him, as it did.''

''Why didn't Amy divorce Marcus?''

George shook his head. ''I asked her that once. She said she'd taken a vow for better or for worse. She considered her daughters were better than Marcus was worse.''

Bram frowned.

''You had to know Amy. Once she gave her word there was no looking back. It would have been different if Marcus had been abusive, but he simply ignored the girls. I promised Dennison I'd look after all of them if his heart ever gave out, but I did a damn poor job of things.''

His regret came from the heart, Bram knew. Hayley had

said Emily and George took in troubled kids. Bram wondered if those kids realized how lucky they were.

The others returned and Bram was relieved to see Hayley looking better than she had a few minutes ago. She came to his side as if it was the most natural thing in the world, and he slid his arm around her waist.

Saul couldn't tell them much until his wife tested the samples, but his exam hadn't revealed anything overtly serious. By the time the couple left, Bram's apprehension had lessened.

"I made up rooms for you both," Emily told him. "Feel free to help yourselves to whatever you need. Hayley knows where things are."

"Thank you, Emily, but I can go back to Heartskeep for the night."

Hayley tensed.

"You can, but I'd like it if you'd stay the night," Emily said.

Bram didn't look at Hayley. He nodded slowly. "All right. Thank you."

She showed them to rooms across from one another. His room obviously had been intended for a couple of "their boys," as the couple referred to their foster charges. At the moment, they didn't have anyone staying with them.

Explaining that he pretty much lived out of his truck while working at Heartskeep, Bram went back out to get his shaving kit and a change of clothing. He set clean clothes on the bed closest to the door and went to take a shower before lying down on clean sheets.

The water soothed his muscles, but not his mind. He'd started to care entirely too much about Hayley. She was stirring to life dormant emotions that terrified him. He'd known from the start that she wasn't the sort of woman he could have a casual affair with. Hayley was the type who would insist on the whole package—love, marriage... children.

His mind balked. He couldn't go through that again. Yet he didn't see how he was going to walk away from her now. Hayley had chipped away the edges of the barrier he'd erected to keep people at a distance. There was a connection between them as tangible as a touch and as deep as his heart.

He kept telling himself it was sex. And sex was definitely part of the draw. Wanting her was becoming a physical ache. She'd brought a zest and exuberance to the life he'd kept wrapped in regret for so long. The energy that poured from her infused him with all sorts of long-buried emotions. He wanted her, but he knew they'd both be hurt when he had to let her go.

Wrapping a towel around his waist, Bram left the bathroom, relieved to find the hall empty.

His assigned bedroom was not.

Chapter Ten

Hayley sat perched on the edge of the far bed, looking nervous but determined. Her hair spilled naturally over one shoulder, touching the peak of her breast. It wasn't a pose, and that only made the effect more erotic. The satin gown of deep pink that Emily had lent her had been an unfortunate choice because the material molded to the generous curves it covered. Already half-aroused from thinking about Hayley, Bram found his body reacting instantly.

"What are you doing in here?"

"Waiting for you."

A light blush highlighted her cheeks. She looked incredibly soft and utterly feminine—a woman waiting for her lover. But he wasn't her lover even though the temptation was becoming harder and harder to deny.

Her eyes changed to smoke. Such expressive eyes. Yearning passion simmered there, barely concealed. Bram didn't need words; he knew exactly what she was thinking.

The same blasted thing he was.

"You shouldn't be in here." His gruff response wasn't as firm as he would have liked.

He could see she was nervous, but the tiny muscles at the corners of her lips lifted them into a smile. Even an angel would be moved by that smile, and those muscles weren't the only things lifting. Bram ignored the stirring under his towel.

"Why shouldn't I be in here?"

Her softly voiced question hummed in his head, blotting out other, more rational thoughts. Anticipation stirred his blood. The top of her gown shifted, sliding over her skin with the barest trace of sound. Bram desperately wanted to follow that shift with his hands and mouth, to glide over her skin exactly as that material was doing.

"Cut it out, Hayley. I'm not going to make love to you." He might die from wanting her, but Bram was resolute on that point.

"All right."

All right? It was anything but all right. His body strained with the fierce longing to touch and caress her. He hadn't even really kissed her yet!

But he wanted to.

Badly.

"Then I'll make love to you," she said quietly.

His heart stuttered to a stop while his mind went to work anticipating every shiver, every silken touch, every erotic taste, until there was no oxygen left in his lungs.

"Later," she added.

Only the slight tremor of her hands belied her calm, and she clasped them together. "Believe it or not, that isn't why I came in here."

"It isn't?" He tore his gaze from the press of her nipples against the thin, pink material as she fidgeted.

"Not entirely. But if you keep looking at me like that, I could change my mind."

So could he. They were on treacherous ground. His fingers were already curled in an effort to resist the craving to stroke the delicate curve of her neck, and to follow that curve to where the lace rested against the slope of her breasts. He longed to trace her skin above that bit of lace.

To dip his finger below the line of her gown and discover if her breasts were as responsive to his touch as he suspected they'd be.

"I've been thinking," she said unsteadily.

"Where you're concerned, that's a bad idea." His voice wasn't supposed to come out sounding coated with desire.

"Thanks a lot. I don't know if it was the sandwich Emily made me eat after the doctor left, or that vitamin B shot he gave me, but something seems to have energized me." A mischievous smile curved Hayley's lips. "Did he give you one, too?"

His gaze followed hers to where his towel clearly displayed his reaction.

"This is a bedroom, Hayley. You're a desirable woman sitting there in a provocative nightgown. I'm a man."

"Yes, you certainly are," she agreed pertly. "I'm glad you want me, Bram. I want you, too."

Bram cursed under his breath. He told himself to stay where he was and keep the other bed between them, but somehow, his intentions never made it to his brain. He was across the room, towering above her, close enough to touch the tempting spill of her hair.

"I told you before I was too old for games, Hayley."

"Not all games, I hope," she whispered.

He stopped her hand when it reached out toward the knotted towel at his waist. "Don't." If she touched his skin it was all over. His resolve went only so far.

Her hand dropped to her lap. "Sorry. I've never tried to seduce a man before."

She couldn't have come up with anything that would have inflamed his senses more. Bram held on to his slipping control with effort.

"When I make love to you, Hayley, I want to know it's completely your decision and not some chemical reaction you have no control over."

"*When* we make love? Well, that's promising, anyhow. But I feel compelled to point out that our response to one another is basically a chemical reaction whether you like it or not. Pheromones have nothing to do with what may or may not be in that bottled water."

"Cute. No wonder some men think education is wasted on women."

"Ha, ha. Bram, I know I've been coming on pretty strong, but I can't seem to help it with you. I look at you and I want to touch you. I touch you and I want to kiss you. I'd like to blame it on the drug, because believe it or not, this is totally out of character for me, but the truth is, I've felt this way since the moment I saw you standing over your forge in the woods. I felt hotter than your fire that night."

Bram gritted his teeth. He was holding on to his sanity by a thread.

"We're guests in the Walkens' house," he said thickly. "They showed us to separate bedrooms, Hayley. I doubt they'd approve of all the things I'd like to do to you right now."

She shivered. Bram felt that shiver to the soles of his feet. That look of total trust was back in her expression. And if that wasn't bad enough, it was mixed with a look of molten desire that nearly scrambled his determination right along with his mind.

Hayley tossed her head. Bram couldn't take his eyes from the ripples in her hair. She was so lovely.

"You're wrong, you know."

Her words washed over him, penetrating slowly.

"Their guest wing is on the other side of the house near their bedroom. They put us together over here so I could have a choice. I've made my choice, Bram. I don't want to sleep alone tonight. May I stay with you?"

Bram closed his eyes. His body was taut with a craving

only she could satisfy. He was tired of playing the martyr. He swore silently as his resolve ebbed away.

"If you came in here expecting more than a quick tumble between the sheets, you'd better change your mind right now, Hayley," he said hoarsely. "I'm not marriage material."

Hayley rose in one fluid, graceful motion that set his heart pounding. "Oh, you're not *that* bad, but I don't remember proposing anything beyond a night together."

Inflamed by the trembling expectancy revealed in her expression, Bram slid his fingers under the silken river of her hair and cupped the back of her head, drawing her mouth to his. He brushed her lips with agonizing gentleness, despite the pulsing need throbbing inside him.

Her delicate hands moved over his bare chest with painful slowness before clasping the back of his neck, leaving every inch of skin they'd touched on fire. Hayley nipped at his bottom lip. Bram stilled. He opened his mouth to tell one of them not to be a fool, and she deepened the kiss with insistent demand.

Rational thought fled. He returned her kiss with a fierce hunger she matched, until their teeth accidentally clicked together. Bram seized on a dangling thread of control. "Stop, Hayley."

"I don't want to stop."

Neither did he. He pulled her against his naked chest, letting her feel the powerful need she'd created. She leaned into him in answer and he covered her lips with his once more. Hayley turned softly pliant in his arms, spurring him on with tiny sounds of pleasure. His body hardened, more firm than the metal he shaped.

"Still think I'm too young?" she whispered shakily against his mouth.

The breathless tremor of her voice ignited every heightened nerve ending in his body. Bram stopped thinking altogether. He lowered her onto the bed and followed her down, feeling her tremble.

Or was he the one who was shaking?

A wild, hot hunger had taken control. He didn't remember ever wanting anyone like this. Holding back even a little bit was a supreme effort. He covered her lips in a soul-destroying kiss, plunging into the hot depths of her mouth to explore and taste at will. Without breaking that contact, he restlessly roamed the satin covering her body with his hands, finding the tight bead of a nipple and rubbing gently until she mewed in pleasure.

He nipped at her earlobe. Found the sensitive spot behind her ear, reveling in the soft sounds of excitement she made and the sensual stirring of her body under his.

When he kissed a path down her throat to the exposed flesh above the lace, she shuddered, staring up at him through passion-clouded eyes. He held her gaze as his finger slipped beneath the edge of lace. Lightly, he skimmed the soft skin of her breast. She inhaled sharply when his fingers shaped, then gently pinched and tugged on the tender bud of her nipple.

"Oh!"

Her eyes closed and she arched her back to give him better access. Bram shoved aside the slippery pink fabric, tugging it down so his lips could close over one rosy tip. Hayley cried out in pleasure. She was going to be a noisy lover. He realized he didn't mind a bit.

Satisfaction sizzled through him as his mouth moved to the other nipple, drawing on it hard. Her hands threaded his hair and she thrashed back and forth, spurring him on. The slick contact of skin against skin was driving him mad.

Sliding his hand beneath the hem of her nightgown, Bram was startled to find her totally naked. The shock sent a wave of intense heat through him as he traced a path along the soft skin of her inner thigh with the flat of his palm. His fingers stopped at her damp passageway.

He cupped her there and Hayley rocked against his hand. "Bram, please!"

"I intend to please," he promised. He crushed her to him, sealing her lips while he traced a pattern through her wiry curls with a finger. She moaned softly, straining against his hand.

Mesmerized by her frank desire, he kissed her hard, dueling with her tongue, the taste of her more heady than any drink he'd ever taken.

"Still want to play games, little girl?" he asked thickly.

"Yes," she whispered urgently into his mouth.

Bram swallowed her sounds of shocked pleasure as his finger slowly probed the soft, wet folds. He should slow this wild pace before he exploded, but Hayley would have none of it. Her fingers slid down over his abdomen, making him inhale as she released the knotted towel at his waist.

"Oh!"

Bram smiled. He was going to have to work on her limited vocabulary.

Later.

Much later.

Her stare tested the limits of his control. Timidly, she traced him with her fingertips. The butterfly caress was exquisite torture. He had to stop her when she took him in her hands.

"My control isn't what it should be, Hayley. I want you too much."

"Yes."

Her simple, breathy acceptance was all he needed to hear. He tugged her gown down and off. Lying back, he pulled her on top of him. Her eyes went wide at the full contact of their naked bodies.

"Are you sure this is going to work?" she asked tremulously.

Bram chuckled low in his throat as he slipped first one, and then a second finger inside her, watching her reaction as she clenched around him.

"It'll work," he promised.

"Oh. Oh, yes."

He smiled and she nipped his shoulder playfully, soothing the spot with her tongue.

"I've never done this before."

"Pretend I'm a horse you're going to ride."

"Yes, I saw the similarities," she whispered, eliciting another chuckle.

He positioned her, trying to preserve a core of sanity. She was so tight. The sensations went beyond fantasy—beyond anything he knew as she began to encase him with exquisite slowness.

Bram claimed her mouth, certain he was glowing as brightly as one of his works in progress. He was close to the edge when she wriggled. Bram surrendered to his body's demand and surged the rest of the way inside her.

The momentary barrier was so unexpected that it shocked him into stillness—much too late. He'd swallowed her startled cry. Now he gripped her shoulders tightly.

"Why didn't you tell me?"

"I just did."

"You knew I thought you meant you'd never tried this position before—not that you'd never done it at all."

"Does it matter?" she whispered. "I wanted you. I still do."

Suffocated by emotions he could barely keep straight, Bram found a single arrogant word dominating his thoughts.

Mine.

Hayley kissed the corner of his mouth lightly. "Please

don't tell me this is all there is after that incredible buildup.''

He choked, not sure if he wanted to strangle her or kiss her. She clenched around him, taking away the choice. ''I'll see if I can't take you to the grand finale.''

But as she began to move over him, it was difficult not to surrender to the urge to plunder what she had so willingly offered. Instead, he cupped her face and kissed her with mind-numbing intensity. She squirmed in pleasure, moving against him with insistent demand—tight, hot, wet.

Bringing her back to fever pitch proved to be an intensely enjoyable task. When her hands began tracing erotic patterns against his skin, he tried to slow the pace once more, but Hayley took the lead until mere thought was no longer an option. He rolled her beneath him quickly, feeling her legs wrap around him eagerly.

Bram kissed her hard, setting free the searing hunger. The bed rocked with the force of each thrust. The sensations were too intense. He couldn't last, but he was determined not to plunge into that abyss of surrender alone. Inserting his finger between their bodies, he watched her expression when he touched her where they joined, barely covering her cry of release in time. Her body clenched around him, and he tumbled over the edge with her.

For a long time, neither one of them moved. Bram was content to listen to the rhythm of her heart as the sweat cooled on their bodies and the scent of their lovemaking lingered in the air.

With a contented sigh, Hayley rested her head against his shoulder. Once again he noticed how comfortably she fit there—as if she belonged.

Holding her seemed too precious a gift to spoil with words, so he kissed her forehead, brushing back the strands of hair. But eventually, contentedness yielded to the recriminations chasing through his head. ''Why, Hayley?''

The soft question punctured the quiet of the room.

She turned her face and kissed his chest lightly. "Because there's never been anyone else I wanted the way I want you."

Her frankness undid him. Bram suddenly understood the urge to beat his chest and shout his satisfaction to the world. Inner demons he wasn't ready to face lay in wait, but for this minute, all he could think was that Hayley belonged to him as she had never belonged to anyone else.

She peered up at him through those long, thick lashes and smiled. "And if you ever say one more word about being too old for me, I promise I'll hurt you."

"Too late. I think you just killed me."

"Good. Death becomes you." She snuggled against him. "This is nice."

A serious understatement. A drowsy, contented sort of lethargy stole over him. Bram wished they could lie like this forever, but even as he had the thought, his brain began listing a litany of problems.

"You know what would be even nicer?" she asked. "If we could magically conjure a sheet to cover us."

"Are you cold?"

"After all that heat? Hardly. I just like to have something over me when I'm lying down."

"We'll have to get up."

"I know, darn it." She kissed him lightly and rolled over. "I need to use the bathroom, anyhow. What happened to the nightgown? Oh, there it is."

Bram watched it settle into place over the sweet curves of her body. "Are you okay?"

She flashed him a brilliant smile. "I've never felt this good in all my life. I think we just found an antidote for that drug. I'll be right back."

Bram rose and tugged down the covers. Hayley had a way of keeping a man on his toes. It was frightening to discover how little he minded. But he'd once felt a similar passion for Helen, and look how that had ended.

Hayley was humming when she returned. "Shall I turn off the light?"

"I'll get it after you come to bed."

"Do you know how long I've waited to hear you issue that invitation?" She hurried to join him, slipping quickly beneath the sheet. Bram hit the light switch, trying to summon the courage to burst her bubble of happiness with reality.

Her voice came softly out of the darkness. "Do you always sleep naked?"

"Yes. Is there anything else you'd like to know?"

The sheet rustled as she stretched. The sound was surprisingly intimate, given the situation.

"I want to know everything there is to know about you."

Bram stared up at the dark ceiling. "Hayley, I tried to warn you not to fill your head with romantic notions about me." The rustling sound stopped. "I'll only hurt you."

"Because of what happened to your wife and daughter?"

"Yes." Bram swallowed remembered guilt. Oddly, the memory wasn't nearly as intense as it once had been.

For a long time, neither of them spoke. He probed at the memory, surprised to find sadness and regret without the usual bitterness that generally accompanied thoughts of Helen and those awful days when he'd waited for his infant daughter to die.

"Bram?"

"Yeah?"

"If the bottled water is drugged, I just want you to know that it wasn't one of those date-rape drugs. My sister was given one of them once. This is nothing like that."

Surprised, he was almost relieved to give his mind something else to focus on.

"I've been thinking," she continued, before he could ask

the questions hovering in his mind. "I don't think the drug was meant for me at all."

Bram rolled over. He propped his head on his hand, resting on his elbow. He stared at her dim shape beside him.

"No one knew I was coming here. Marcus has always drunk bottled water. He doesn't like the taste of well water. Eden told me he was in the early stages of dementia. But what if he isn't? What if that's what continued exposure to this drug is supposed to simulate? I can certainly vouch for the confusion part. A doctor who didn't know Marcus, and wasn't looking for drugs, could easily be fooled into thinking his behavior is due to a mental condition."

Her words made sense.

"As a nurse, Eden has access to drugs and needles right there in the house."

"What does she have to gain, Hayley?"

"I don't know. That's what I can't figure out. I'm sure she knows Marcus doesn't inherit Heartskeep, but as his wife, Eden can expect to inherit *his* estate."

Bram lay back down against the pillow. "Does Marcus have money of his own?"

"I don't know. He was a doctor, but I'm not sure how successful he was. I once overheard my grandfather tell someone that Marcus married my mother for her money. I know he's been drawing against the estate as a trustee, but he must have some money of his own after all these years. He never had to pay rent or food or any of the normal expenses. The money he earned as a doctor has to have gone somewhere. He's still a relatively young man, so he could live a long time. Eden must know she might have a long wait to gain anything—unless he's declared legally incompetent and she becomes his guardian."

Bram rolled the idea around in his head. "I think it's weak, but I'll concede the idea has merit."

''Jacob told me there have been a number of rumors going around town about Marcus over the years.''

''What sort of rumors?''

Bram listened in silence while she related Jacob's gossip. ''Jacob's been a busy boy, hasn't he? No wonder you thought I might be here for revenge.''

She laid a hand on his chest. ''I never believed that, Bram. I knew it wasn't true. Only a crazy person would wait so long to take revenge, and you're the sanest person I know.''

He snorted. ''Given the sort of people you seem to know, I'm not sure that's a compliment.''

She nudged him in the side in retaliation. ''Even if you had come here for some sort of twisted revenge, you would never use me to get it.''

Her complete trust was as astonishing as it was naive. Such blind faith scared him. ''I appreciate it, but you really don't know me, Hayley.''

''Yes, I do.''

Her words carried a conviction that cratered his heart. No one except his family had ever had that sort of blind faith in him. It was humbling. And scary.

Bram changed the subject. ''Jacob isn't a chemistry major by any chance, is he?''

''No. He did take chemistry at one point because his mother wanted him to go into medicine, but he wasn't interested. He said there was too much studying involved. He majored in computers.''

''So he could have been the one who doctored that photo you found.''

''Well, yes. But I've been thinking about those pictures. Whoever was going through my bag must have dropped the one you found in my room. Jacob wouldn't have had any reason to go through my bag.''

''From what you told me, no one would have.''

"True. Eden or Marcus could have been looking for the letter the lawyer sent me, to find out what it said. Or Paula or Mrs. Norwhich could have been looking for valuables. But what would any of them be doing with a doctored picture of Leigh as a teenager?"

"You said you thought Marcus was refusing to pay blackmail."

"It sounded that way when I followed Eden out in the maze the other day."

"Hayley, you and Eden weren't the only one in the maze that morning. I followed Jacob in there, as well."

"You never told me that!" She sat up on her elbow.

Bram shrugged.

"Why do you dislike Jacob?"

Bram could hardly tell her he resented the way the younger man looked at her. "Call it instinct," he growled.

"I thought men liked to refer to it as a gut feeling."

The thread of amusement in her voice coaxed a reluctant smile from him. "Only the insecure ones."

"Well, that definitely leaves you out. I've never met a more secure person in all my life. Jacob doesn't like you, either," she added, before he could decide if she was complimenting him or chastising him.

"I'm crushed. How does he feel about Marcus?"

Hayley sucked in a breath. "You can't suspect Jacob of tampering with the water."

"Sure I can. I suspect every single person connected to that sorry house."

"But Jacob didn't even arrive at the estate until after I did."

"So he claims. Remember, you said you thought someone else was in the house with you right from the start. Why couldn't it have been Jacob?"

Hayley sat up all the way. "He would have come forward when I called out."

"Maybe." Bram sat up, as well.

"I would have seen his car."

"Did you check the garage?" Her long silence was answer enough. "You've got a blind spot where Jacob is concerned, Hayley."

"You may be right," she said slowly. "He asked me to marry him tonight."

"What?"

Bram groped for the lamp. Hayley blinked in the sudden light. She tossed her hair back over her shoulder, smoothing it behind her ear in a familiar, nervous gesture.

"I know. I couldn't believe it, either. I had no idea he thought of me that way." She plucked at the sheet, then went back to swiping at her hair. "We've known each other all our lives."

"What aren't you telling me?"

Her head jerked up. "Why did you ask that?"

"Because I'm coming to know you very well. When you start toying with your hair like that, you're nervous about something."

Immediately, she released the strand of hair she was tormenting. Silently, Bram vowed to have a few private words with Jacob. "Maybe you'd better finish telling me exactly what else happened tonight."

"Nothing, really."

"Tell me."

Several times during her hesitant recital, he had to bite back questions and comments. His tension was acute when she finally finished. He flexed his fingers, trying to relieve the anxiety building inside him.

"You can see why I've been doubting my sanity."

"Stop it, Hayley. There's not a thing wrong with your sanity," he said fiercely.

Hayley blinked at his tone. "Thanks, but unless the drug

causes hallucinations, too, I'd like to know how I heard that pantry door close when there wasn't anyone inside.''

''Isn't Mrs. Norwhich's room right off the kitchen? You were upset and drugged, remember? Maybe it was her door you heard.''

He watched Hayley testing that theory in her head. ''I suppose it could have been.''

''She could also be the one drugging the water, Hayley. Who has better access to the kitchen?''

''What would she have to gain? Next you'll suggest Paula Kerstairs.''

''Okay, she can be next.''

''Get serious. What reason would either one of them have? Eden just hired them.''

''Who knows? If the rumors Jacob was spouting have an iota of truth, more than one person may have a reason to hate Marcus. For all we know, Paula or Mrs. Norwhich might be your father's lover.''

After a shocked second of silence, Hayley began to giggle. ''You have to be joking.''

He allowed himself a brief moment to enjoy her amusement. The idea *was* pretty ludicrous. ''Okay, but like I said, they're all suspects. Even your father.''

''Marcus?'' Hayley gaped at him. ''But it's his bottled water!''

''Exactly. We've been assuming someone put a toxin in those bottles. What if it's medication instead?''

Her lips parted in astonishment.

''It's possible Marcus has been injecting something into the water himself. You said everyone else uses tap water.''

''I never thought of that possibility.''

Neither had Bram until the words came out of his mouth. ''My point is we need to keep an open mind about everyone. We should know more when Rhea finishes running her tests.'' He snapped off the light, plunging the room into darkness once more. ''We'd better try to get some rest.''

Hayley lay back down against the pillows. ''Bram? Do you think we could go to Heartskeep in the morning? Real early. Before anyone is awake.''

His body tensed again. ''Not a chance. I'll drive over and pick up your purse and anything else you need, but you're not going near that place until we find out what is going on.''

''Eden won't let you in.''

''I wasn't planning to ask permission.''

''Oh.''

''What's wrong?'' he asked in the sudden silence.

''Shall I make you a list?''

His lips twitched.

''I was just wondering if you knew how to pick a lock.''

He definitely didn't like the sounds of that. ''What is going through that Machiavellian mind of yours now?''

''We should check out Marcus's office.''

Fear sunk talons deep in his gut. ''Absolutely not!''

''Yeah. We really should. For one thing, he has a lab. It's small, but he's got a lot of equipment.''

''Equipment, not chemicals,'' Bram pointed out.

''We don't know that unless we look.''

''Hayley, even if it was a fully stocked chemical lab, he isn't going to leave the drug lying around for us to find.''

''Why not? Where would it be safer? No one goes in there except Marcus and Eden. Remember, Paula said she isn't even allowed in there to clean. We might learn a lot from his files. You said yourself if Jacob's rumors are true, there's bound to be more than one person who has a reason to hate Marcus.''

''Forget it. That's something for the police to investigate. This is not up for discussion.''

But already his mind was busy thinking about what Marcus might be hiding behind locked doors.

"Bram, did you say Marcus found you on the Internet? What if he didn't? What if it was Eden who found you? What if she heard the same rumors Jacob heard? Maybe she's the one who started them. What if she convinced Marcus to hire you because she wanted to set you up?"

His pulse rate took a flying leap. "How could she do that? I don't have access to the house or the bottled water."

"No, but you had a wife who died at the hands of an incompetent doctor."

"It wasn't Marcus. The doctor was a much older man. I don't remember his name, but the hospital would have a record of who it was, and Eden would know it wasn't Marcus."

"You're right, but I keep feeling like Eden is trying to set you up. Remember when she left you a note telling you to go up to the house, and then she warned you away from me?"

"I don't know who left me the note."

"Eden," Hayley said firmly. "She told Jacob she found you roaming around inside the house on more than one occasion."

Hayley had his full attention now.

"That's a lie, Hayley."

"I know that. But Jacob warned me to be careful around you because his mother was worried. What do you want to bet she's told other people how worried she is about you? What if she's planning to kill Marcus and set you up for his murder? What if she's the one who killed my mother seven years ago?"

Chapter Eleven

Neither of them got much sleep after that. Before the sun was nibbling at the horizon, they were both up and dressed. Bram scribbled a brief explanation for the Walkens while Hayley struggled with a ponytail. She was so nervous her fingers didn't want to cooperate.

She joined him in the kitchen, extremely conscious of her unconfined breasts in the lime-green T-shirt. Last night it had seemed naughty and daring. Today it felt naked. However, the flash of heat in Bram's expression when he first looked at her was reassuring.

Did he see how well they complemented one another? Could she make him see that this connection between them was more than biological pheromones, or would she always come up against the pain of his loss ten years ago? Hayley heaved a mental sigh.

"All set?" he asked.

"Yes."

It had taken her a long time to convince him that a quick look inside Marcus's office might give them some much needed information, but Bram still wasn't happy about it.

Following him out to his truck in the dark, she thought again that she could happily spend the rest of her life with Bram. They would argue a lot—both of them being so strong-willed—but he had plenty of self-control, which was a good thing, given her tendency to be impulsive. They could make a relationship work. She knew they could.

"This is a bad idea," he said as he started the engine.

"No, it isn't."

"I'd rather be making love to you than taking you back to that house."

A thrill ignited inside her. "Really?"

His arms snaked out, pulling her against him. His mouth covered her squeal of surprise in a kiss that left no question about his desire.

"I still can't believe I let you talk me into this," he muttered, kissing the curve of her jaw and finally releasing her to put the truck in gear.

"We'll be in and out before anyone knows we're there," she soothed.

"From your lips to God's ear."

"What?"

"One of my father's favorite expressions."

Hayley smiled. "I like it."

"I'm sure he'll be pleased to hear that. Just remember our deal. You stay close to me and do what I tell you."

"Yes, Bram."

He shot her a disgusted look. "Meekness does not suit you."

"I know."

She was still grinning when he pulled into the clearing by the barns. But when Hayley would have opened the door to get out, he stopped her with an iron grip on her arm. "Wait!"

He was out of the truck before she could ask why. He paced the campsite slowly, examining the place without touching anything. His features were dark and forbidding when he returned to the truck and opened the door without getting in.

"What's wrong?"

"Someone's been here," he said.

Her stomach plunged. "Are you sure? Is something missing?"

"My two-pound hammer. The piece I was working on last night was moved. Some other pieces have been disturbed. I don't like this, Hayley. I've got a feeling things are on the brink of exploding around here. I want you to wait. I'll go have a quick look around and get your purse."

Hayley scrambled down from the truck. "I'm not staying here alone."

Bram's expression turned thunderous, but she held her ground, braced for a fight. After a moment, he nodded curtly.

"If anything happens, you are to come straight back here, get in the truck and drive to the Walkens'. Agreed?"

He handed her the keys. A chill swept over her at his bleak expression. "You sense it, too, don't you?"

Bram shifted. "Sense what?"

"Something bad is going to happen."

"That does it! We're going back to the Walkens. Come on, get in the truck."

"I don't think it will make any difference," she said softly.

"What are you talking about? Don't you dare start getting weird on me."

She shook her head, gazing up at him. She could read so many emotions in his expression—including the one she most needed to see. Hayley surprised both of them by reaching up to stroke the side of his face.

"Sorry. My sister's usually the one with the imagination." She pressed his lips closed with her fingers. "We have to go inside, Bram. You know we do. There's only one reason a person would take your hammer. They plan to implicate you in a crime."

Bram stepped back and swore. "Let's get this over with." He took her hand and started down the path.

Heat was already gathering strength for its assault on the day. Though she'd had little sleep, Hayley realized her head felt more clear than it had in days. Only the muzzy sensation had been replaced by a desperate sense of urgency she didn't understand.

At the house they discovered the doors had been locked for the night.

"My keys are in my purse," she apologized.

Bram looked as if he'd expected no less. "We'll go in through a window. You're certain the alarm system doesn't work?"

"Positive. Last year they told Marcus the system needed to be completely rewired. I'll bet that's when he got the idea to put grills on the windows."

Bram crossed to the parlor window farthest from the main door. He hadn't put up bars here yet. Pulling a tool from his pocket, he tapped the glass gently above the lock. To Hayley, the sound was horrifically loud, but Bram didn't look concerned. None of the front rooms were occupied, so he was probably right not to worry, but her nerves were doing a tap dance inside her.

Wrapping a handkerchief around his hand, Bram reached through the broken pane to unlock the window. Seconds later, he was helping her climb over the sill. Broken glass crunched beneath their feet.

The house was deathly quiet, as if waiting in gloomy silence for the sun's rays to strike. Hayley was vividly reminded of the night she'd sensed a presence in this room. Now the entire house seemed filled with menace. The urge to turn around was strong, but Bram was already moving across the floor. He tested the doors leading to the front hall. Locked. Going around the desk, he reached for the door leading back to the offices. The handle twisted freely.

A chill galloped straight down her spine. Bram shot her a tight look. She knew what he was thinking. This was too easy. It was as if someone *wanted* them to go inside.

"Are you sure no one is up yet?" he whispered in her ear.

"Even Marcus doesn't get up this early."

Bram stepped into the narrow hallway. Two closed doors faced them, and another was to his immediate right. Bram looked at her questioningly.

"Closet," she mouthed, pointing to the door on his right. "Bathroom," she whispered, pointing straight ahead. "Lab. Exam rooms. The office is at the end of the hall."

She'd only been back here once as a kid. Some new equipment had been delivered and Marcus was out front arguing with the delivery men. No one else had been around and the doors had been standing wide open, so she'd dared Leigh to explore with her. They'd crept inside like a pair of thieves—exactly as she and Bram were doing now.

She hoped this situation would have a happier ending. She was pretty sure Marcus wouldn't settle for yelling at her this time.

"What's that smell?" Bram whispered.

Hayley shook her head. A strong chemical odor lingered in the air. "Cleaning solution?"

Bram scowled. He bypassed the closet and headed for the lab. Hayley wasn't surprised. If Marcus had something to hide, it would be in there or in his office. The door was locked, but there was no keyhole, just a small, round hole. Bram reached above the frame with the handkerchief still wrapped around his hand. Puzzled, she watched as he felt along the molding and pulled down a shiny object.

"What is that?"

"Key," he whispered back.

Unlike the original heavy wooden doors, these were hollow, the type carried by most hardware stores. Fascinated, Hayley watched him insert the device into the tiny round hole on the knob. The door opened with a small click.

"How did you know that was there?" she whispered.

"Builders usually put them there for safety in new construction."

Impressed, she followed him inside. The chemical smell was stronger in here. He hit the light switch. The fluorescent lighting seemed overly bright after the darkness of the hall. Hayley peered around the cluttered room. "Someone's been using this."

Bram nodded. He surveyed the room without moving. An almost invisible layer of dust showed signs of being recently disturbed. Hayley started to run a finger over the counter when Bram stopped her.

"Put these on first."

Reaching into a box of surgical gloves, he yanked one free without touching anything else. After pulling it on, he removed three more and handed her a pair.

"We don't need to worry about fingerprints," she protested. "I own Heartskeep."

"You do. I don't. We'll argue later. Put them on."

Hayley did so as Bram began opening drawers and cupboards. He stopped when he came to a drawer containing an open box of needles and syringes. Selecting one, he placed it inside a clear plastic bag he'd found in the drawer.

"What are you doing?"

"I want to see if this makes the same size mark as the one on the water bottle."

"Oh."

Minutes ticked past. He opened every door and drawer. Marcus had a lot of equipment. He'd done some in vitro fertilization as well as cryosurgery here in his office.

"What's that?" Bram asked, indicating a tiny cupboard-like box on the wall between the lab and the bathroom.

"A pass-through for urine specimens."

"Right."

It never would have occurred to her to check inside, but Bram did. He withdrew a tightly sealed bottle containing a perfectly clear liquid.

"What is it?"

"We'll have to ask Rhea."

Taking a clean hypodermic needle, Bram deftly withdrew a sample of the liquid. Carefully, he replaced the bottle. Now she saw the sense in not leaving prints. He didn't want to contaminate possible evidence. When he opened the refrigerator in the corner, she tapped him on the arm.

"I'm going to have a look in his office to save time."

Bram scowled. "I want us out of here in ten minutes or less."

Hayley was tempted to point out that ten minutes wasn't enough time, but the tension in his expression made her nod and hurry to the end of the hall. Because he was usually so calm and unflappable, Bram's nervousness added a layer to her own.

She realized that if the office was locked, she wouldn't be tall enough to take down one of those handy little key things. Surprisingly, the office was unlocked.

Distinctly uneasy now, she stepped inside. The chemical smell was strongest in here. The odor was enough to give her a headache.

The single window behind the desk would allow only a minimal amount of light in the room once the sun came up. Unlike the lab, which didn't have any windows, lights turned on in here would be clearly visible to anyone outside. There wasn't any choice. She didn't know what time Mrs. Norwhich started her day, yet surely not before five-thirty or so. Hayley turned on the lights.

Marcus hadn't practiced medicine in a long time, but someone was still using this office, as well. Curiosity propelled Hayley toward the heavy maple desk. A computer and printer sat on the credenza behind it. Ten minutes would never be enough time to search everything, so she decided to ignore the machine and the tempting desk drawers and concentrate on the cherry filing cabinets against the far wall first.

When she opened the top drawer, the pungent chemical smell nearly overwhelmed her. The files were orderly, but damp, as if they'd been sprayed with an atomizer.

Her first thought was that Marcus had called in a fumigator to spray for bugs. It wouldn't be the first time they'd needed help against pests that had wanted to set up housekeeping indoors. But this smell was different. And the files were so damp they must have been sprayed very recently.

Maybe someone *was* awake at this hour. Fear sent Hayley's heart racing. A noise in the hall made her freeze until she realized it was Bram opening the closet door. She was about to go and tell him what she'd discovered when one file caught her eye.

MYERS, Helen.

The file sat there, silently accusing.

Bram had said Marcus wasn't his wife's doctor. Hayley believed him, despite this evidence to the contrary. Tugging the file free, she saw it looked different than the files around it. She flipped it open and realized the file was a fake. Nurses generally recorded preliminary information, then the doctor would write his notes regarding medications or treatments. Only one person had written on the sheets of paper inside. Hayley had been right after all. Someone was trying to frame Bram.

Or were they trying to set him up so she would distrust him?

It disturbed Hayley to realize she wouldn't recognize Eden's or Marcus's handwriting. How sad to think she'd grown up with a father who had never signed a permission form or a birthday card.

Before she could compare the file with the writing in one of the others, there was a noise in the hall. Something fell. A door slammed. Hayley ran to the doorway to see Bram picking himself up off the carpeting. Blood streamed down the side of his face from a gash on his forehead.

As she hurried toward him, he swayed, his hand going to the injury. It came away red with blood. Terrified, she dropped the file and tried to support his weight. He pushed her away, toward the exit. "Go!"

"You're hurt!"

"Get out of here! Now!"

He was bleeding profusely. She reached for him again and her heart threatened to stop when he sagged heavily against her. Her gaze landed on an object on the carpeting near their feet. Bram's hammer, splattered with his blood.

"Bram!"

"Leave it!" He straightened weakly.

Her eyes and the back of her throat began to sting. The chemical smell was suddenly overwhelming. The doors to the waiting room were closed, but something wet was spreading in a dark evil stain beneath the door.

Terrified, she reached for the knob. It wouldn't turn. She spun toward Bram. He leaned against the wall of the lab with his eyes closed.

"The door's locked!"

And the air at her back exploded with a whoosh of sound.

The force sent Hayley careening against him. They went down together as a thick cloud of noxious smoke billowed to the ceiling. There was a loud crackling sound in her ears and an incredible burst of heat at her back.

Overhead, the smoke detector deafened them with its

wail. Hungry flames were suddenly everywhere, lapping at the walls and racing along the baseboards.

Bram grabbed her head. He shoved her toward the flames!

Hayley struggled futilely. He'd gone mad! But instead of pitching her into the fire, he shoved her into the tiny bathroom.

Shutting the door behind them with his foot, he thrust her head toward the sink and turned on the water. Only then did she understand. Her ponytail was on fire!

Bram doused the flames and started to cough. Her own lungs were raw and irritated. The sound of the fire raged, even over the blare of the smoke detector.

"We need to block the door," he gasped between coughs.

She could barely hear over the din, but she had no trouble seeing the smoke pouring in beneath the door. There was nothing in the small room to use!

Bram stripped off his shirt. He wet it down and stuffed it against the bottom of the door. Smoke filled the room, trapped there with them.

"There's no other way out!" Hayley shouted.

The only exit to this string of rooms was the door where the fire had started.

Bram rested his hand on the wall next to the sink. She thought he was about to collapse, but then she realized he was testing it for heat.

"What's on the other side of this wall?" he demanded.

"The ballroom."

"Stand back."

Grasping the sink, he kicked at the wall with frightening force. His foot tore a hole right through the wallboard. Hayley realized what he was trying to do, but there wasn't enough room for both of them to work. She could only watch as he continued kicking, widening the hole.

When it was large enough, he began tearing at the wallboard with his bare hands. He had to keep stopping to wipe his eyes as blood ran into the one near his wound.

Grabbing the hem of her skirt, Hayley tried to tear off a strip of fabric from the bottom. The movies made it look so easy, but the sturdy material resisted her best efforts.

The room was darkening as more smoke seeped inside despite Bram's shirt. He stopped working and grabbed for her hem. An open pocket knife appeared in his hand. The small blade sliced through the skirt. They were both coughing, struggling to draw a breath.

Rinsing his handkerchief, Bram pressed it against his wound while Hayley wrapped the torn strip from her skirt around his head to hold the handkerchief in place.

They could actually feel the fire's heat. The wall on the lab side was warm. The fire was already next door! Hayley had no idea what sort of combustibles might be in the lab, but it didn't take a genius to know the whole place could explode if there were any volatile chemicals.

As Bram renewed his efforts, Hayley wondered where everyone was. Surely the alarm had awakened the entire household. Only they'd be seeking their own escape from the fire. They had no way of knowing anyone was in here.

Bram began kicking at the wall on the ballroom side. This was harder, because the angle was more difficult. The leg of his jeans ripped when it caught on a nail, but a hole finally appeared.

As the second hole widened, Bram grappled with the drywall, punching and pulling at it with superhuman strength. Hayley could see the ballroom floor on the other side. Bram kept at it until the space looked big enough for them to crawl between the studs.

''Go!''

Hayley started through. Her skirt caught on something, trapping her. She felt Bram's hands at her back. There was a tearing sound. She realized he was using his knife to cut her free. Suddenly, she was loose. She scampered through the hole in the wall, crawling along the polished floor. Her skirt dragged in her wake, torn practically off her body.

"Bram! Hurry!"

But the opening wasn't large enough for his broad shoulders. Hayley wanted to scream as he backed up and began kicking once more. On her side of the wall, she started ripping at the tough material. The plastic gloves hung from her hands in obscene tatters, like her skirt. She paused to pull the gloves off.

Her fingers were raw and bleeding, but she barely noticed. Heat and smoke poured through the opening. Bram stopped kicking and forced his broad shoulders through the hole. Hayley tugged at him in a frenzy to get him clear, sobbing frantically in her panic.

Then he was free, sprawled on the floor, his scraped, bloody chest heaving as coughs racked him.

"Get up! Get up! We have to get out of here!" She tugged at him until he rose unsteadily. Hayley ran to the heavy wood doors that opened into the main hall. They were locked. So was the other set of doors, and they weren't the flimsy, hollow doors of the converted offices. These were solid cherry.

Looking at Bram, she realized he wouldn't have the strength to kick down another wall. Besides, there wasn't any more drywall. These were the original walls of plaster. With bars on all the windows and fancy gates covering the doors opening onto the patio, they were still trapped. They had just traded one prison for another.

For a long moment, Bram bent over, hands on his thighs, coughing hard. Hayley coughed as well, until her chest ached from the effort. Smoke billowed in through the hole they'd made. She didn't have to touch that wall to know it would be hot. She could hear the crackle of the flames.

"The fire's spreading!" Her words ended in a fit of choking.

Bram straightened unsteadily. Blood seeped beneath the bandage, trickling down his soot-streaked face. His chest was filthy—scraped and matted with blood.

Terrified, Hayley grabbed his arm. Together, they staggered across the floor to the far end of the room. Their only hope lay in someone outside seeing their plight.

"We're trapped."

Bram shook his head. "Open…window."

"That will just make the fire spread faster."

Bram shook his head again.

What did it matter? The air was so foul they'd pass out if they didn't get fresh air soon, and maybe she could scream for help and someone would hear them.

She fumbled with the catch. The lock was jammed. When she would have smashed the glass with her bare hand, Bram nudged her aside. Yanking down one of the huge drapes hanging there, he used it to protect his hand, smashing out several windowpanes. Air reached them—far from cool, but their starving lungs didn't care.

Using his pocket knife, Bram forced the stiff latch and opened the window. Pausing to cough, he ran his hands along the left side of the bars. It took her a minute to realize what he was doing. Several small, nearly invisible catches were built into the metal. He was releasing them.

"Fail-safe," he told her with a weak smile.

To her amazement, the grill swung out and away from the window on invisible hinges.

"You *are* a superhero!"

Bram grabbed her around the waist and boosted her up and out. He doubled over with a coughing fit, then managed to half climb, half fall out of the window beside her.

Together, they staggered across the lawn.

Chapter Twelve

''Ms. Thomas?''

Hayley looked up quickly.

''I'm Dr. Ravens. I understand you're Mr. Myers's fiancée?''

Hayley removed the oxygen mask from her face, swung her legs over the side of the gurney and nodded anxiously.

When Bram had suddenly collapsed a short distance from the house, she'd panicked. The house, the fire, the sound of approaching sirens had all faded to insignificance as she'd tried to rouse him without success. Not until she saw the cluster of people running toward her did she realize she was screaming.

Surprisingly, it was Marcus, fully dressed, his hair standing on end and a forbidding scowl on his features, who reached them first.

''Move aside, girl,'' he snarled.

''Hayley, come on! Your dad's a doctor!'' Jacob's hands had pulled her away. She'd struggled, but a coughing spell drained her strength. Jacob was wearing cutoffs and a pair of mismatched socks. The others were all in various stages of undress as well. Obviously, the fire alarm had caught everyone by surprise.

When Jacob pulled her against his naked chest, she'd pushed her way free and turned back to Bram. Eden, in a nightgown and robe, bent beside Marcus, shouting orders to Paula and Mrs. Norwhich. Both of them, Hayley noticed, were fully dressed, but disheveled.

"Mom!" Jacob yelled. "Hayley's hurt, too."

Hayley tried to tell him she was fine, but her lungs wouldn't cooperate. They were busy trying to purge the smoke she'd inhaled.

"What's wrong with that stupid woman?" Eden snarled as she hurried over to them.

Hayley realized Eden was talking about Paula Kerstairs, not Hayley herself. The thin, bony woman stood there wringing her hands, looking scared to death.

"I told her to run down and open the gate," Eden continued in exasperation.

"I'll do it," Jacob offered. "Just take care of Hayley."

"Let's see where you're hurt, girl," Eden demanded as Jacob sprinted away. "How'd you get all scraped up like that? Burned off half your hair, too. Don't see any burns on your skin. Where's Odette? I told her to fetch the first-aid kit from the barn."

Flames burst through the barred window of the office, shattering the glass. The fire department appeared a few minutes later, sirens screaming up the driveway. And the morning became filled with shouted orders.

"I'm a doctor," Hayley heard Marcus snap at one of the paramedics. "This man has a concussion. Get that oxygen over here. He's got a nasty scalp wound. There may be pressure on the brain. The cuts and burns appear minor, but I haven't rolled him over yet to see what other damage he's done. One of you better see to the girl, as well."

Pressure on the brain.

Horrified, Hayley allowed an oxygen mask to be clamped over her face while she watched the paramedics and Marcus minister to Bram's injuries. This was a side of Marcus she'd never seen before, but her attention remained on Bram. He could have permanent brain damage, and it was all her fault! If she'd listened to him—

"Never mind whose fault it is," Eden snapped, abruptly filling her vision. "You just answer the man's questions. Where are you hurt?"

Hayley stared at her blankly. She tried to tell Eden she was fine, that it was Bram who mattered, but she began to shake. Her body felt so cold that she knew she'd never be warm again.

"Shock," she heard someone say.

Another voice yelled that they needed to move these people back. It all seemed far away, like a bad dream. Everything except Bram lying motionless in the grass.

"Oh, God, please!"

A soothing voice tried to assure her he was going to be okay. That she needed to calm down and breathe slowly. Hayley ignored the voice and closed her eyes.

She remembered little of the trip to the hospital, but she finally pulled herself together enough to realize they wouldn't let her see Bram unless they were related. She told the attendant she was his fiancée, hoping the lie would work as it had in an old movie she'd seen. It didn't. They wheeled Bram down one hall and her to a bank of cubicles in a different hall.

Time had little meaning. No one around her seemed to feel the same sense of urgency she did. She answered a million questions, but no one would tell her about Bram's condition. All she got were empty promises to check on him. She'd been sitting there fretting alone forever, it seemed. She didn't care what anyone said, she was going to find Bram. That was when Dr. Ravens had appeared.

"Where's Bram? Is he okay?" A fit of coughing stopped her flood of questions. The doctor came over and firmly but kindly replaced the oxygen mask.

''Mr. Myers is going to be fine,'' the doctor assured her. ''He's conscious and equally concerned about you.''

Relief left Hayley weak and shaken. ''Thank God.''

''Yes. You should. From what I understand, you were both very fortunate in many ways. Do you know what could have happened if the fire department hadn't been so close by, finishing an earlier call?''

Hayley didn't care. ''I need to see Bram.''

Dr. Ravens nodded. ''Mr. Myers is also quite agitated over your condition. If you're feeling well enough, you can come with me and reassure him that you're all right.''

Hayley was off the gurney so fast the doctor had to steady her.

''A bit slower, if you please. Would you like a wheelchair?''

''No. I don't need a wheelchair. I just moved too fast.''

''Are you sure? I need you to reassure him, not scare him by passing out in front of him,'' Dr. Ravens scolded. ''We have every reason to believe Mr. Myers will be fine. However, anytime someone is unconscious for several minutes after a serious head trauma, it's best to take precautions.''

''Oh, my God.''

''Ms. Thomas, you really do need to calm down,'' the doctor said sternly. ''I can't let you in to see him if you're going to be this agitated.''

''All right. Okay. I'm all right. I just want to see him. Please.''

The woman pursed her lips, but finally resumed leading her down the hall. ''Your fiancé is refusing to let us take him down for X rays. He insists on leaving right away. We can't force him to cooperate, so I'm hoping you can convince him to let us do our job.''

''But you said he'll be okay.''

''I believe so. A CT scan is precautionary, but highly

advisable. We put thirteen stitches in his scalp. The wound was deep and located close to his temple. Do you know specifically what caused the injury?''

''I didn't see him get hurt,'' Hayley replied honestly, but in her mind, she saw the bloody hammer lying on the carpet. ''We were trapped by the fire. Bram had to kick through two walls to get us out.'' She stopped as another bout of coughing overtook her.

''Go ahead and cough. I know it hurts, but coughing is the body's way of expunging the smoke from your lungs. I'll have the nurse bring you both something to ease it a bit.''

Hayley nodded her thanks, too out of breath to respond. Then she heard the reassuring rumble of Bram's voice. He sounded as hoarse and scratchy as she did. He also sounded determined to get his way.

''Try to convince him to let us run the CT scan,'' Dr. Ravens urged.

''I will,'' she promised. ''It may take chains and a unit of marines, but I'll see to it he does whatever is necessary.''

Dr. Ravens smiled and patted her shoulder. ''Good luck. I'll give you a few minutes to talk alone.''

''Thank you.''

''Go ahead and get up again, Mr. Myers,'' a nurse was saying. ''I'll just have the orderly put you back in bed after you pass out.''

''I am not—''

A fit of coughing choked off his protest. Hayley squared her shoulders and stepped into the room.

''Don't worry about, Bram,'' she told the nurse, trying to sound jaunty. ''He thinks he's a superhero.''

The older woman clamped an oxygen mask over his face and winked at Hayley. ''Does he now? I'll bet he looks real cute in a pair of blue tights. But even a superhero should know enough to accept help when he needs it. Now you just keep that oxygen on your face for a few minutes,'' she admonished Bram. ''You've got yourself a live one here,'' she told Hayley as she left.

''Are you all right?'' Bram demanded, reaching up to pull off the mask.

Hayley covered his hand. ''Leave it there. It really does help. I'm fine, thanks to you. You made a great superhero.'' She tried to sound light and upbeat when what she wanted to do was burst into tears.

Pain had etched tired lines around his eyes. A stark white bandage covered one side of his face. They'd cleaned the area to stitch his wound, but smoke and dried blood were still in evidence. His bare chest was more dirty than clean.

''I was coming to find you,'' Bram said.

''Well, here I am, so sit back.''

''We need to go.''

''After you let them take a CT scan,'' she told him firmly.

Bram shook his head, winced and raised his hand to the bandaged area. His hands were cleaner than the rest of him because several clearly visible burns and cuts had been treated there. She wanted to cry for his pain, but Bram needed strength from her now, not pity.

''What do you have against CT scans?''

He yanked off the oxygen mask. ''I don't have insurance, Hayley,'' he told her frankly. ''I can't afford a huge hospital bill.''

''Well, fortunately, I can. And before you pitch a fit based on pride, let's get something clear here. You just saved my life. I *owe* you.''

''Hayley—''

''No, darn it. I've got pride, too, you know. And I've got plenty of money. I can afford to pay your hospital bill. This is not charity, you stubborn fool, so let's not waste time arguing about this, all right?''

Laying her hand on his grimy chest, she blinked back the tears that were scalding her eyes. ''Please, Bram. I was so damn scared. Please let them make sure you're okay. Do it for me, please.''

Another dose of coughing punctuated her plea, choking off the rest of her words. When she finished, Bram reached for her, pulling her against him in a tight, reassuring hug. ''Don't cry. I'm okay.''

She swallowed hard.

''It's you I'm worried about,'' he said against her hair. ''That fire was set deliberately. I don't know what the accelerant was, but I should have realized that something was wrong when we first went in and smelled that odor.''

He let her go and coughed, pressing his hand to the bandage until the spasm passed.

''I was there, too, remember?'' she said. ''I thought it was insecticide. Why should you have known what it was?''

''Someone tried to kill you,'' he said.

Her heart raced. ''Not really. The accelerant was already there before we got there.''

''A technicality. The person who hit me knew we were in there. He locked us in and lit the fire. We were supposed to die.''

The fear that never seemed to be far away rushed back. ''Who?''

''I don't know. I was looking in the closet when I heard a noise behind me. I thought it was you. I started to turn my head and it felt like it exploded.''

Dr. Ravens cleared her throat, moving to stand in the doorway. ''Well, Mr. Myers? Do you want the release forms, or are you willing to let us make sure your brains haven't all leaked out?''

''According to my fiancée, I don't have a say in the matter.''

He coughed, and cringing at the word *fiancée,* Hayley covered his mouth and nose with the oxygen mask.

"I'll have an orderly wheel him down to X-ray before he changes his mind," the doctor told Hayley.

"Could we have a few more minutes, please?"

"It will take me a few minutes to locate an orderly," she said. "If you wouldn't mind filling out the paperwork? And I'm afraid there's an officer waiting to ask you both some questions about the fire."

Bram tensed. Hayley covered his hand with hers, then quickly let go when he winced. She'd touched an angry burn whose blister was starting to seep. "Shouldn't this be bandaged?" she asked the doctor.

Dr. Ravens nodded. "Mr. Myers hasn't exactly been cooperative since he woke up."

"He will be now," she promised.

Once again Bram pulled off the oxygen mask, looking fierce.

"I'll send the nurse back in to tend to those burns while I call down to X-ray," the doctor said as she disappeared.

"Hayley—"

Lightly, she stroked his face and touched the stark white bandage. "They said it took thirteen stitches to close this."

"My lucky number."

"Bram, please let them take the scan. You could have swelling of the brain. I...I couldn't stand it if—"

"I've got a hard head."

"Thick," she said, holding fresh tears at bay with an effort. He cupped her face so tenderly, two tears escaped. Bram brushed them away with his thumbs.

"That, too. But I'm not leaving you alone again. Not for a minute."

"We're in a hospital full of people, so I don't think it's an issue. Besides," she added quickly, "as soon as they take you to X-ray I'm going to call the Walkens and ask them to come pick us up. I'll ask them to stay with me. You know they will. Please, Bram."

"You promise you'll stay with them?"

"If you'll go have your hard head x-rayed, I'll promise you anything you like."

"Now, there's an offer," he said with a crooked smile. "To be honest, my head isn't feeling all that hard at the moment. Whoever slugged me did a good job. The blow must have scrambled my brains. I don't even remember getting engaged to you."

Hayley felt her face flame. "I can explain that."

He looked toward the open door. Hayley heard someone approaching.

"I'll look forward to that—later," he told her. "Call the Walkens right away, Hayley. I don't want you to be alone for even a second."

"I won't. I promise."

He studied her face. "You aren't to blame for what happened, Hayley."

"Not for the fire, maybe, but if I hadn't insisted on going there this morning—"

"He might have burned down the entire house instead of just that wing. Whoever it was must have been inside one of the exam rooms when we got there. He was probably getting ready to torch the place when we interrupted."

"He?"

"A generic he."

"He hit you with your own hammer," Hayley told Bram. "I saw it on the floor right before the fireball exploded. You even told me to leave it."

Her heart raced in remembered horror.

"I don't recall that."

"Excuse me," a voice said from the doorway. "Mr. Myers? I'm here to take you down to X-ray, sir."

"I'll be here when you get back," Hayley promised.

''And I'll call the Walkens right away. Is there a telephone I can use?'' she asked the orderly.

''Right over there, miss.'' He indicated a bank of pay phones across from them.

''Oh! I don't have any—''

Bram was already digging through his pocket. He handed her his wallet and some change. From another pocket, he retrieved the bag containing the evidence he'd taken from the lab. Hayley had forgotten all about it. Her body blocked the orderly's view as she took the plastic bag and held it against her hospital gown.

Hayley signed her discharge papers and filled out the paperwork for Bram, listing herself as the person responsible for his bills. He would probably argue with her once he was back in fighting form, but she looked forward to that. It would mean he was feeling better.

The police officer was too young to have been on the force when her mother disappeared, but Hayley kept her answers simple, anyhow. She and Bram had gone into the office to look for something she'd misplaced. They had smelled something right away, but they hadn't realized what it meant. She didn't know who had started the fire or what had happened to Bram's head. She had no idea why anyone would want to do such an awful thing. She didn't actually live at Heartskeep any longer.

Hayley couldn't tell what he was thinking, but caution kept her from showing him the bag of evidence or giving him any details. Her distrust of the local police ran deep.

It was a relief to see Emily and George striding toward her as the police officer left. They hugged her tightly.

''I thought you might be needing these,'' Emily said, holding out a plastic sack. ''We aren't exactly the same size, but the blouse was too big on me, so I'm thinking it might fit you. And the shorts have an elastic waist. Would you like some help?''

Hayley gave her another hug. "Please. I don't know why I'm feeling so teary."

"It's perfectly understandable after what you've been through."

Hayley pulled out the bag she'd hidden beneath her ruined blouse and handed it to George Walken. "Bram took this from Marcus's lab before the fire. He wants Rhea Levinson to test the contents of the one syringe. It may be whatever was in the water. He took the other one to see if the size matched the hole in the bottle he gave her."

George and Emily exchanged looks. "I'll take care of it," George promised.

"Why don't we go find a rest room? Come on, Hayley," Mrs. Walken said, leading her to the bathroom next to the bank of pay phones.

With most of the smoke and grit washed off her skin, and dressed in clean clothing, Hayley felt marginally better. The T-shirt was a bit tighter than she would have liked, considering she still didn't have a bra to wear underneath, but the shorts were a good fit, and Emily Walken had even included a pair of sandals.

"Much better," she said. "It's a shame about your hair."

"Thank you, Mrs. Walken. My hair's the least of my worries right now."

"Good girl. I think you should call me Emily, don't you? Would you like me to help you pin your hair up for now?"

"Yes, thank you."

Her husband was coming down the hall when they left the ladies' room.

"I wandered down to X-ray," George told them. "They're running Bram through the scanner now. The waiting room is empty at the moment, so why don't we go down there and wait for him?"

Sitting in the smaller, more private waiting room, George

told Hayley what Rhea had learned about the water she'd already tested.

''The bottle had been doctored, all right, but it wasn't a standard drug. Someone with a knowledge of chemistry created whatever was in there. Rhea doesn't think it will cause any lasting effects, but the symptoms you described were consistent with her findings.''

''Eden thought Marcus was suffering from dementia, but it's really just due to being drugged, isn't it?'' Hayley asked.

''Sounds that way,'' George agreed.

''Did you have a chance to tell Bram?'' Hayley asked.

''Yes, while I was waiting for you and Emily. Bram and I agree it's time to turn all this information over to the police. I know how you feel, Hayley, but there isn't much choice now. The person nearly killed the two of you. The police will have to investigate.''

''Like they investigated my mother's disappearance?''

''It won't be like that this time,'' he promised. ''We've got hard evidence of a crime now.''

''I wish I had your faith.''

And it was difficult to think of Marcus as a victim after all these years. But Marcus had rushed to help Bram. Hayley leaned back and closed her eyes. Even Eden had tried to help. Had it all been an act so no one would realize Eden had just tried to burn them alive?

''Have you seen Marcus?'' Emily asked.

''Not since the fire. I haven't seen anyone since they brought us here. I assume everyone is still at the house. We need to warn him about the water.''

''I don't think it will be a problem right away,'' George said. ''The fire department isn't going to let anyone back in the house until they complete their investigation.''

''Where will they go?''

''The Inn, more than likely,'' Emily replied. ''But we'll

check and be sure they have a place to stay. You and Bram will stay with us.''

''Thank you. Both of you. I don't know what I'd do without you.''

They returned to the Walken estate late in the afternoon. Dr. Ravens had reluctantly agreed to release Bram after looking over his CT scan.

Stress and a lack of sleep had caught up with Hayley long before they arrived. Her throat was too raw to do more than choke down some soup and sherbet before she stumbled upstairs with Bram and fell into bed in the room they'd shared the night before. She was asleep before her head hit the pillow.

As Bram followed her into sleep, he was relieved that the Walkens didn't seem upset with their sleeping arrangement. When he awoke some time later, the other side of the bed was empty.

Fear brought him to a sitting position. Pain made him wince, and set off a coughing spell, but not before he heard Hayley's voice in the hall and realized she was talking with Emily. Everything was all right. They both came running to check on him and he sank back down, spent from coughing, and fell back asleep.

Nightmares stalked his dreams. It was almost a relief when Hayley woke him with a tray of food some time later.

''You didn't need to bring this upstairs. I can go downstairs to eat,'' he told her.

''Well, you can, but we already ate.''

His stomach growled as the scent of soup roused it to life. ''I need to use the bathroom first.'' Every fiber of his body protested his movement and he groaned.

''Exactly,'' Hayley said sympathetically. ''And I'm not the one who kicked my way through two walls. Want to lean on me?''

''Isn't that supposed to be the superhero's line?''

"Maybe later. Right now, I bet even I could take you down."

"No bets."

He would have liked to tell her he could manage, but the truth was, he was so stiff and sore it would have been a lie. His head hurt the worst, but every burn and scrape screamed for a share of attention. His throat was raw and his chest felt so tight that each breath was painful.

The food tasted wonderful, but halfway through the meal, his eyes gave up the battle to stay open. Bram mumbled an apology as Hayley removed the tray, and he sank back against the pillows.

Emily roused him the next time. It was full dark and his gaze quickly turned to his side. He relaxed when he saw Hayley curled beside him, sound asleep. He swallowed some water and the medication the doctor had prescribed, thanked Emily and went back to sleep.

Sunlight woke him next. It was morning and Hayley was gone. Bram suffered a moment of panic until he realized she was probably downstairs having breakfast with George and Emily. Getting up, he discovered there wasn't a spot on his body that didn't hurt, but his legs no longer felt like rubber. He was reassured when he stepped into the hall and heard voices drifting up from downstairs.

A shower helped the stiffness, but it made his burns and cuts sting like crazy. And it was hard to keep the water away from his bandages. Still, the effort was worth the inconvenience. It felt good not to smell like smoke anymore. He wondered if he would ever get the scent and taste of it out of his nose and mouth. Dressed in the last of his clean clothing, he made his way gingerly down the stairs.

George sat at the oversize kitchen table. A woman he introduced as Nan bustled cheerfully about the kitchen, setting a plate of sausages and eggs in front of Bram on a colorful place mat.

"I hope you're hungry," George said ruefully.

"Hungry, yes. Capable of chewing? Only time will tell," Bram said. "I think my muscles are on strike. Where's Hayley?"

"You just missed her."

His heart skipped a beat.

"It's okay. Emily is with her. They made an appointment to see Emily's hairdresser. Emily promised not to let Hayley out of her sight. Hayley was fretting over her hair and not having any clothing, which I think you'll agree is a healthy sign. They'll be surrounded by people at all times. Don't worry."

But Bram did worry. Anxiety left the food tasteless in his mouth.

"The fire marshal and a police officer are on their way over to talk with you. I think it might be best if Hayley isn't here when we talk to them. Understandably, she doesn't have a lot of faith in the local authorities, and Officer Crossley is related to the police chief."

"Is that wise?"

"Maybe not, but we no longer have a choice. I asked Rhea to join us. She's going to bring the lab results. And for your peace of mind, Emily promised to check in with me every half hour."

Bram knew he should be reassured, but he wasn't. Hayley drew trouble worse than a magnet. He wasn't going to feel secure until they arrested the person who had set the fire.

The doorbell rang as he pushed aside his plate. Stiffly, he rose to face the local authorities. The first time Emily checked in, Bram bit back a demand to talk with Hayley. When the phone rang half an hour later, George suggested he should answer.

"Hi, Bram!" Hayley said cheerfully in his ear. An image

of her grinning up at him like some impish pixie made him relax. "How are you feeling?"

"Where are you?"

"Grumpy, huh?"

"Hayley," he said warningly, and then ruined it by coughing.

"I'm doing better than you. My cough isn't nearly that bad. Emily and I are walking into Aurora's Clothes Closet as we speak. I knew you'd be worried, but we're fine. You can relax."

"I'll do that when you get back here."

He was aware that four sets of interested ears were listening to his every word.

"I love you, too. We'll be home shortly. Bye."

Bram sat there listening to the dial tone. What did she mean? *I love you, too.* It was just an expression, right? He didn't want her to fall in love with him.

Did he?

"Everything all right, Bram?"

He focused on George. Rhea Levinson and the two officials watched him with interest. "They're at a clothing store. They'll be home shortly."

"Good. Go on with what you were saying, Rhea."

Bram tried not to brood, but the men had to repeat several questions before they registered. The officers wanted to talk with Hayley, so they said they'd return later.

The policemen had been cordial, even friendly. Wyatt Crossley was a few years younger than Bram and seemed competent and professional. If he felt any animosity toward Hayley and her family, he didn't let it show.

George took the next two phone calls from his wife. The women had decided to stop and have lunch, since it had gotten so late. Bram decided he would throttle Hayley as soon as he saw her again. If she was trying to show him how much he'd come to care about her, she'd succeeded.

He brooded over that as he and George ate lunch in the kitchen.

Bram was pacing the floor when they finally called to say they were on their way home.

"They have one more stop to make," George said reluctantly. He quickly raised his hands, palms out. "And remember, I'm just the messenger here. Do you play chess?"

"No."

"Then I'll teach you."

The next half hour came and went without a phone call. When another fifteen minutes passed, both men gave up the pretense that they weren't worried.

"They probably forgot to keep an eye on the time," George said, but he picked up the phone and called Emily's cell phone. No one answered.

"Something's wrong," Bram told him, getting stiffly to his feet.

"My car's out front," George said.

"Did they say where they were going after lunch?"

"No, but we'll find them," George said forcefully. "The town isn't that big."

And for no reason at all, Bram suddenly knew exactly where they'd gone. Hayley had been fretting about her purse. "They went to Heartskeep."

"Emily wouldn't take her there."

Bram regarded him wryly. "How well do you know Hayley?"

"Not as well as I know Emily."

"Uh-huh. Well, I knew better than to take her there yesterday, but you see how well I held out against her. She wants her purse. When she sets her mind to something—"

George swore. "I'll have us there in five minutes."

Bram prayed it would be soon enough.

Chapter Thirteen

"I suppose Bram is insisting on meeting us at Heartskeep?" Hayley said as Emily returned from the ladies' room. She replaced the cell phone in her bag.

"I didn't tell them where we were going."

"Smart thinking." Hayley swung her head, loving the freedom of the new, shorter hairstyle. She hadn't realized how heavy her long hair had been until it was gone. Spotting her reflection in a shop window as they strolled to Emily's car, she was surprised to realize how much she now resembled the picture she'd shown Bram. She wondered what his reaction would be.

"Hayley! There you are! I've been looking ev—" Jacob stopped dead, surveying her with openmouthed surprise. "Hayley?"

Delighted, she smiled. "It's me."

"You cut your hair!"

He sounded appalled. What was it with men and long hair?

"Do you like it? I think it gives me a sophisticated look. I didn't have much choice, since so much was singed in the fire. What do you think?"

"I, uh, wow. It'll take a little getting used to."

"Emily's beautician says this style's quite popular again."

Jacob looked at Emily. ''Hi, Mrs. Walken. I didn't mean to ignore you. I was just, uh, sort of, you know, surprised. I mean, Hayley looks...so different. Good!'' he added hastily. ''But, uh, different. That's a new dress, too, isn't it?''

''Uh-huh. We've been shopping this morning.''

''Oh. Well, you look good. Great! So you're really okay, then?''

''As I told you on the phone yesterday, I'm fine other than a scratchy throat, a cough and a bit of tightness in my chest.''

''I was worried.''

''I appreciate it, Jacob.'' She took a step back so he wasn't standing quite so close.

''Have you been out to see the house yet?''

''No.'' Hayley exchanged looks with Emily. She'd just spent their entire lunch hour convincing Emily to drive her past the house. ''Is the fire marshal letting us back inside yet?''

''I don't know. I haven't been out there today. I don't see why he wouldn't. I mean, the fire only damaged the one wing. That's pretty much totaled, I'm afraid, but you weren't planning any fancy-dress balls in the near future, were you?'' he asked with a disarming grin.

Hayley managed a weak smile in return. The memory of being trapped in that ballroom was one she couldn't stand thinking about.

''How much damage was done to the ballroom?''

''Mostly smoke and water, I think. Your dad's office was completely gutted and so was the front parlor. Marcus is wild, but Mom says he hardly ever used it anymore. Not since...well, you know.''

Hayley knew.

''I couldn't believe it when that alarm when off. Scared the heck out of me. I thought it was a false alarm until I got out in the hall and smelled the smoke. We were really lucky that fire truck was so near. If they'd had to drive all the way out from town, you might have lost the whole house.''

Hayley wasn't so sure it would have been a loss. She couldn't imagine ever being comfortable living there again.

''I'm just glad Bram had the foresight to devise an emergency exit through those bars Marcus had him put on all the windows,'' Emily said.

''Yeah. That was a lucky break. I'm really glad you're okay, Hayley,'' Jacob said again, laying a hand on her arm.

''Thanks.'' She shifted the packages she was carrying so that his hand fell away. ''Bram's going to be okay, too.''

His smile faded slightly. ''Good. That's good.''

''Hayley, Jacob, I hate to interrupt,'' Emily said with a meaningful look at Hayley, ''but we really need to be running along.''

''You're right, Emily. I'll talk with you later, Jacob.''

He frowned. ''Okay. Look, I'll give you a call, all right? Maybe we could have dinner together tonight.''

''I'm sorry, Jacob. I can't,'' Hayley said firmly.

The frown deepened, becoming almost a scowl.

''It was nice to see you again, Jacob,'' Emily said, leading a grateful Hayley away.

''Yeah. Uh, you, too, Mrs. Walken. I'll talk with you later, Hayley.''

Hayley smiled and waved and kept walking. ''Thanks,'' she said when they were safely out of earshot.

''I know it's none of my business, Hayley, but if I didn't know better, I'd say your stepbrother was acting like he'd developed a crush on you.''

''I wish that was all it was. Would you believe he asked me to marry him?''

Emily stopped walking. ''He did?''

''The other day, completely out of the blue. I've known Jacob forever, and I'm usually fairly savvy when it comes to guys hitting on me, but I swear I didn't have a clue. I never suspected he had any romantic feelings for me.''

Emily looked thoughtful as she started walking again. ''I can see why Bram was worried.''

''Oh, Bram's not worried about Jacob. At least, not in that way. Bram knows exactly how I feel about Jacob.''

''And does he know how Jacob feels about you?''

''Yes, I told him.''

''Hmm. The male of the species tends to be quite territorial, you know.''

''That's kid stuff. Bram is no kid. He knows he doesn't have to worry about Jacob.''

Emily didn't respond. She had a pensive look on her face.

''What are you thinking?''

''Does Jacob know you inherit Heartskeep?''

They reached the car and began loading their purchases inside.

''Now you even sound like Bram. I don't know who knows what about my inheritance, but Jacob isn't the least bit interested in the estate. He told me himself that he doesn't even like Heartskeep.''

''The estate is only part of it,'' Emily said as she unlocked the car and climbed in.

Hayley got in as well. She realized she hadn't really thought about the money that came with her inheritance. The truth was, she'd always taken money for granted.

But maybe Jacob didn't.

''You and Bram have a thing about Jacob. I think Eden is the one we should be watching out for,'' Hayley said stubbornly. ''Jacob wouldn't have any reason to drug Marcus or destroy his files.'' She fastened her seat belt as Emily started the car.

''What would Eden gain by destroying her husband's files?'' Emily asked. ''And why set fire to the house?''

''Good point. Jacob told me Eden loves Heartskeep.''

''Hmm. It's quite a muddle, isn't it?'' Emily frowned, chewing on the inside corner of her lip. ''Perhaps we shouldn't drive past the house, after all, Hayley.''

''We don't have to get out of the car, especially if they won't let us inside to get my purse, but I'd still like to see how bad the house looks.''

The last thing Hayley wanted to do was put Emily in danger—or get her in trouble with George and Bram. But she did feel a sort of morbid curiosity about the damage.

''Well, I can't see how driving past would hurt anything, but we'll have to make it quick.''

''We will.''

Police tape stretched across the front porch, blocking access to the house. Surprisingly, a cluster of officials were on the scene, probing the rubble. Hayley's car still sat in front, covered in a fine layer of soot.

''Do you think I could ask one of those men to run inside and get my purse?''

Emily nodded reluctantly and parked. Hayley scooted from the car before she changed her mind. She heard Emily get out, as well. The scent of wood smoke hung in the air, sending a shiver right through Hayley.

''Excuse me. I'm Hayley Thomas. I was wondering if I could trouble someone to go inside and get my purse? I have a bedroom on the opposite side of the house.''

''If you'll just—'' The young man's gaze traveled past her and his face lit in a smile. ''Hey, hi, Mrs. Walken!''

Emily joined her, smiling at the young officer.

''Hello, Jim. How's the family?''

''Great. The baby's walking already.''

''Wonderful! You and Carolyn should stop by one day. We'd love to see all of you again.''

''Maybe we'll do that. You and Ms. Thomas can drive around to the back. The fire department has some men inside. The left wing is roped off, but we're letting the family in to get personal effects from the safe areas.''

''Thank you, Jim. Say hi to Carolyn for me.''

''Will do.''

Emily did not look happy as they returned to the car.

''We don't have to go inside, Emily. I can get the purse another time.'' Hayley's gaze riveted on the blackened interior she could see through the empty sockets of the burned out windows.

''We're here now. The men won't be happy, but there can't be any danger with all these people around. We just need to hurry. Your Bram strikes me as the sort who'll be worried stiff until we get home.''

''You're right.''

''I like him, Hayley.''

''So do I.''

Emily parked alongside several other cars. Hayley recognized Marcus and Eden's large Cadillac and her heart sank. She didn't want a run-in with them right now. She wanted to grab her purse and flee.

''Bram's name's rather unusual,'' Emily was saying. ''Is he related to the Peppertons, by any chance?''

''It's okay, Emily. I know all about Bram's marriage to Helen Pepperton.''

Emily smiled in obvious relief. ''I'm glad he told you. It was such a dreadful tragedy. They say Dr. Lonnigan never got over it. He committed suicide less than a year later.''

Hayley gaped at her. ''You knew her doctor?''

''Not personally, but he'd been in practice for years around here.''

''Emily, right before the fire I found a file someone had faked to make it look like Marcus had been Helen Myers's doctor.''

Emily inhaled sharply. ''Why would someone do that?''

"I'm not sure. Either it was put there to make me doubt Bram, or it was part of a plan to frame him."

"Frame him for what? The fire?"

"Maybe. I've been thinking about that. Bram was hit with a hammer someone stole from him. What if whoever set that fire intended to lure Marcus in there first and kill him with Bram's hammer?"

"Dear heavens. Hayley, I know how you feel about the police, but I think you and Bram need to sit down with them and tell them everything."

Hayley nodded. "I think so, too."

"Let's get your purse and go home."

Looking up at the house, Hayley found she was strangely reluctant to step back inside. If Emily hadn't been with her, she would have left.

Inside the kitchen, the smell of smoke was surprisingly strong. If the house had seemed sinister before, it was downright spooky now. A haze drifted in the air, thick enough to make Hayley queasy and start her coughing again.

"Hayley, I'm not sure this is such a good idea."

"I'm sure you're right, but I'm okay."

Heartskeep had been in her family forever, but as she climbed the back stairs ahead of Emily, Hayley knew that she would never be able to live here again.

Could she decline her inheritance? If she did, would the house revert to Leigh? Hayley needed to call that lawyer as soon as she got back to the Walkens'.

"I can't get over how dark it is up here," Emily commented as they reached the second floor. A strip of yellow tape blocked off the hall to their left. A man in a hard hat looked up and nodded at them.

"I remember when your grandfather had these walls installed," Emily told her. "This was all open, of course. The design was completely unique. Today, it might not be all that unusual, but back when it was built there wasn't another house like Heartskeep. Poor Dennison was terrified that once you and your sister started walking, one of you would fall over the balcony railing and break your neck."

They rounded the corner and Hayley found herself hurrying. "You mean the balconies that go around the living and dining rooms aren't just there for architectural show?"

"Of course, you wouldn't have known, would you? There used to be a step-down onto the balcony that encircled both rooms. I believe the pillars are the support columns for them. You used to be able to look straight across to the other wing from up here. Or you could peer down at the rooms below, or gaze up at the sky. I have pictures somewhere. I was only up here on this level once, but the house seemed so light and airy back then despite all this dark paneling. I remember thinking it must be a bear to heat this place in the winter, even with all the fireplaces going, but it really was something to see. The way it's closed in now...the upstairs reminds me of a gloomy hotel."

"I agree." Hayley turned the knob and stepped into her bedroom. It seemed eons since she'd last been inside. Everything reeked of smoke, including her purse. It sat in plain sight, right where she'd left it.

"I'd like to see those pictures. I'm going to have the walls torn down again," she told Emily as she pulled a few things from her drawers and stuffed them into her overnight case. "But I have to tell you, owning Heartskeep has lost all appeal for me."

"Oh, dear. Don't make any hasty decisions, Hayley. You've been through a lot since you came home."

"That's part of the problem. Heartskeep isn't home anymore."

Emily crossed to the window. "Give it some time. You

might see things differently later on. Goodness, I can't get over how much the mazes have grown."

"You mean, become overgrown, don't you? All Marcus seems to have taken care of are the roses."

"What a shame. Your mother and grandfather were so proud of the gardens. And speaking of Marcus, isn't that him?"

As she picked up her purse and her case, Hayley glanced outside. "I don't see him."

"He just disappeared behind that tree."

Hayley shook her head. "Figures. I bet he plans to garden today as if nothing was wrong. You know something, Emily, whoever was drugging his water wasted their time. I think he lost touch with reality long ago. Let's get out of here."

It was all Hayley could do to keep from bolting back downstairs to reach the sunshine. The house was oppressive and the smell of smoke was irritating her throat and making her cough harder again.

"Are you okay, Hayley? Here, suck on this."

Gratefully, she accepted the piece of hard candy Emily held out to her. In the kitchen, they bumped into Mrs. Norwhich carrying a bulky suitcase. She scowled suspiciously at Emily and eyed Hayley balefully. "You look quite fit for someone who nearly died."

"I'm fine, thank you. This is our neighbor, Emily Walken. Emily, Mrs. Norwhich."

Odette Norwhich inclined her head.

Belatedly, Hayley realized she hadn't given a thought to the two women since the fire. "Do you and Paula have a place to stay?" she asked.

"Mrs. Norwhich and Paula are staying at The Inn with the rest of us," Eden said, striding around the corner. She, too, had obviously returned for her personal effects. "Emily," she acknowledged curtly.

"Hello, Eden. It's a terrible shame about the house."

Eden glared at Hayley. "Yes, it certainly is. Marcus is already looking into contractors to start the repairs."

"One of our former boys, R. J. Monroe, runs a construction firm now. You might want to give him a call," Emily suggested.

Hayley remembered R.J. as a tall, nice looking guy a few years older than she and her sister.

"Do you have his telephone number?" Eden asked.

"I have a few of his business cards in the car," Emily told her.

"I'll walk out with you, then. Hayley, your father wants to speak with you."

That would be a first.

"He's out back near the fountain, checking on some of his precious roses," Eden added in disgust.

"Uh, Hayley, we need to be getting back," Emily cautioned.

Eden sniffed. "Don't worry. He won't snap her head off for starting the fire."

Hayley and Emily exchanged looks. They weren't about to get into a discussion with Eden over who had started the fire.

"I'll call him later," Hayley promised. "Emily, I think I'll drive my car instead of riding with you. That way Bram and I can return for his truck later on. I'll meet you back at your place."

Emily didn't look happy, but she reached for her cell phone and nodded as she led Eden over to her car. Hayley started to walk around the house then saw Mrs. Norwhich getting into a car. A memory that had been tickling her brain since yesterday suddenly emerged.

"Mrs. Norwhich? May I speak with you?" The stocky woman paused as Hayley hurried over to her.

"Do you remember the other day when Bram carried me inside?"

"'Course I do. Nothing wrong with *my* mind."

"Good, because you said something as I was running outside that morning. Something about a fire in the gardens or something."

The woman's eyes narrowed in rejection.

"I don't remember exactly what you said, but you implied I wasn't the only one who'd gone running outside."

"You weren't."

When she didn't elaborate, Hayley continued, "You said something like, 'first the mister, then the missus, then the boy and even the hired help.' Did you mean Jacob and Bram?"

"Everyone went rushing out there," she agreed.

"Do you remember in what order?"

"What order?" She managed to look affronted. "I've got better things to do than keep track of all the comings and goings around here, missy."

"I know you do, but this might be important. I went out there after Eden. Bram said he followed Jacob into the maze. Do you know if Jacob went out before or after Eden?"

Mrs. Norwhich surprised her by taking time to think about the question. "You know, I don't remember. I think the boy went out after his mother, but it might have been the other way 'round. You might ask Paula Kerstairs. She was out there, too, and that one doesn't miss much."

Paula had been out in the maze that morning?

"Thank you. If you need anything, you can reach me at the Walken estate. I don't know if Eden has said anything to you, but you and Paula will collect your regular pay while we wait for the fire marshal to let us move back in."

"The missus didn't say a word except that she'd let us know when to come back."

"Well, I'll be speaking with the lawyer in charge of the estate this week, and I'll be sure to mention this to him. If there's any problem with your pay, please let me know."

Her sour expression softened the slightest bit. "You can be sure I'll do that."

As Hayley said goodbye, she turned and saw Marcus walking from the fountain toward the start of the second maze. In his hand was a familiar bottle of water. Her first instinct, born of years of avoidance, was to head in the opposite direction, but she knew she could never live with the guilt if she didn't warn Marcus not to drink any more of the water. Eden was still talking to Emily, so reluctantly, Hayley went to intercept him.

Marcus stopped when he saw her approaching. His skin paled visibly. For a split second, something that could have been fear crossed his features.

"Are you all right?" she asked, wondering if he was ill.

"Hayley?" he said tentatively.

It was the first time she could ever remember seeing Marcus look vulnerable. He was staring at her hair as if it were full of snakes.

"It's me. I had my hair cut because of the fire. Did you take that bottle of water from the house?" She was relieved to see the cap looked unopened. "May I see it?"

He struggled to compose himself, but she'd never seen such a mix of emotions on his face before. He gripped the bottle tightly. "How did you find out?" he demanded.

Stunned, Bram's words replayed in her head.

It's possible Marcus has been injecting something into the water himself.

"You knew there was something in the water?" She'd never seriously believed that. Why would he want to make himself disoriented and confused?

Marcus reached for her arm. His grip was punishing.

Hayley dropped her overnight case, feeling the first twinges of fear at the ugly look on his face.

Paula Kerstairs burst from the maze. Her features were more animated than Hayley would have thought possible. The expression took years off her age, though she still reminded Hayley of a wraith in baggy clothing.

"Come with me! Hurry!"

Still clutching Hayley's arm, Marcus turned them both to face her.

"Someone's destroyed your roses!"

Marcus made a sound like a low growl. He shoved Hayley in Paula's direction, into the maze. Hayley stumbled and nearly fell before she caught herself. Paula was already disappearing. Marcus's expression was so thunderous it sent a sharp thrust of fear straight through Hayley.

He had never laid a hand on her or her sister, but he looked perfectly capable of anything at the moment. Her arm throbbed where he'd grabbed her, and he now loomed between her and the safety of the yard.

Knowing she couldn't push past him, she followed Paula. Marcus wouldn't hurt her in front of the housekeeper, Hayley reasoned, and when she reached the spot where two of the mazes converged, she could dart down the path that would bring her back out by the fountain.

But Paula didn't lead them in that direction. She waited for them near the first junction and pointed toward a path that eventually wound up in a dead end. Hayley realized it was the place where she had first seen Marcus talking to his roses.

"It's horrible. Wicked. Evil."

Paula was so agitated, Hayley half expected her to start wringing her hands. Marcus pushed past both of them. Hayley nearly bolted back the way they had come, but Marcus gave a low bellow of rage and began to run. As he came to the dead-end circle where the roses were, he pitched forward without warning, sprawling facedown in the clearing.

Hayley gasped. Every flower and every rose bush had been hacked to tiny pieces. The clearing was littered with the remains and there was an overpowering odor of chemical weed killer.

Marcus moaned and started to rise. Hayley came out of her shock. She took a step forward and tripped. A length of fishing line had been strung across the path. She pitched forward and landed hard, sprawled across Marcus.

Enraged, he shoved her to one side. Thorns and branches jabbed at her exposed skin. Marcus scrambled to his feet. Hayley started to stand in turn when she heard two muffled coughs. Marcus doubled over, clutching his stomach. He fell to the ground again and began to groan.

Bewildered and horrified, Hayley regained her feet.

"Don't move!"

Fear corkscrewed inside her. Paula stood in the opening, but gone were the stooped shoulders and frail appearance. Her entire demeanor had changed. She stood tall and erect. There was nothing the least bit wraithlike about her now. Her eyes glittered with satisfaction and a shrewd intelligence. Hayley couldn't take in the abrupt change. It was like looking at a completely different person.

Marcus writhed at their feet, moaning in agony. Horrified, Hayley made the connection between the large red stain spreading across his cotton shirt and the woman's thin, bony hand holding a gun with an elongated barrel.

"You shot him!"

"Very good," Paula told her. "That's a silencer on the end. No one will hear a thing, but you'll be dead when I pull this trigger. I can't miss at this range."

"I don't understand."

"Dr. Thomas understands, don't you, *Doctor?*" Viciously, she kicked him.

"Stop it!" Hayley demanded.

"Stand still!"

The gun barrel was pointed at her face. Hayley could see the woman meant to pull the trigger. She stood perfectly still.

"I won't stop until I destroy him and everything he cares about," Paula told her.

Hayley had never seen such hatred on a human face.

"I nearly killed you once before, you know," she continued calmly. "The night you arrived. I thought it would be poetic justice to kill his child, since he killed mine."

The nastier rumors claim he may have lost a few of the babies on purpose, Jacob had told her.

"But your boyfriend came in so I decided to wait. Then his wife came home and her brat showed up and the two of them started whispering together. I decided to wait for a better time."

The whispers that had woken Hayley that first night! She hadn't dreamed them, after all. Paula had been the silent watcher she had sensed.

"Only, I discovered he wouldn't care at all if I killed you. Do you know your own father hates the very sight of you? There wasn't much point then, was there? All you had to do was stay out of my way, and you'd have been safe. But you couldn't do that, could you? You and that boyfriend of yours had to go poking around and prying into things that were none of your business."

This couldn't be happening. The sun was shining brightly. They were only a few yards away from all sorts of people who could help.

They might as well have been standing on the dark side of the moon.

"I needed a D & C to get pregnant. It's a simple operation. Doctors perform them every day. Any qualified gynecologist can do it—anyone except *him.*"

Paula's words began to flow more quickly as her rage built. Marcus moaned. His breathing was becoming labored. Hayley tore her eyes from him and darted a glance to her right. There was a slight gap in the yews forming the maze. It was only a few feet away, but Hayley knew she'd never reach it before Paula shot her.

Marcus needed help, and he needed it fast. Was there any chance Emily might notice her overnight case lying there by the mouth of the maze? Hayley spotted her purse on the ground near the bench, out of reach. It wouldn't have made much of a weapon, anyhow.

"He botched that simple surgery," Paula was saying bitterly. "He left me sterile! My husband swore it didn't matter. He lied! Of course it mattered! I didn't want to adopt some stranger's baby. I wanted *my* baby!"

Hayley took a cautious step back. Paula didn't notice. Her voice continued to rise in a crescendo, spitting fury.

"Every time I saw a baby, I broke down and cried. I couldn't concentrate at work so I lost my job. Downsizing, they said, but I knew better."

Hayley inched closer to the hedge.

"They said I was crazy. My own family had me locked up!"

Paula rushed on as if these words had been bottled inside her too long.

"My husband divorced me. He married a woman who could give him babies!"

Her gun never wavered.

"It was all his fault!"

A humming seemed to fill Hayley's head. Paula was working herself into a frenzy. Hayley knew if she couldn't diffuse the situation somehow, Paula would pull the trigger and she and Marcus would both die, right here among the roses Paula must have just finished destroying.

"I knew what I had to do. I needed to weaken him first.

It took a long time to devise a formula he wouldn't suspect—something colorless and odorless that wouldn't last. I wanted him aware at the end. And you are, aren't you, *Dr. Thomas?*''

Marcus stirred. Hayley took another step back. ''You've been drugging his water.''

''Of course. I am a trained chemist, you know,'' she said with a proud lift of her chin. ''It was there in my file. Oh, but you never saw my file, did you? I found it and destroyed it as soon as I took this job. Then I heard you and your boyfriend talking about computers. I realized he probably kept backup files there. I couldn't leave anything like that for the police to find, now could I?''

''You set the fire.''

Paula beamed. Her smile was more terrifying than her fanatical stare.

''I set out to destroy everything he ever cared about, and I've succeeded. I planned it so carefully. I wanted him weak so I could beat him to death with your boyfriend's hammer, knowing the police would blame him. Everyone knew about what happened to his wife. That's what the boy told you. Only I couldn't find her file in his office, so I had to make one. I wanted to leave it where it wouldn't get burned, but that would have been too obvious. Besides, it wasn't important. Making *him* pay is what's important.''

''Didn't Marcus know who you were when he hired you?''

Paula's expression turned sly. ''How could he? I changed my hair, and my makeup and it's been seven years since he butchered Lydia Carpenter, successful businesswoman. He never looked twice at Paula Kerstairs. She was only a lowly maid, after all.''

She laughed, a chilling, cackling sound.

''You realize you have only yourself to blame. You left

me no choice. First I'm going to kill you and then your boyfriend.''

''Hayley!''

It couldn't be Bram's voice. He was safe at the Walken estate!

Paula lowered her gun arm as she darted a glance over her shoulder. Hayley didn't give herself time to think. She threw herself sideways, pushing through the gap in the hedge. Paula screamed in rage. The coughing sound came again.

Expecting to feel a hot flash of pain in her back any second, Hayley began to run.

Chapter Fourteen

George covered the distance between the two estates as if trying to break a speed record. When they arrived, Hayley's car still sat out front. An official waved them around to the back, where Emily and Eden stood talking beside Emily's car. Hayley was nowhere to be seen.

Bram's heart dove for his feet. He was out of the car and running before George brought the car to a complete stop.

"Where's Hayley?"

Guiltily, Emily pointed toward the garden. "Jacob went to look for her. I tried to call, but my cell phone's battery went dead."

Hayley's overnight case lay on the ground in plain sight. Bram heard another car pulling in behind George, but he didn't turn to look. Bram began to run.

Somewhere in the garden, a woman screamed in rage.

Hearing Jacob yelling for Hayley to wait, Bram pushed his tortured lungs and screaming muscles forward. He had to reach Hayley before Jacob did.

"HAYLEY! Wait!"

Hayley heard Jacob as she ran, but she couldn't see him. She had no idea where she was in the maze—or even which maze she was in. Ahead of her, three paths intersected, and she paused as a coughing fit seized her. Vainly, she tried to muffle the sound against her dress.

"Hayley!"

Jacob rounded a corner. Hayley tried to wave him off. "Get help! Paula's got a gun!"

Jacob kept coming.

Hayley realized someone was running toward her from another path. Where was Paula?

She'd started toward Jacob when something rustled the bushes a few yards in front of her. Abruptly, the branches were pushed apart as Paula forced her way through the dense hedge, gun in hand.

BRAM LOST JACOB in a fit of coughing that left him weak and spent and too winded to call out. He heard Hayley coughing somewhere ahead of him.

"Hayley!" Jacob called again.

The man was to his right. Bram had taken a wrong turn somewhere.

"Go back! Paula's got a gun!"

Adrenaline gave Bram a surge of new energy. He ran forward, catching sight of Hayley moving down a branching path. Paula Kerstairs suddenly emerged from the middle of the hedge to block Hayley's way, aiming a gun right at her.

Bram's lungs strained for air. He wouldn't reach Hayley in time! But Jacob raced up behind Paula and yanked on her shoulder. The gun spat flame and smoke. As Paula and Jacob began to struggle, Bram closed the distance, grabbing Hayley and shoving her behind him.

The gun fired. Jacob's lips parted in shock. He staggered and fell back. Paula twisted toward Bram, gun in hand. At this distance, she couldn't miss.

"Hey! You! Over here! Hey!"

Hayley was behind him, yet her voice came from the left.

Distracted, Paula jerked and half turned as she pulled the trigger. The bullet whizzed harmlessly into the thicket beside Bram. He dove at her in a hard tackle that took them both to the ground. The gun sailed from her hand.

Paula went wild, kicking, clawing, screaming obscenities, but the clearing filled with people who pulled her away. Coughing so hard he could barely see, Bram let hands pull him to his feet. Eden was bending over Jacob. George and a policeman were trying to pin the crazed woman, while Hayley was being hugged by her exact duplicate.

"You said everything was okay," he heard the woman who must be Leigh accuse.

"I lied." Hayley hugged her sister, then turned and threw herself into his arms.

AFTER A LATE DINNER that night, the three of them sat in the Walkens' cozy living room, still trying to make sense of it all. The police were gone, George was taking a telephone call and Emily had gone out to the kitchen for something.

Marcus had died among the ruins of the roses he loved. Jacob was in the hospital with a hole through his arm as a result of his heroism, and Paula was in jail, smugly mute, but unbowed, having achieved her ultimate revenge.

Bram tugged Hayley more tightly against his side, feeling every one of his almost thirty-five years. His chest ached painfully, while his head throbbed in concert with assorted muscles, scrapes and burns. He didn't care. Hayley was safe.

Unconcerned that her sister was sitting right there, he kissed the top of her hair. Hayley smiled up at him and settled her head against his shoulder, while Leigh stared in bemusement from the chair across the room. Bram was getting used to looking at the stranger with Hayley's face. Despite their identical features, he had no trouble telling them apart. It had nothing to do with Leigh's longer hairstyle or the difference in their clothing. Distinguishing the two of them would never be a problem for him. Leigh might look exactly like her sister, but there was only one Hayley.

"I'm still confused," Leigh complained.

"Welcome to the club," Hayley said. "When Bram told me he suspected everyone at Heartskeep of tampering with the water bottles, including Paula and Mrs. Norwhich, I thought he was nuts. I was so sure Eden was behind everything."

Bram felt a tiny tremor course through her, and he smoothed back a strand of her hair. "I owe Jacob an apology," he told her.

"A big one," she agreed. "He saved my life."

"I know."

Bram would never forget his terror when he saw Paula aiming that gun at Hayley and knew he wasn't going to reach her in time. He had known such helpless fear like that only once before—when his infant daughter had struggled for her life.

"So this Kerstairs woman is insane?" Leigh persisted.

"I don't know," Hayley said. "I got the impression she'd spent a couple of years creating that stuff she put in the water. She knew exactly what she wanted to accomplish, and bided her time until she was ready. That doesn't sound like a crazy person to me."

"Then you showed up and ruined everything," Leigh said. "So was Paula blackmailing Marcus?"

"I'm not sure anyone was," Hayley replied. "Marcus may have been talking to himself that day. He was doing that the first time I saw him—when he told Mom her roses were doing well.''

Both women shuddered, and Bram stroked Hayley's arm. She rewarded him with a wobbly smile.

''Do we know why you saw Eden sneaking into the maze that day?'' Leigh asked.

Hayley shook her head. ''Mrs. Norwhich said Paula was out there, too, that morning. I think it's a safe bet Eden was following her.''

''I saw Jacob acting weird and followed him,'' Bram told Leigh, ''but I lost him and had to blunder my way back out. He was following either his mother or Hayley.''

''We'll ask him about it later,'' Hayley said.

''I'm surprised you didn't all fall over one another.''

Hayley shook her head. ''The mazes are a mess. There could have been half a dozen people moving around in there.''

''Oh, no you don't,'' Leigh protested. ''There are already too many people wandering around in there in my imagination. What about those pictures you found? I don't understand how they fit in, but I'd like to see them. You'd think I'd remember talking to some man outside that café in New York, even if I didn't know my picture was being taken. And as you can see, I do not have short hair, though I have to admit I love the way yours looks.''

''Bram showed me how that was done on the computer,'' Hayley told her.

''We'll have a look for the picture file when the police let us back in the house,'' Bram promised.

''We can't,'' Hayley stated. ''Paula did something to the machine and now it wants a password. Jacob's not going to be happy. I think it's his computer.''

''I'll have a look at it,'' Bram promised.

''Bram used to work with computers before he was a blacksmith,'' Hayley told Leigh.

"Really? We'll come back to that in a minute," Leigh promised. "I still have some questions. Like why did Paula clean the library and take the telephone books?"

"To keep me confused, I think," Hayley told her. "She knew I was drinking the water, so she felt safe coming in while I was sleeping. Want to bet she was the one who went through my bag that first day?"

"But why? I still don't understand the point."

"She was trying to create as much chaos and confusion as possible."

Bram nodded. "She wanted Hayley to go away, but if she didn't, Paula wanted to make Hayley seem so confused that no one would believe anything she said."

"It's all so hard to believe," Leigh protested. "I leave the country for a short vacation, and look what happens."

Neither woman smiled.

"I still believe Paula's plan was to lure Marcus into his office and kill him after she spread the accelerant," Hayley commented.

"You think she wanted him to die in the fire?" Leigh asked.

"Paula said Bram and I ruined her plan," Hayley said thoughtfully. "I think she intended to hit Marcus with Bram's hammer and set the fire so that the police would blame him."

"Is that why she made up the phony file on Bram's wife?"

"It's possible. She overheard Jacob telling me what happened to his wife."

"I don't think so," Bram told them. "I think Jacob or Eden created that file to make you doubt me, Hayley. I think Paula expected the police would think I hit Marcus when he caught me rifling through his office. And it could have worked. Most nights I wouldn't have had an alibi."

"Geez, what a thought," Leigh protested.

Hayley stroked his cheek. "When we interrupted her setting the scene she must have panicked and hit you to escape. In retrospect, she was the only person who looked totally terrified when everyone was gathered around us out front, after we got out."

"She couldn't be sure I didn't see her when she hit me."

"Is that why she decided to kill Marcus in the garden, after destroying his roses?" Leigh asked.

Hayley nodded as Emily entered the room with a platter of cookies.

"Can I get anyone anything else to drink?" Emily asked.

"No, thanks. Sit down, Emily," Hayley insisted. "You don't have to wait on us."

Emily smiled. "I know. The one point that still troubles me about what happened is why Paula attacked you and Marcus with all of us standing only a few yards away."

Bram laced his fingers with Hayley's, reassured by the warmth of that contact. He would have nightmares about today for a long time, he was sure.

"I think she heard me trying to warn Marcus about the water, and felt she was out of time," Hayley told Emily.

Bram scowled at her. "If you'd done what I told you and stayed with people—"

"I did stay with people," Hayley protested. "Just the wrong ones."

Leigh smiled wryly. "If you want Hayley to do something, you have to tell her she can't. I could tell you stories—"

"Don't even think about it," Hayley warned her sister.

They all looked up as George Walken strode back into the room. Emily rose and crossed to her husband's side. He slid an arm around her waist and smiled at her fondly.

"Sorry for the interruption," he told them. "That was a friend of mine who works for the fire department. Were either of you aware that Marcus had a hidden room off his office?''

''What?'' Hayley and Leigh exclaimed in unison.

George nodded. ''They found a small surgery with a concealed entrance from his office and a hidden exit to the outside.''

''You're joking!'' Leigh said.

''I wonder if Mom or Grandpa knew.''

''I doubt it,'' George said. ''The only reason he'd need a hidden room was if he was doing something illegal. Dennison wouldn't have stood for that.''

They all fell silent.

''Maybe they'll find some answers in Marcus's files or on his computer,'' Emily suggested.

''I'm afraid not,'' George told her. ''Everything in that wing is a total loss.''

Bram shook his head. ''Maybe not. Hard drives are pretty close to indestructible. It's possible to retrieve a lot of the information, even after a fire and water damage. I have a couple of friends in New York who do that sort of thing for a living. It's expensive and time consuming, but it's often possible.''

''Will you call them, Bram? See if they'll try? There are still so many unanswered questions.''

''I have another one,'' Emily offered. ''How is it you managed to time your arrival so perfectly, Leigh?''

''Good question,'' Hayley agreed. ''What *are* you doing here?''

''Are you kidding? I knew something was wrong the minute you called me in England. It didn't take ESP, you know. You and Marcus in the same house without a referee? As soon as you said he was putting up bars, I knew the fur would be flying. I couldn't get a plane home fast enough. And believe me, getting one at the last minute like that wasn't easy. I was so frantic by the time I got to the airport that security did everything but strip-search me. And the only reason I didn't get a jillion speeding tickets on my way here from the airport was because I think I broke the sound barrier. Radar traps probably wrote me off as a UFO.''

''My cautious, careful sister, speeding?''

Leigh tried to stifle a yawn and failed. ''Can we discuss the error of my ways after I get some sleep? I hate to be a party pooper here, but I've been up for a day and a half already. Or is it two days? Whatever. I'm wiped.''

''I think we all need some sleep,'' Emily said.

''I have one last question for Bram,'' Leigh said as she got to her feet. ''At the risk of sounding weird—which is redundant around here—what are your intentions toward my sister?''

''Leigh!'' Hayley protested.

''Hey, from the looks of things, this is a whole lot more intense than your relationship with Peter Vonnavitch.''

''Who's Peter Vonnavitch?'' Bram demanded.

''The guy she dumped a couple of months ago,'' Leigh said. ''So answer the question.''

''Leigh, shut up,'' Hayley said. ''It isn't *his* intentions you should worry about. At the risk of offending the Walkens, I can tell you that *my* intentions are highly immoral and are not being acted on right now only because we are guests in this house. Now, shut the heck up and go to bed.''

Leigh blinked and started to smile. She looked to Emily and George. ''And here I thought all the excitement was over. Looks like this situation is just starting to heat up. Good night, everyone.''

George nodded. ''It's been a stressful day for all of us.''

''You're right, dear.'' Emily snatched up the plate of cookies. ''Sleep well.''

The room emptied with unnerving speed.

"One thing you can say for Leigh, my sister knows how to clear a room," Hayley said lightly.

Bram held her in place when she would have stood. "Hayley, I knew this would happen. I warned you I wasn't the marrying kind," he told her gruffly.

"At least twice," she agreed.

"But you are."

"Did I ever once mention marriage?" she demanded.

"You aren't the sort of woman to have affairs."

"Really? And here I thought I was doing a pretty good job of it, considering you were my first seduction. I'll improve with practice. Wait until you see the underwear I bought in town today."

"Hayley—"

"Don't, Bram. We are not having this conversation right now. Like George said, it's been a long day. We're both tired. My chest hurts, and you must be hurting everywhere. We can talk in the morning." She pulled free and stood. "Just remember one thing. Loving someone isn't a disease."

"No, it isn't. But some people aren't very good at it."

"Like everything else, love takes practice. Good night, Bram. I'll be using the room across the hall tonight so you can get some rest."

HAYLEY STOOD by the window of the dark room and wished she hadn't made such a stupid declaration. What was she doing in here when she could have been snuggling with Bram? It was never a good idea to give a man too much time to think.

She wished she could cry. She would have liked to shed a few tears for the mother and the grandfather she missed so much, and for the death of a father who couldn't love her. But especially for a man who wouldn't let himself love her.

Would she ever be able to push past the barrier that death had erected? Bram loved her. She knew he did. They were meant to be together. She couldn't imagine a life without Bram. But how could she make him see that?

The bedroom door opened quietly at her back. She'd been half expecting her sister, so she turned around. But it was Bram who stood silhouetted in the open doorway.

"I do love you, you know."

His hoarse, raw words left her shaken.

"You'd be better off with Jacob," he continued as he stepped inside and closed the door firmly. "Or anyone else who doesn't come with a lot of baggage."

She lifted her chin while her heart soared. "I don't want anyone else."

He crossed the room silently, a looming shape in the darkness.

"You'll change your mind, Hayley. I carry more baggage than you know. I'm dead broke, my father is dying of cancer and I've got a mound of debts to pay off."

"I have plenty of money. I could help."

He stroked the side of her face. Moonlight etched the planes of his features.

"I won't take a dime from you. I'm only telling you this to show you why there can't be an 'us.' I'm trying to help one brother get through school, another one get through a messy divorce, and—"

"Wouldn't these things be easier if you let someone share the burden?"

"Not when that someone is an heiress. I've been down that road before."

"Don't you dare start making comparisons! I'm not Helen."

"No, you're nothing like Helen."

"Then stop thinking with your pride, Bram. Start thinking with your heart."

His hands reached for her, his fingers tangling in her hair. She turned to kiss his palm and got his wrist instead.

"What am I going to do with you?"

"I have a couple of suggestions," she said, breathless with new hope.

He made a soft sound of amusement in the back of his throat. "I know all about the sort of suggestions you tend to make."

"Good."

"Hayley, I don't want to hurt you."

"Then don't. Life doesn't come with guarantees. It comes with chances and opportunities. All we can ever do is make the best of what we have."

His eyes were dark pools.

"I love you, Bram. I'll love you even if you walk out on me. But if you do, I'm giving you fair warning that I'll hunt you down."

"You'd do it, too."

"Bet on it. I think what we have is worth at least a try, don't you?"

He drew her into his arms. She listened to the sound of his heart beating with hers. Bram was a proud man. Her man.

When he bent his head, she raised her face. The kiss was pure magic and she sighed in satisfaction.

"Want to see what I have on under this gown?" she whispered.

His fingers found her breast. "Feels like nothing."

"Exactly."

The kiss deepened with an edge of urgency. Bram backed her against the bed and stopped.

"We shouldn't do this here."

"Okay. My car's out front."

He choked on a low chuckle. "I love you, Hayley."

Her heart sang with joy. "I know."

"I should walk out that door and keep going."

"But you won't."

Getting past his pride and the memories that haunted him wouldn't be easy, but they'd make it work, somehow.

Bram searched her gaze for an endless second. The smile started in his eyes, crinkling the corners, then curved his lips with wry humor.

"No," he promised, "I won't. I guess someone has to keep you out of trouble. But the tights and the cape are officially retired, got it?"

Laughter bubbled in her throat. She threw her arms around his neck. "They weren't really your best color, anyhow," she whispered against his mouth.

Laughing out loud, he followed her down on the bed.

RM PB Sin
The firstborn /
Walkerton Public Library
3451

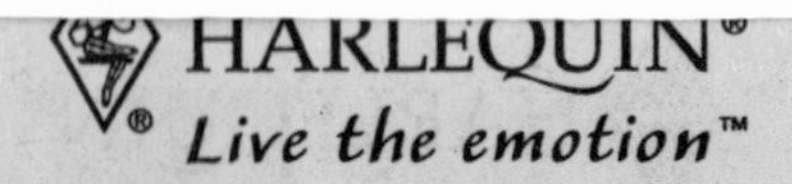
HARLEQUIN®
Live the emotion™